Beara: Dark Legends

The Beara Series - Book One

Also by Brian O'Sullivan

The Beara Trilogy:
    BEARA: Dark Legends Book 1
    BEARA: Dark Legends Book 2

The Fionn mac Cumhaill Series:
    FIONN: Defence of Ráth Bládhma
    FIONN: Traitor of Dún Baoiscne
    FIONN: The Adversary
    FIONN: Stranger at Mullán Bán
    FIONN: The Tightening Trail
    FIONN: The Betrayal

The Irish Woman Warrior Series:
    Liath Luachra: The Grey One
    Liath Luachra: The Swallowed
    Liath Luachra: The Seeking
    Liath Luachra: The Metal Men
    Liath Luachra: The Great Wild
    Liath Luachra: The Consent

Short Story Collections:
    The Irish Muse and Other Stories
    The Celtic Mythology Collection 1
    The Celtic Mythology Collection 2
    The Celtic Mythology Collection 3

Beara: Dark Legends

The Beara Series - Book One

BRIAN O'SULLIVAN

IrishImbas Books

ISBN: 978-1-0670637-0-2 (ePUB)
ISBN: 978-1-0670637-1-9 (Paperback)

A **pronunciation guide** for the Irish Gaelic names and placenames in this book are available at the Irish Imbas Books website. A copy of the **book notes** (not available in the digital version of this book) can also be downloaded at that site.

Prologue – Part One

West Cork, Early 1960s

By midnight, the boy's limbs had lost all sense of feeling. Crouched in the same excruciating position for several hours, the pain in his legs had finally blunted, the ache at the curve of his back dulled from nerve ends worn numb by tension.

Despite his physical distress, the boy was still too scared to move, too frightened to swallow the mucus lodged in his throat, for fear of the sound it would make. His terror was mingled with a primal instinct, an unconscious 'knowing' that the slightest noise would draw the *Púca* to him.

And he could still feel it out there.

Seeking him.

The *Púca* came when the boy's father was absent on one of his increasingly frequent visits to the O'Sheas. Two brothers in their late thirties, the O'Sheas scraped a meagre living from a patch of stony soil lodged in a cleft of the Caha Mountains. It was a precarious existence, one supplemented, by necessity, through the sale of *poitín*. The illicit still was hidden between two boulders at the back of the property. The clear, tongue-numbing liquid it produced was served from the *síbín*, a ramshackle lean-to located closer to the house. Here it was dished up to local farmers desperate for company and a few hours' respite from the rigours of working their unproductive lands.

Despite their isolation – or perhaps because of it – the brothers were renowned for their love of fresh gossip, often stalling the departure of their visitors with extended hospitality and fresh offers of drink or black tobacco. It was not unknown for people to extend their visit for many hours – or, in some cases, days.

The boy's first sense of the *Púca* was intuitive rather than perceptive, a sudden awareness of an astringent presence like a pungent stench inside his mind. Startled, he dropped the toy soldiers his father had made him – lifelike figures carved from the rough cuts of an abandoned building project – and stared uncomprehendingly around the room. Although there was nothing to be seen or to be heard, he could feel an aberrant presence closing in, clenching around him like a tightened fist.

A warm gush of urine streamed down the inside of his trousers, and he whimpered in terror, huddling into a ball among the soldiers strewn useless as a defeated army on the floor around him.

As the boy sensed the physical source of the intrusion draw closer, some instinctual measure of self-preservation finally kicked in. Scrambling across to the corner of the room, he tore a small heap of dusty furniture aside and ripped up the tattered carpet. A ragged gap was revealed in the floor, overlain with three loose boards. Clawing the planks aside, the boy pushed himself into the darkness below.

The rocky niche in which he found himself was small, a narrow, natural fissure beneath the floor of the building that had been overlooked or simply ignored during its original construction. Approximately five yards in length, its deepest extremity was less than a yard and a half in height. From there, it sloped upwards at a thirty-degree angle, tapering to a narrow flat just below the opening.

Wheezing with fear, the boy crawled to the furthest end of the cavity where further progress was impeded by a flat section of rock. There, he clamped both eyes shut and pressed against the cold surface, desperately willing himself to be absorbed into its intractable solidity. Despite his frantic heartbeat, he attempted to slow his breathing, instinctively knowing that the *Púca* could close in on such giveaway physical traces, his own body's terror treacherously exposing him.

Little sound penetrated the rocky space from the room above. For a time, nothing could be heard other than the distant rattle of a window shifted by the wind. Gradually, however, he thought to hear something new among the low cacophony of the house's habitual creaks and groans: a faint rustle in the passage, a slither on the floorboards overhead.

It went quiet again for several minutes, but he could still feel the malignant presence, surveying the room, attempting to locate him, searching, honing in on any noise, any physical flicker of fear or panic.

Too terrified to do anything else, the boy simply faded away.

And ceased to exist.

***

The boy did not know how much time had passed when he finally returned, for no daylight passed through the hole at the far end of the cavity. His first sensation confirmed the absence of hostility within the house: all trace of the entity had vanished as though it had never been. The sense of relief was so intense that for several seconds he could hardly breathe.

It took another two hours before he finally emerged from his hole in the ground, constrained by both an overwhelming caution and the pain raging through his cramped legs. Despite his conviction that the danger had passed, the child remained too scared to leave the room and spent the rest of the night beside his refuge in the floor.

His father discovered him there at noon the following day, shivering, covered in dirt and in obvious distress. Although reeking of alcohol, he had the wit to recognise that the boy was traumatised and used his most gentle persuasions to convince him to step away from the hole. After an hour of reassurances and several unsuccessful attempts to learn what had happened, his father resorted to hugging him.

'It's all right now. You're safe. You're a good boyeen. 'Twas just a dream. A bad oul dream.'

Exhausted, and calmed by his father's embrace, the boy relaxed and was on the verge of sleep when a sudden realisation sent a shiver up his spine and he knew that he could never, ever, sleep soundly again.

He had been lucky. The cold breath of sunlight had cleansed his home and the *Púca* had departed.

But it was only a matter of time.

Before it returned again.

Prologue - Part Two

Munich, 2008:

Volunteer Nina Hilleke first noticed the gentleman with the bouquet by the congested hospital entrance. A middle-aged man with blond hair, a tidy beard, and old-fashioned spectacles, he was standing nervously to one side of the automatic doors, wielding a leather briefcase like an ineffective shield against the passing crowds. She stopped to stare for there was something in his bewildered manner that appealed to her, some unthreatening, childlike quality that stirred a maternal instinct within her heart.

And she had a big heart.

A sentimental woman with a weakness for romantic novels and soap operas, Hilleke had often experienced disappointment at seeing the passionate accomplishments of fictional characters absent from her own existence. Over the years, the prolonged absence of physical and emotional intimacy had instilled her with a growing emptiness, one that she'd subconsciously tried to fill through voracious overeating.

This, at least, was what her counsellor, Doctor Drey, had informed her during their sessions. Her unappeasable appetite, he insisted, was not a disorder but a symptom, a symptom of her loneliness and low self-esteem.

Hilleke sniffed in annoyance.

That was all very well and good of course. Nevertheless, knowing the reason behind her craving hadn't provided much practical benefit in countering them.

She brushed such thoughts from her mind as she waddled towards the distressed visitor, determined to fulfil her role of 'Leader of Hospital Hospitality' to the best of her ability.

'Good evening, sir. Can I help you?'

The man peered at her, eyes dropping from her face to the hospital badge on her left breast. The sight of the authoritative title seemed to reassure him for his frowning expression transformed to one of relief.

'Oh! Oh, dear me. Yes!' He removed a handkerchief from his coat pocket and paused to pad his brow. 'I'm afraid I'm a little lost. I haven't been to a hospital for several years. Ever since … well since my wife died.' He stared out through heavy, pebble-glassed spectacles with all the vulnerability of a deserted puppy. 'It's all a little … overwhelming.'

Hilleke's heart melted. She offered him a sympathetic pat on the arm.

'I understand,' she assured him. 'Hospitals don't usually bring back happy memories, but everyone says this is one of the best in the country. It might look higgledy-piggledy at first but there really are processes in place to take care of everyone. And the staff are very efficient. There's a method in our madness.'

She tittered at the age-worn joke, but he just stood there blinking helplessly.

'Now, how can I help you, Mr …?' Hilleke raised her eyebrows expectantly and he responded on cue.

'Guttmann. Ernst Guttmann. I'm here to visit my niece, Sara Guttmann but I …' his voice trailed off as he looked around the bustling reception area, his eyes finally settling on the crowded reception desk.

Hilleke, who'd been following his gaze, understood his trepidation. To the uninitiated, the reception area could appear chaotically disconcerting. On the far side of the counter, a small army of hospital administrative staff in white uniforms was hectically occupied fielding an array of beeping telephones and frantic enquiries from concerned friends and family members. The commotion, she conceded, was somewhat off-putting.

'Please don't worry, Mr Guttmann. I'll take care of this.'

Stirred by the challenge of a fresh humanitarian goal, Volunteer Hilleke plunged forward into the melee, brushing through the assembled crowd with an ease facilitated by a commanding air and her awe-inspiring bulk. Reaching the counter, she leaned forward and grasped a blue clipboard lying beside a neatly stacked pile of files. The wooden structure creaked disconcertingly as it took her weight but slowly reassumed its former shape as she straightened up and returned to the anxious Mr Guttmann.

Hilleke flipped through several sheets on the clipboard.

'Guttmann. Was that right?'

'That's right. Sara. Such a lovely girl. Happy-go-lucky.' The frown reappeared, tightening his features. 'So terrible to see her in such a place.'

Hilleke loosened her own smile in sympathetic support. 'Yes, well at least you can be assured that if she's in this hospital, she's being properly taken care of. The doctors and staff here are just wonderful!'

She studied the clipboard again.

'Do you know what department your niece would be in?'

'I believe it's the oncology department.

Hilleke was unable to disguise her concern. 'Oh dear, I'm so sorry. I'd assumed it was an accident or something like that.'

'No, no, it's all right,' the gentleman assured her. 'She's in remission. All the family are allowed to visit her again.'

'Oh!' The relief was evident on her face. 'Oh well, that's excellent news. I'm very happy for you.' She glanced at the clipboard again. 'Ah, Guttmann! Here it is.'

She pointed at the floor, directing his attention to a rainbow array of coloured circles embedded in the large, square tiles beneath their feet. A thin line of identical colour protruded from each circle and streaked across the shiny surface in several different directions. Two of them, the blue and the green, led directly to the lift shafts in the central foyer.

Hilleke calmly issued directions with the ease of practised repetition.

'If you take the lift to the second floor and follow the blue line, it'll lead you directly to the Oncology Ward. I think it's a short stroll of about … three minutes.' She punctuated the latter statement with a nod as though concurring with her own calculation. 'It's certainly no more than that.'

She glanced down at the clipboard again.

'According to my chart, your niece is currently in Room 274. If by some chance she's not there, the ward nurses will be able to tell you where to find her. She won't have gone far.'

She beamed with the satisfaction of a job well done. 'Is there anything else I can help you with, Mr Guttmann?'

'No, please. You've been so kind already, Miss …' Mr Guttmann peered again at the badge pinned to her blouse.

'It's Hilleke. Nina Hilleke. I work here as a volunteer supervisor on the weekends. You know, organising the volunteers, making tea for the patients, helping visitors and such.'

'That's very considerate of you.'

'Oh, well! I do feel it's important to give a little back to the community.'

'You're a very generous person.'

Volunteer Hilleke felt an unexpected blush flood her features. Unaccustomed to such compliments, she drew herself up decisively, struggling to regain her composure.

'Enjoy your visit, Mr Guttmann. If you need any more assistance, please don't hesitate to come back and find me.'

'Thank you again, Miss Hilleke.'

With a grateful smile, Guttmann turned and proceeded to the central foyer, stepping into the first vacant lift that became available. Emerging on the second floor, he followed the blue line as instructed, strolling at a leisurely pace as it led him through a labyrinthine system of white-walled corridors decorated with a recurring series of generic watercolour prints. Finally, as Volunteer Hilleke had indicated, he found himself before a pair of swinging doors with the words 'ONCOLOGY WARD' printed overhead in bright green letters.

Pushing through the double doors, he entered the ward. The office of the ward nurse, at the far end of a long corridor, appeared temporarily deserted but as the nearest door to his right had the number 268 inscribed on it, locating his destination proved little challenge.

Tutting quietly to himself, he continued down the corridor to Room 274. With a gentle knock, he opened the door and peeked inside.

As anticipated, the door opened into a private room. Clean, uncluttered, and minimally furnished, the sterile surfaces of its white walls were relieved only by pieces of medical equipment and a single window overlooking a small public park. A girl of about sixteen or seventeen lay on the large, metal-framed bed in the centre of the room. She was a pretty thing, blonde hair and delicate features, but her thin frame and pinched face were clear evidence of the invasive medical treatments she had endured.

Mr Guttmann stepped inside and closed the door, then locked it firmly behind him. As he stood observing the room's single occupant, a strange transformation overtook him. The faint stoop eased from his shoulders, and he straightened perceptibly, instantly increasing his height by almost half an inch. When he moved towards the bed his movements assumed new purpose, as though he'd shed some corporeal burden of indecision.

Placing the bouquet of flowers on a small bedside cabinet, he removed his overcoat and draped it over the back of a wooden visitor's chair. He opened the briefcase, removed a sketchpad and two pencils then pushed the chair closer to the bed. When he was sitting comfortably, he removed his thick spectacles, rubbed his eyes and silently studied the sleeping young woman before reaching out to stroke her hair.

Her eyes flickered open.

Startled, he drew back but she continued to observe him without expression, her gaze drowsy and dim from medication.

'You're awake!' Her visitor smiled. 'Sara, my name is Dr Casper. I'm sorry to come and disturb you.'

Sara Guttmann stared at him without emotion.

Dr Casper bent forwards, cupping both hands around his left knee. 'You can't imagine how pleased everybody was to hear the positive prognosis. I saw your father earlier, Sara. He's like a new man! Excited, reinvigorated ...' He stopped and patted her tenderly on the cheek. 'Mind you, that's understandable. You're his golden girl. The apple of his eye.'

He chuckled softly.

'I think the poor man's suffered just as much as you throughout your treatment.'

The girl moaned softly and attempted to lift her hand.

'Shhh.' He stroked her forehead. 'You need to save your strength.'

They remained there for several minutes without speaking, the girl dozing in and out of consciousness, Dr Casper sitting quietly, sketching her likeness on the drawing pad with a series of deft pencil strokes. Finally, leaning forward, he shook her shoulder softly before holding up the pad and displaying his handiwork.

The results of his efforts were impressive. The girl's fragile likeness had been accurately and sensitively transferred onto the crisp white surface.

'What do you think?'

She blearily regarded the paper before her, and Dr Casper was rewarded with a sleepy smile. Satisfied, he returned the pad and pencils to his briefcase. When he was finished, he addressed the girl once more.

'Sara, I know you have to rest, but first I have something to tell you, and it's very important that you concentrate.'

The girl's eyes opened again and settled on him. Her gaze was a little clearer and she appeared to be observing him with greater focus.

'Good girl. Now, Sara, I want to talk to you about your father.'

Dr Casper paused momentarily to remove his handkerchief from his pocket and started to clean the lenses of his spectacles.

'I'm sure you're already aware what a unique man he is.' He sat back in his chair and pensively formed the shape of a steeple with his fingers.

'You see, most human beings are a self-centred lot. Your father, however, has that rare capacity to extend his compassion beyond his immediate circle. People like your father are special. They're leaders of social justice, human rights activists, future engineers of social change.'

He stopped and replaced the handkerchief in his pocket. The girl's eyelids were growing heavy again and he realised that she would not be able to remain awake for much longer.

'Individuals like your Papa don't go unnoticed. Such people often come into conflict with oppressive governments or commercial organisations fearful his activities that might be detrimental to their interests.'

He shrugged.

'But that's neither here nor there. At the end of the day there's not a lot these entities can do about it. In civilised countries like ours, we have laws that constrain them and besides, such people are too conspicuous in the public eye to interfere with publicly.'

He shook his head decisively. 'No. If they did want to stop him then they'd have to do so through other less obtrusive, less conspicuous means.'

He looked at her and smiled sadly.

'And that, I guess, is where I come in.'

Leaning forward he stroked the girl's face once more then stood up and removed one of the pillows from under her head. Taking it firmly in both hands, he placed it over her face and pressed downwards. At first, there was no reaction but then her body responded to its predicament, self-preservation instincts kicking in as she began to struggle. Over the next minute or two there was a sustained, albeit weakening, resistance. Under Dr Casper's steel embrace, the outcome was inevitable. The girl's body shuddered violently one last time and went limp.

Dr Casper continued to hold the pillow down for a full three minutes after all movement had ceased. Finally, removing it from the girl's face, he put it aside and checked her wrist for a pulse.

Another minute passed before he was satisfied and let her hand drop back onto the bed.

Picking up his briefcase, he removed a thin membrane that had covered the external surface, instantly transforming it from a battered 'hold-all' to the prized accessory of a business executive. He approached a hand basin in the corner of the room and stared at himself in the mirror for several seconds before raising his hands to remove the blond wig loosely glued to a bald pate beneath. He deposited the wig in the briefcase, peeled the false beard from his chin and added this as well. Removing a striped silk tie from his other jacket pocket, he did up the collar button of his shirt, put on the tie and knotted it firmly. The coat he had laid on the chair turned inside out to reveal a suit jacket matching his pants. Slipping it on, he brushed the sleeves and removed a loose thread that he also placed in the case.

He studied his face in the mirror, concentrating on relaxing his facial muscles. Soon his features lost their intensity, softened and became almost kindly. He practised several quick smiles and when he found one he was happy with, he held it there for over a minute.

Leaving the mirror, he did a rapid but efficient once-over of the room to make sure he had left no trace of his presence behind. Finally, he approached the door, opened it, stuck his head outside and quickly surveyed the corridor. There was nobody in sight.

With one final glance at the body on the bed, he stepped into the hall and closed the door firmly behind him.

***

The well-groomed businessman who strolled boldly through the main door of the hospital bore little resemblance to the mouse-like Mr Guttmann who'd entered some thirty minutes earlier. Casting a surreptitious glance towards the reception counter, he noted the presence of Volunteer Hilleke engaged in conversation with a white-coated member of staff. Prompted by some inexplicable intuition, the community volunteer suddenly raised her head and stared in his direction. He suppressed a quick smile of triumph as her eyes washed over him, empty of any recognition.

Exiting anonymously amongst the hordes of mid-day visitors, he paused only when he noticed several young women on the concourse in front of the building, collecting for a local cancer charity. Adjusting his course, he ambled towards them, drawing to a halt before an attractive young woman with blonde hair. Smiling politely, he pulled his wallet from his pocket, removed a fifty Euro note and slipped it into her collection box.

The girl's eyes widened as she realised the value of his donation and she beamed in gratitude. 'Thank you, sir!' 'That's extremely generous of you.'

Dr Casper smiled gallantly.

'Have to do our bit,' he said.

Chapter One

Cork City, 2008

The rain had been falling for four days. It was a typical Cork downpour, a cold, grainy torrent that drove all activity from the streets and washed all colour from the world. An incessant, mean-spirited deluge, it trickled into every corner, seeped into every cranny and left nothing untouched by its damp and dreary fingers.

Late in the evening on the fourth day, a solitary figure in a herringbone overcoat and a flat cap pulled low over his forehead appeared at the junction of the Grand Parade and St Patrick's Bridge. Silhouetted against the swirling grey backdrop of mist and rain, he traversed the bridge, head bowed, and shoulders hunched against the wind. Halfway across, he halted abruptly, leaned over the balustrade and peered down at the river below. The *Laoi*, roused to an unnatural frenzy by the sheer volume of water flushed in from its various tributaries, thundered beneath, a churning, frothing, cappuccino-coloured flood of eroded soil, diluted effluent, and industrial contaminants.

The man remained where he was for almost a minute, apparently oblivious to the rain cascading upon him. With abrupt decisiveness, he straightened, crossed the remainder of the bridge with a brisk step and hurried up the ascending pavement to MacCurtain Street. Outside the grim exterior of McCarthy's Bar, he paused to catch his breath beneath a malfunctioning streetlamp. There, he appeared to hesitate for several moments, flickering in and out of darkness until, finally stepping across the threshold of the doorway, he disappeared inside.

Shaking the rain from his overcoat, Muiris O'Súilleabháin stepped in out of the night, shadows clinging to his flapping coattails as though reluctant to give him up. Brushing the more resistant drops from his sleeves, he removed the coat, folded it over one arm and passed into the lounge bar through a thick, loosely swinging door.

The interior of McCarthy's Bar was dim, bathed with a weak, musky yellow light thrown down from ancient light fittings that looked as though they'd congealed to the ceiling. Directly inside the door, a teak counter stretched for several metres through a fug of cigarette smoke, stale body odour and spilt whisky. It ended abruptly at a sharp corner, where the L-shaped room branched into a narrow area containing two tables and a raised platform used during the establishment's infrequent music sessions.

An elderly man with a chaotic mop of frizzy, grey hair stood behind the counter, wiping a beer glass with a tattered cloth. Nodding in greeting, he placed it on the shelf behind him with an array of similar glasses.

'Evening, Mos.'

'Michael.'

'Bad oul night.'

Mos grunted in response, divesting himself of the saturated overcoat by tossing it onto a nearby barstool.

Michael McCarthy, proprietor and barman, placed a glass tumbler on the bar, pulled a bottle of whiskey from beneath the counter and slowly unscrewed the cap. He took his time as he poured, observing with professional detachment the amber liquid slowly ascend to the lip of the glass. When it was level, he slid the glass effortlessly across the counter. Not a single drop was spilled.

'Get that down ye. It'll burn the chill off.'

Mos reached forward to take the glass and raised it to his lips. He relaxed perceptibly as the liquid burned down his throat, curling comfortably in the depths of his stomach.

'Weren't you supposed to be doing a site up in Mayo?'

Mos stared at the barman. 'Cancelled,' he said curtly.

McCarthy shrugged. Recognising when it was time to leave a customer to the pleasures of solitary drinking, he withdrew, losing himself in the routine of emptying, cleaning, wiping and filling glasses.

Mos, meanwhile, searching for his wallet, had discovered a folded sheet of paper in the pocket of his jacket. Curious, he flattened it on the counter then winced in recognition. It was the title page of a draft archeological report prepared for the Mayo site he'd been working on, the same site where his contract had unexpectedly been terminated.

Crumpling the paper into a little ball, he tossed it into a bin beside the door then proceeded to tap an irritable finger scale along the edge of the counter. He looked up as McCarthy returned to fill a fresh glass of whiskey.

'Are ye still in a foul mood, Mos?'

For a moment Mos glared at him, then his shoulders sagged and he slumped wearily on the barstool.

'I'm sorry, Michael. It's been a shit of a day. I shouldn't come in here crying at you like me Mammy.'

McCarthy shrugged.

'I'm not your Mammy, Mos. I'm your barman.'

He leaned forward and refilled the glass with quiet precision.

'There, now! Swallow that drink, and it'll make it all better.'

***

If there was a single silver lining in the folds of the inclement thunderclouds, it was probably that the pub was sufficiently deserted for Mos to withdraw to the comfort of the 'Cavern', a cave-like cubicle to the left of the lounge entrance. Little more than a slab of unpolished oak bolted to a stone wall that curved out around it on either side, the resulting enclosure was large enough to hold seven or eight tightly packed individuals. Despite its odd shape and unattractive walls coated with yellowing newspapers reporting events of some thirty years earlier, the resulting niche appealed to his warped sense of decorum and his desire for privacy.

Dropping his cap and coat onto one of the chairs, Mos took a seat at the table and brooded in silence as he savoured the raw burn of whiskey on his tongue. Occasionally, his eyes would flicker over a discarded copy of the *Examiner* left behind by some previous occupant. It was a measure of his own distraction that he absorbed the headlines of murders, strikes and a racial assault in Patrick's Street with little reaction or interest. He scowled.

He was tired.

Tired and cranky.

In a bastard of a mood.

Nothing new there then!

In retrospect, he realised, it hadn't been a particularly brilliant idea to venture out on such an evening. Then again, at the time it'd seemed like the right thing to do. The stifling solitude of his house had done little to alleviate the anger eating away at him because of the Mayo contract's termination. His dark reflection had been further compounded by the fact that it was the anniversary of his father's death, a date that always provoked some unwelcome soul searching.

Earlier that afternoon, he'd spent several hours alone in the dining room pretending to read a seven-page archaeological paper. Later, at four o'clock, when he realised that he had read the document several times and still had no idea what it was about, he knew he was only fooling himself.

As the evening drew in, the walls of the house had closed around him. His mood had deteriorated still further when he became aware of a subtle tension beneath the skin at the back of his neck. This was a familiar symptom from a condition that had plagued him since childhood, but it had been two years since he'd last experienced it. To have it reappear so suddenly, at that specific time, added strongly to the impression that fate was going out of its way to challenge him.

Finally, he could take no more. Throwing on a coat, he'd stomped out into the plunging rain without any particular purpose or destination apart from a vague intention of walking the anger off, driving it out through his system and into the sodden earth beneath his feet. He had walked for over half an hour and if the deteriorating weather hadn't forced him into the shelter of McCarthy's Bar, he'd still be trudging along some isolated side road, half-way to Blarney.

A glacial blast rushed up the length of the bar and there was a flurry of laughter and voices as a merry band of revellers surged in through the door.

Mos flinched as the draught brushed over him and tightened the woollen scarf that was wrapped about his throat. He watched from the shadows as the ebullient newcomers spread out, heralding their arrival with a bustle of flapping coats, dripping umbrellas and hearty exclamations at the severity of the weather.

McCarthy, face a mask of concentration, stepped forward to deal with the unaccustomed activity although it was evident he was struggling to cope with the orders barking at him from all sides. One of the newly arrived punters, a portly individual with silver hair, broke away from his comrades and stood in the centre of the room surveying his surroundings with ostentatious bonhomie.

Mos groaned.

Ah, shite!

The silvered-haired figure removed his sopping overcoat to reveal an expensive jacket, a bright red waistcoat and dickey-bow beneath. Casting the coat onto a barstool with a melodramatic flourish, he regarded the saturated garment with disdain and loudly declared in a theatrical voice, 'A curse on you, foul bloody weather!'

His companions laughed, clearly accustomed to this flamboyant behaviour. Buoyed by their appreciative response, he released a withering glance around the bar as though holding its occupants personally responsible for his sodden condition. His gaze slid up the length of the room, halting only when it fell on the cubicle where Mos was observing him coldly over the lip of a tilted pint glass.

'Muiris O'Súilleabháin!'

He bounded towards the cubicle with surprising alacrity, slid through the narrow entrance and planted himself on the bench opposite its occupant. He stared at Mos with undisguised satisfaction. 'Well,' he declared. 'This is a fortuitous occurrence.'

'Hello, Desmond.'

Mos slowly placed the glass on the table and gestured across at the increasing clamour around the bar counter.

'What's all this? The *illuminati* of Cork slumming it downtown tonight?'

'Just a little tipple after the show.'

Desmond Hegarty's grandiose mood was not to be undone, although he did regard Mos with a slightly askew expression.

'The show at the Opera House. Given the subject matter, I'd assumed you'd know all about it.'

Mos raised his eyebrows.

'*Tóraíocht Dhiarmada agus Gráinne.*' Hegarty clarified. 'The Pursuit of Diarmaid and Gráinne. They were performing a revisionist version.'

Mos shrugged.

'Yerra, I need to get out more.'

'Never mind that, Muiris! I'm just delighted to see you. I've been trying to contact you all week.' The alcove's new occupant laughed out loud in apparent amusement at the vagaries of fate. 'There I am, resigned to the fact that you've disappeared from the surface of the planet when, lo and behold, you turn up right before my very eyes.' He frowned then and regarded Mos critically with both of those very eyes.

'You know, you really ought to get yourself a mobile phone, Muiris. Or at least set up an answer phone so people can leave you a message.'

Mos considered Hegarty with a wry expression. It wasn't generally known, but his home phone was a mobile, one to which his landline number had been assigned. It just happened that he never actually bothered taking it out of the house with him.

'Ah, but if I did that, Desmond, every annoying Tom, Dick and Penis would be ringing me up.'

The silver-haired man nodded sagely.

'Of course. Of course.'

Mos watched without surprise as the sarcasm coursed off his companion, finding no grip on his slick, unblemished exterior. Previous association with Hegarty had adequately demonstrated his imperviousness to sarcasm or criticism. The man had a skin thicker than a rhinoceros encased in bubble wrap, a characteristic that had aided him substantially throughout his professional career.

'Tell me, Muiris,' Hegarty, all business, leaned forward and brushed the debris of small talk aside. 'Are you still working with Milo on that Ros na Rian site up in Mayo?'

'No, Desmond. My input was terminated a few days ago.'

'Really?'

Hegarty tapped the tabletop thoughtfully as he considered that.

'That's what I'd heard through the grapevine,' he said at last. 'Frankly, I didn't believe it. Not really my area of expertise, of course, but word on the street suggests the findings have the potential to rival the Céide Fields.'

'You've got a particularly good grapevine for something outside your field. But you're right. It does have that potential.'

'So why was your contract terminated? I'd have thought you'd be the obvious candidate to advise on the excavation.'

Hegarty glanced down and brushed an imaginary piece of fluff from the knee of his pants before continuing.

'I assume you identified the site in the first place?'

Mos' stare was cold.

'Creative differences.'

Hegarty nodded sagely as he digested this response.

'I see. Please don't be offended, Muiris, but to be honest, I'd heard you were simply being difficult.'

He glanced across at Mos, who simply smiled back at him without responding.

'That you were unwilling,' he pressed, 'to follow direct instructions.'

This time the response was a sarcastic chuckle.

'You know I don't follow directives I don't agree with, Desmond. Milo's instructions would have contravened fundamental tenets of the Moron's Guide to Archaeology.'

'Hmmm. Yes.' murmured Hegarty. 'And yet I recently read an article stating Milo was widely considered to be one of Irish archaeology's best hopes for the future.'

'Which would suggest Irish archaeology is pretty well fucked.'

Mos laughed at the expression on Hegarty's face.

'Come on, Desmond. He's a competent enough archaeologist but you know as well as I do, that he's lost interest in archaeology since he started developing political aspirations. The only things on Milo's mind these days are backroom deals and ballot boxes. He's only involved with the Mayo excavation because he's got such a hard-on for the county nomination in next year's elections.'

'What does the Mayo excavation possibly have to do with the election?'

Mos gave a tight smile. Hegarty was being deceptively naive. Behind the masquerade of 'baffled academic' was one of the most manipulative and self-interested minds he'd ever encountered. His one-time mentor, and long-time Professor of Philology and History at the Centre for Celtic Studies at University College Cork, Hegarty was one of the few academics who had thrived in the increasingly competitive and corporate environment of modern-day tertiary institutions. Flamboyant but astute, what he lacked in ability he more than made up for in bravado and sheer political cunning. University Deans had come and gone, but after two decades, Hegarty remained, enduring and as permanent as the stones of Brú na Bóinne.

Mos held Hegarty's gaze as the silence stretched on, neither man willing to relent or look away. He understood that there was a game being played here: Hegarty's 'grapevine' was firmly rooted in Milo's garden. No one else was aware that his contract had been terminated and although their encounter here at McCarthy's had probably been coincidence, Mos didn't doubt Hegarty had been seeking him industriously for several days. For a moment, he considered telling the academic to stick his head up his ass, but curiosity prevailed and he decided to play along.

'The importance of the site means that once the initial findings have been processed, the media will be over it like flies on a fresh turd. Milo intends to use the coverage as the launching platform for his political career. He'll set himself up to take all the credit associated with the discovery, then portray himself as the "saviour" of Irish heritage. That'll go down a treat with Seán and Sheila Public and he'll be a shoo-in for the party nomination.

Mos pushed the empty pint glass away from him, replacing it with the whiskey.

'Milo's problem is one of timing. He needs the results of the excavation to be made public in time for next year's nominations. If the site management followed normal practice, those results won't be published for several months after the nominations have been allocated. That's why he's desperate to speed up the excavation. A little bit here, a little bit there. Just enough to make sure the results are released on time but more than enough to compromise the analysis of the findings.'

He raised his glass in a mocking salute.

'In the end, it all comes down to the age-old contest of "doing what's right" versus "doing what's right for you". In that respect, working with him was a lot like working with you.'

Hegarty quickly dismissed such unpleasantness with a shrug of his shoulders.

'Really, Muiris! That's unfair. I understand you're upset with Milo but that's no reason to attack me. I've always felt our collaborations were a major success.'

Mos regarded his ex-colleague wearily.

'You have balls, Desmond. I'll give you that. Desiccated, reptilian testicles with all sorts of fucked-up, mucous-coated knobbly bits – but at least you have some.'

Hegarty glared at him in outrage but bit his tongue. Their one and only 'collaboration' had been when Hegarty was acting in his official capacity of academic overseer for Mos' Master's thesis. During the final term, Hegarty had essentially published Mos' research and analysis under his own name. An embarrassing lawsuit had been avoided only because of Mos' refusal – to the consternation of his colleagues – to initiate legal proceedings. Quietly accepting the proffered degree, he had left academic life and ensured that he never worked with his ex-mentor again.

Mos rubbed his eyes, suddenly tiring of Hegarty and his small-minded machinations.

'What do you want, Desmond? What do I have that you'd risk crawling back to ask for?'

'Really, Muiris! I—'

'I mean it. You know how little I think of you, and we operate to incompatible value systems.'

He shrugged.

'So, tell me, Desmond. What is it?'

Hegarty was staring down at his hands. When he looked up again, his eyes expressed a depth of bitterness that Mos had not seen before.

'Ah yes! The great O'Súilleabháin obsession with the truth. Tell me, Muiris, do you never tire of being such a paragon of historical virtue? Do you never stop, just for one moment, and wonder whether there's any chance, any chance at all, that you might possibly be wrong or that there might be other needs involved?'

'No, I don't. Now, tell me what you want or fuck off.'

Hegarty blinked, his indignant composure undercut by the vehement gauntlet tossed down on the table before him. Mos watched him mentally working through his response, conscious that his ex-colleague was weighing up the minimum he could tell him while retaining any degree of credibility.

'An opportunity has arisen,' he said at last.

Mos gave a cynical laugh then stood up to leave.

'See you, Desmond.'

Hegarty stared panic-stricken but before he could support his pitch, several members of his group converged on the Cavern, invading the dim recess in a flurry of boisterous laughter and movement. Mos halted in momentary bemusement as the intruders swept in around him, staking their claim to the cubicle through the deposition of beer glasses, coats and umbrellas and the annexation of tables around its immediate entrance. With a shake of his head, he gathered up his belongings and was turning to leave when he felt a hand grip his arm. He glanced down to find Hegarty looking at him with uncharacteristic desperation.

'Please, Muiris. Don't go. This is serious. I really need to talk with you.' He glanced around the rapidly-filling cubicle. 'In private.'

From the corner of his eye, Mos noted the lounge door swing open as yet another drenched patron entered, wiping rain drops from his hair and face. Just before the door closed, he caught a glimpse of the bleak street-scene outside – streetlamps shuddering in the wind, horizontal rain.

Despite his best instincts he found himself wavering at the thought of the long walk home.

'Please,' pleaded Hegarty.

Breathing deeply, Mos nodded reluctantly.

'Oh, fuck it! All right.'

For an instant, relief flooded Hegarty's face, and he nodded with what looked like genuine gratitude. Mos dubiously noted the reaction and wondered if he'd somehow been outmanoeuvred. He briefly reconsidered his decision but by then circumstances seemed to be conspiring against him. At that very moment, a fresh crowd of people poured in through the entrance of the pub, congregating in a tight mob outside the cubicle and effectively locking him in.

With a sigh, he silently resumed his seat.

Newly energised by Mos' acquiescence, Hegarty reverted once more to his habitually expansive nature. As the assembled group and various hangers-on made themselves comfortable around the table, he cheerfully assumed the role of master of ceremonies and started to introduce his companions. At first glance, they appeared typical of the retinue with which Hegarty habitually surrounded himself; a melange of local *intelligentsia*, artists and academics, supported by a fan base of drooling students in *de-rigueur* uniform of jeans and woolly jumpers.

'Muiris.' Hegarty gestured towards an attractive woman with brown hair set in an impish 1920s Louise Brooks-style bob who'd somehow managed to squeeze her slim frame onto the seat beside him. 'This is *Mademoiselle Giselle Talibat* from Bordeaux. She's the current writer-in-residence at the Karilee retreat.' He took her hand, raised it to his lips and kissed it with mock reverence. 'She's writing a brilliant new work which will have the critics salivating at her feet. Am I not right, Giselle?'

The Frenchwoman smiled, revealing a set of brilliant white teeth. Her eyes were bright and had a mischievous quality that made her look younger than she probably was.

'But of course, Desmond. I have always been a literary genius, unrecognised in my own country. But now I will make them pay.'

Her English was flawless and had it not been for the precise inflections that marked the diligent second language student, it would have been impossible to identify her as a non-native speaker. She reached across the table and shook hands with Mos. 'Hello,' she said.

'Always a pleasure to meet a fellow genius.'

She gave him a startled look but said nothing.

'Beside her,' continued Hegarty, 'we have Dr Connor Boyle from the English literature department and his wife Mary. Mary's a painter.'

The Boyles, a heavy-set individual with a grey beard and his beautiful, matchstick-thin wife, nodded cordially but had no time to get a word in as Hegarty moved along the table.

The next person to be introduced, a stocky man in his thirties with a thin moustache and a matching goatee, was bent forwards over the table, nursing a double whiskey. He looked up in irritation as Hegarty leaned forwards to disrupt him but then shrugged and swallowed a mouthful of liquid from his glass.

'This handsome devil is Dennis O'Donoghue. You might have heard of him. He writes a column for the *Irish Age* newspaper and I think he was runner-up in the latest media awards, eh, Dennis?'

O'Donoghue gave a desultory wave as Hegarty went on to introduce the remainder of the group around the table. The students, mere bystanders with insufficient social standing, were consigned both physically and metaphorically to the edge of the group, on the outer fringes of the cubicle and surrounding tables where they could, assumedly, hang on every word that was spoken.

Then, to his horror, it was Mos' turn to be introduced.

'This gentleman,' Hegarty informed the table, 'is Mr Muiris O'Súilleabháin – an old student of mine. As you can see –' He patted his paunch. '– the years have been a lot kinder to him than to me. That simple lifestyle and all that clean living just doesn't do it for me.'

Mos forced himself to tolerate the subsequent round of laughter. Moments later, Hegarty was called to the end of the table to resolve a dispute between two individuals on some element of the play which they had just been to see.

Madame Talibat leaned forwards, placed both elbows on the table and directed an inquisitive stare at Mos.

'Are you a history lecturer too, then, Mr O'Súilleabháin?'

'No.' Mos shook his head. 'I'm more of an antiquarian.'

'Ah! You collect antiques.'

Mos made no attempt to correct the assumption.

'Something like that. All enmeshed in the study of history and the practice of archaeology.'

The Frenchwoman smiled. You know, I've never completely understood the distinction between history and archaeology. Is there really a difference?'

Mos stared at her, surprised by the question. Trapped within the confines of the alcove, he realised he'd be obliged to make small talk until Hegarty returned.

Perhaps I should feign death.

Resigned to the situation, he took a sip of whiskey before responding.

'Yes, there is. I suppose the main difference is that historians usually focus on written records to understand the past. Archaeologists, on the other hand, study a wider range of materials, everythin from physical remains to recovered artefacts and so on. That's why they're able to study prehistory, that grey area of historical science where written records don't exist.'

Her full lips sipped from a long-stemmed cocktail glass and left a soft smudge of lipstick on the rim.

'When you say "pre-history", do you mean in the sense of "before history"?'

'That's right. Irish history prior to the fifth century.'

Mlle Talibat tossed her head, flicking her fringe away from her eyes. It was, thought Mos, a particularly Gallic gesture.

'I didn't realise history had an official starting point.'

Several of the nearer students laughed dutifully. Curious, Mos glanced over and caught a glimpse of the main instigator – a gormless-looking youth with red hair who was enthusiastically nudging his friends on either side.

He frowned and was about to respond when his attention was drawn to an exotic-looking young woman sitting behind the student. Slightly older than her scholarly companions – probably in her late twenties – she had thick black ringlets that cascaded down around her shoulders and onto the wide collars of a stylish, double-breasted red jacket. She was seated at an odd angle, facing slightly away from the others as though not fully committed to the group.

He returned his attention to Mlle Talibat.

'The generally accepted rule is that official history begins when you have enough information to work out whether something's true or not. The official history of every nation's different, but in Ireland the official records start after the fifth century – probably well after 431 AD – when the Christian Church arrived and introduced writing skills. There aren't any remaining written records on Irish society prior to the sixth century, if any ever actually existed, and in terms of physical pre-fifth century materials – buildings, tools and so on – there's bugger all apart from various burial sites and their contents.'

He shrugged.

'That's the beauty of pre-history, though. It's a time that's full of mystery: mythological heroes, vague classical references and, in some cases, complete fabrication. It's exotic. It's like a foreign country you've heard about but have never been to.'

'I'm sorry, I don't quite get that.'

Dr Boyle, who'd been listening to Mos' explanation with interest, gave a slightly condescending smile.

'If so, little actually remains from before the fifth century, how can we possibly know anything about it?'

He seemed impressed with his own reasoning, as some people did when they stumbled upon this particular argument. Mos' response was tinged with impatience.

'There's not much evidence in terms of hard archaeological artefacts but there's plenty of evidence from other, more indirect, sources.'

He halted briefly and glanced up as one of the students appeared at his shoulder and replaced a round of drinks for those sitting at the table. A tall man, who'd been introduced earlier as a radio presenter, ostentatiously waved the student over and handed him several euro notes.

'There were a number of writers from contemporary cultures,' he continued. 'Greece, Rome, and so on. Places where literacy existed before it came to Ireland. Occasionally individuals from these cultures took the time to comment on Ireland. Their comments weren't particularly complimentary, but they help give some indication of what life would have been like around that period.

Apart from that, there's also the descriptions passed down through the Christian scribes. From the early seventh century onwards, many of those scribes wrote down oral accounts from the local communities that had probably been doing the rounds for hundreds of years. They mightn't have been completely accurate but, again, if you compare them with the other evidence and snippets of information, you can make a tentative reconstruction of what life was like before the fifth century.'

He took a fresh sip of whiskey from the glass the student had deposited in front of him.

'Then, of course, there's the Irish folk narratives.'

There was a snort of derision across the table.

All eyes turned to O'Donoghue, the journalist, who was slouched back in his seat. He regarded Mos with a cynical expression.

'I hadn't realised fairy tales were an exact science.'

'Don't be silly, Dennis,' countered Hegarty, who had returned to join them. 'He said folk narratives, not fairy tales.'

O'Donoghue shrugged as though this only supported his point.

'Whatever you think,' Mos continued. 'The study of narratives is a science. It's a systematic study not only of religious, spiritual and mythic systems, but the everyday traditions and rituals of Irish culture.'

O'Donoghue made a point of yawning. 'That's still a pretty broad brushstroke.'

Mos considered the journalist coolly. He'd come across O'Donoghue's column in the local newspaper on occasion and although the writing was certainly competent, he'd always found the articles acerbic and too self-indulgent for his liking.

'So's life. You have to study a mishmash of the esoteric and the mundane elements of ancient cultures in order to understand how they worked. Otherwise, you can't even start to put historical findings into context or make sense of how different events affected people's behaviour.'

'So, no fairy tales,' commented Mlle Talibat.

Mos glanced at her, uncertain if it was a genuine question or whether she was simply mocking him. He decided to assume it was the former.

'No,' he confirmed. 'No fucking fairy tales. At least, not in the conventional sense of the word.'

He sensed a slight discomfort at his easy use of the F-word in such a scholastic discussion. They were a sensitive bunch, he decided.

'What about the annals?' asked Boyle. 'I thought they went back well before the first century.'

The Frenchwoman's eyes widened.

'I'm sorry. The annals?'

Boyle frowned.

'Well, as far as I understand, the annals were some kind of historical record initiated by the Western Church.'

He turned to Hegarty.

'Have I got that right, Desmond?'

'Absolutely!'

Hegarty was only too happy to provide confirmation.

'They were originally based on the Church's Paschal tables and used to work out the order of the liturgical feasts and religious festivals back in the Middle Ages.'

He offered a contented smile, enjoying the attention.

'In the original manuscripts, the annual dates weres separated from each other by a blank space. After a while, the clerics started filling them in with notes of their own about important events between the festivals. Over time, they developed into a rather useful chronological record.'

'So, wouldn't they be an excellent source of information?'

Mlle Talibat redirected the question back to Mos.

'You'd think so,' Mos acknowledged. 'Unfortunately, in Ireland the Church didn't start that tradition until the end of the seventh century. And human nature being what it is, the compilers couldn't help themselves from filling in all those irritating gaps in the pre-Christian records. They gathered all the information on the pre-fifth century they could find, collated them with their own views of what might have happened, then set the finished product in a rough chronological order using the Christian church annals as their template. In that respect, the early Irish annals read as though the clerics had first-hand knowledge of the historical events whereas, in fact, they were rewriting them to align with their own religious prejudices and beliefs.'

There was a thoughtful silence around the table. Mrs Boyle, who hadn't said a word until then, was the first to renew the conversation.

'So, does that mean the annals are incorrect?'

Mos shrugged.

'Well, the pre-fifth century material is dubious to say the least.'

'I don't understand.'

Her husband's forehead creased into a series of deep furrows.

'Seathrún Céinn and many of the earlier Irish historians believed the church annals were accurate.'

Mos put his glass on the table.

'That's a common problem with older works. Their age tends to give them an unfounded credibility in many people's minds. That's what happened with works used by Cétinn and his peers. They made the assumption that everything in the older documents was fact, simply because it'd been written a long time ago. They accepted the content without questioning it and didn't take the historical circumstances or the social context into account. That was a big mistake as any writer, no matter who they are or what age they live in, suffers certain biases or prejudices.'

He leaned back in his chair and breathed deeply.

'Unfortunately, the expression "don't believe everything you read" holds just as well for ancient manuscripts as it does for the latest media release from some dubious weekly rag.'

He glanced meaningfully at O'Donoghue who responded with a petulant glare.

'Good Lord!'

The Frenchwoman plonked her glass on the table with Gallic melodrama.

'So how in God's name did people ever find out what happened?'

'That's easy,' said Mos. 'It's because, as a race, we started becoming more cynical. And we finally started seeking the truth.'

***

Mos studied his fifth whiskey with the clouded intellectual insight achieved only on the downhill slope of inebriation. Drunkenness, he concluded, was a goal sought only by the solitary drinker. For everybody else it somehow seemed to sneak up unawares, clobbering them mercilessly from behind while they were distracted by its more pleasing side-effects.

He considered the whiskey glass standing on the worn, wooden counter. The amber liquid flickered pleasantly in the subdued lighting.

An important milestone in the night's activities had been attained, he realised. Wearying rapidly of the conversations with Hegarty's party, he'd ended up consuming more alcohol than he'd intended as fresh rounds were ordered around the table. During the course of the various discussions, Mlle Talibat had 'accidently' put her hand on his knee, and he'd realised with belated insight that she was flirting with him.

O'Donoghue, conversely, grew colder and more antagonistic, and it was only as Mos was leaving and noticed the journalist sidle into the seat he'd been occupying that he finally understood the reason. O'Donoghue had a crush on the Frenchwoman and had perceived Mos as a potential adversary for her affections.

When he'd finally succeeded in extracting himself and left the Cavern, Mos had felt Hegarty's eyes burning into his back. Despite his earlier urgency however, Hegarty had neglected to take the opportunity to pull him aside and discuss what was troubling him.

He stood by the bar, surprised to discover that his temper had softened. If nothing else, the conversation had been an effective diversion from the thoughts smouldering at the edge of his consciousness that evening. Now, he felt sufficiently calmed to put his glass down, walk out the door and go home.

'Mos.'

Mos looked up to find McCarthy standing opposite him on the other side of the counter.

'You've been staring at that glass for over five minutes.'

'I'm focusing, Michael. Drinking's a serious matter.'

McCarthy laughed, a kind of hollow bark that passed for mirth.

'Much as I respect your conscientiousness, Mos, I still think you're one drink short of half-steamed.'

'Well spotted, Michael. Now, if you'd leave me feckin' concentrate, I might be able to complete that particular fraction.'

McCarthy grinned and opened his mouth to respond when a sudden thunderclap shook the building, drowning out his witty riposte. The pub lights flickered and the hum of conversation throughout the room faltered.

'Jesus, Mary and Joseph!'

McCarthy blessed himself, the automatic response beaten into him from years of a Catholic upbringing. 'That's some fierce weather!' He shook his head unhappily. 'You mark my word, Mos, it's a night of portents. Something bad is coming.'

A brilliant burst of lightning flashed through the window as though to underline McCarthy's melodramatic prediction. All colour was momentarily ripped away from the world, and they blinked to rid themselves of the white afterimage. A moment later, the flash was followed by another, lengthy growl of thunder.

The punters' conversations slowly stuttered back to life, but the talk was muted and a few glanced at the window with each new flash or crack of thunder. After a few minutes, however, the storm's intensity had noticeably diminished and the volume within the pub slowly returned to normal.

'The storm's moving on,' said Mos.

'They always do.'

'Leaving desolation in it's wake.'

'Fuck, Mos. You're veering dangerously close to a "glass half-full" perspective.'

Mos laughed harshly.

'Muiris.'

He straightened up and turned to find Hegarty standing at the counter beside him.

'Hello, Desmond. What's up? Are you deserting your friends?'

Hegarty grimaced and made a dismissive gesture with his hand.

'Can we have a quick word?'

Mos shrugged listlessly, momentarily distracted by a flurry of hailstones against the window.

'Do you recall me mentioning how fortuitous it was to run into you?'

'No,' Mos lied.

Once again, Hegarty's massive egotism appeared to deflect the veiled insult, reducing its impact to that of a bee sting on an armoured vehicle.

No reaction from d'oul bollix. Must be losing me edge.

'I mentioned that an opportunity had arisen, Muiris.'

He hesitated for a second or two.

'I've got a proposal for you.'

Hegarty looked around as though fearful of being overheard, then made a deliberate point of staring at McCarthy. The barman shook his head in disgust but, taking the hint, moved to tend a keg at the end of the counter.

Reassured, the plump academic leaned forward with conspiratorial air.

'Two weeks ago, I was contacted by an old colleague, an historian called David Coffey. I worked with him in Oxford years ago. He's a charming man. Did some excellent work on late medieval English manuscripts.'

Mos shuffled impatiently.

'Is there a point to this?'

'I'm coming to it,' answered Hegarty, his voice slightly shrill. 'Anyway, these days, he's based in London, working for a private American institution. Last week, he rang me out of the blue, wanted to know if I knew of anyone with detailed expertise on *An Fianaigecht*. I hope you don't mind, but I mentioned your name.'

Mos rolled his eyes. 'Jesus, Desmond! If you've given my contact details to some coven of new age ...'

'No, Muiris. It's nothing like that. These people are completely legitimate. They call themselves the Opus Foundation and they run a charitable institution that deals in the acquisition and conservation of western antiquities. From what David tells me, they've got their hands on some artefact and need some help verifying its authenticity.'

'I don't get it. Why would an American conservation organisation be looking for expertise on *An Fianaigecht*?'

'Because the artefact's of Irish origin, Muiris. And ...' Hegarty looked meaningfully at him. 'David says that it has some association with the Fenian stories.'

Mos thought about that for a moment. *An Fianaigecht* was an enormous body of poems and tales relating to Fionn mac Cumhaill that covered many locations and time speriods so it was imposible to know what the relation could be.

'So, what is it? What's the artefact?'

'I have no idea.'

Mos winced.

'Well, have they dated it?'

'They've had an initial analysis carried out but it's only a rough estimate at this stage. All I know is that it's pre-twelfth century.'

Mos was unable to conceal his surprise. Early medieval artefacts weren't exactly commonplace but to discover one with a potential link to the Fenian narratives was … well, that was a rarity indeed.

'They're sure it's of Irish origin?'

'David seems convinced that's the case.'

Hegarty coughed delicately and cleared his throat.

'However, they're willing to pay a substantial sum to whoever can confirm that and advise them on certain related aspects.'

'How much?'

Hegarty told him. Mos whistled in surprise.

'Naturally', continued Hegarty, 'I could do an adequate job of assessing the content to help confirm its provenance and authenticity, but they seem to think some in-depth expertise on *An Fianaigecht* would be helpful to assign an accurate time period.'

'Uh-huh.'

'I should add they've explicitly indicated a preference for someone not directly associated with the universities or the national research institutions.'

Mos stared at him in surprise.

'Why don't they want to involve the universities?'

'They said they weren't at liberty to tell me. Shit, who cares, Muiris! They're willing to make a four-figure payment just for turning up to talk with them for a few hours.'

Mos regarded his old colleague with suspicion.

'So, what's your angle, Desmond? What are you getting out of this?'

Hegarty regarded him with a hurt expression.

'Do you think so little of me, Muiris?' he asked sadly. 'Do you really think me incapable of a single act without guile or profit?'

'Yes.'

Hegarty's face flushed through a remarkable variation of purples and reds.

'Very well,' he said tersely. 'If you must know, I'll be receiving a fee for the authentication. And there's a finder's commission for you, of course. A man has to cover his costs.'

That, apparently, was the sum of what he was willing to share. He fixed Mos with a stern eye. 'Are you in, Muiris?' he asked gravely.

Mos leaned back against the bar and pensively stroked the stubble on his chin. The money involved was impressive but the real carrot – as Hegarty was most certainly aware – was the artefact's purported *Fianaighecht* connection. Any item that could shed new light on any context of the Fenian narratives, or even confirm existing theory, was literally priceless from the perspective of a Fenian scholar. To someone like Mos it was intellectual gold.

He regarded the eager expression on the academic's face and his misgivings returned. The downside in this proposal was the fact that it was Hegarty dangling the carrot. Previous experience had adequately demonstrated he couldn't be trusted. For that reason alone, the project was almost certain to be tainted in one form or another.

'Opportunity doesn't knock twice,' Hegarty urged.

'I just like to know who's on the other side before I open the door.'

Hegarty flung his hands in the air in exasperation. 'For God's sake, Muiris! Honestly, I just don't understand you. Sometimes it's as though you go out of your way to rub people up the wrong way!'

Mos shook his head doubtfully.

'I'll tell you what. Let me have an oul think about it and I'll come back to you.'

'Muiris, there isn't much time. Haven't you been listening to me? I've already said …'

Mos ignored him. 'The thing is, I'd planned to head the Gaeltacht for a week or two. It's about time I brushed up on my Gaelic. *Tá sé in am uisce íor an tobair a bhlasfaidh.*' It's time to taste pure water from the well.

Hegarty glowered, clearly furious but unwilling to push too far.

'Honestly, you *gaelgoirs* are a pretentious lot.'

Mos sipped his drink and eyed him coldly.

'Pretentious,' he said. '*Mise?*'

***

Hegarty apparently hadn't appreciated the joke for he'd stalked off in a huff, muttering bitterly of missed opportunities. Although genuinely intrigued by the story of the Irish artefact, Mos wasn't particularly perturbed. Familiar with Hegarty's *modus operandi*, he knew that if there was any substance to the story, Hegarty wouldn't give in. If Mos' particular expertise was required, Hegarty would be back to pester him.

He picked up the untouched whiskey glass. Swirling the contents, he raised it to his lips then paused as he noticed a young woman on the stool to his left, bent forwards over the counter as she helped herself to some ice cubes from the ice bucket. She had removed her red jacket, but he recognised her as the woman he'd seen with the students in the Cavern.

At a guess, he'd have said she was of Middle Eastern – or perhaps South American – descent. Whatever her origins, she was striking. As tall as Mos – about five foot nine – she had small breasts and the lean, powerful build of an athlete. Long, dark curls fell onto a purple, open-necked shirt and framed a face with smooth skin and high cheek bones. Her classically attractive features, nevertheless, had a stillness and austerity about them that bordered on the severe.

Retrieving the ice, she dropped it into her glass. Sensing his attention, turned to look at him. He was struck by the solemnity of her scrutiny, the lack of any identifiable emotion behind that unruffled evaluation.

He nodded in acknowledgement. She offered him a cool smile.

'Ah, the antiquarian!'

'Ah,' he countered. 'The appreciative audience.'

'The captive audience,' she countered right back. 'You must be the official pub philosopher. I'd been told Irish pubs were crammed wall to wall with philosophers and poets.'

He looked at her in surprise, thrown by the accent, which seemed at odds with her looks. Her English was perfect, but the inflection was slightly French or Spanish and had a trace of a brogue or something similar in there as well. The overall effect was further confused by a voice that was surprisingly husky – deep and almost masculine, but also oddly appealing. He sat on a barstool and allowed it to wash over him.

'Ah, that'd probably have been an Irish Tourism Board ad you saw when you were high. They tend to …'

He stopped, momentarily distracted by an unusual tattoo running down the side of her neck.

'Samoan.'

'What?'

'The tattoo. A Samoan design. Or, if I'm being honest, a design based on a Samoan tattoo.'

She regarded him with an impatient expression, and he realised, belatedly, that his reaction was probably one she'd encountered on a thousand earlier occasions.

'Are you Iranian?'

This time it was her turn to look surprised. For a moment he thought she wasn't going to respond but then, slowly, she raised her hands and, mockingly, clapped four times.

'Very good. No, I'm not Iranian. But my mother was.'

'I have an ear for accents,' he lied. 'And there was that, of course.' Mos pointed to the compact knapsack he'd just noticed on the floor beside her stool. A miniature of the Iranian tricolour with its conspicuous central emblem was sewn into the outer lining.

She gave a careless shrug.

'Picked that up in Teheran a few years ago when I was visiting family.'

Mos replaced his glass on the counter.

'Are you in Cork for long?'

'Not for long. I'm pursuing the sun through Western Europe. Running towards the West. Ireland is as far as I can go.' She paused. 'Good enough?'

Mos shrugged.

'I've heard dumber reasons.'

He pointed to the window.

'It went that way.'

Her laugh, pleasantly at odds with her aloof disposition, was subdued and settled around them like the final chords of a melancholic piece of music. She held out her hand and a collection of copper bangles hidden under the sleeve of her shirt slid to her wrist with a series of metallic clinks.

'You can call me Ailbhe.'

'Why. Isn't that your real name?'

She looked at him as though surprised by the question.

'No. But it will suffice.'

He accepted her hand and was surprised at the strength of her grip and the calluses on her palms. As they shook, the copper bangles encircling her wrists clinked noisily.

'Muiris O'Súilleabháin. Naturally, that's not my real name either. Just call me Mos.'

She gave a quizzical expression but said nothing. Either she'd missed the humour or simply did not find it amusing.

'When did you decide to become Cormac's better daughter?'

This time her left eyebrow arched in a puzzled manner.

'Ailbhe. It's the name of Cormac Mac Airt's other daughter. Aren't you familiar with the events of *Tóraíocht Dhiarmada agus Gráinne*?'

She shook her head and he stared at her, confused.

'But weren't you at the play with …' he nodded in the direction of the Cavern where Hegarty's group were still firmly embedded.

'No. I came in through the door at the rear of that group. They left a single seat. I have been talking with some of them, but I don't know them. And I know nothing of any play.'

'Oh. Well, Fionn Mac Cumhail—' He stopped. 'You know who he is?'

'I know who he is.'

'Right then.' He paused and regarded her with curiosity before continuing. The lack of expression on her face made her difficult to read and he was unsure if he was simply boring her. 'According to tradition, a marriage was arranged between Fionn Mac Cumhail and Gráinne, the daughter of Cormac Mac Airt, the High King of Ireland. Unfortunately, as it turned out, Gráinne was an unwilling bride. On the night of the wedding reception, she drugged the entire company and placed one of Fionn's warriors – Diarmuid Ua Duibhne – under a magical prohibition that obliged him to elope with her.

'When Fionn and his warriors woke up and came to their senses, they immediately gave pursuit. Diarmuid and Gráinne became lovers and there was a great chase, or *tóraíocht,* that lasted for several years before it all came to a drastically tragic end. As part of the subsequent peace process between Cormac Mac Airt and Fionn, Cormac offered him the hand of another of his daughters. He chose Ailbhe.'

'Not the main character, then?'

'I wouldn't worry about it. Tradition says Ailbhe was the smart one.'

'How nice. What th-'

The girl was thrust backwards as a tall figure roughly forced his way between them and grasped two pints of Guinness that had been placed on the counter. In the ensuing scuffle, the intruder's feet tangled in the straps of the knapsack, and he stumbled, spilling some of his drink over her.

Ailbhe stared down at the large stain growing on her shirt. When she looked up her expression was distinctly hostile.

Startled, Mos stared at the newcomer, astonished to recognise O'Donoghue. The journalist had apparently been drinking even more heavily since Mos' departure. His cheeks were flushed, his eyes glassy with repressed belligerence. He stared impassively at the stain on the girl's shirt.

'Mind where you put that feckin' bag,' he growled at last, punctuating this conclusion with a kick to the offending article that sent it skidding under her stool.

Mos moved off his own barstool. Catching the movement from the corner of his eye, the journalist immediately jerked around to face him.

'You!' he snarled. 'What the fuck do you want?'

Mos said nothing but held up two conciliatory palms and carefully backed away. The journalist stared at him for two or three seconds then grunted, took his drinks, and stumbled off in the direction of the cubicle.

Mos and the woman watched as he forced his way through the shifting crowd. When he'd disappeared from sight between into the shuffle of bodies, they turned to consider one another.

'Thanks for all your help,' she said icily.

She bent down to retrieve her knapsack from the floor.

'Ach, you were grand. He was drunk. You could have taken him easily.'

She gave him a long look then turned and walked away, ringlets bungy-jumping down behind her; a black curtain on her exit.

***

He'd stayed too long, of course.

Over the years he'd developed a relatively effective strategy for avoiding confrontation. This strategy usually consisted of avoiding the locations or occasions where it was most likely to occur and, for the most part, it had been successful. Although sufficiently realistic to recognise he couldn't have pre-empted the sequence of events leading up to the evening's abrupt conclusion, the incident had effectively stirred up a vengeful stew of emotions, nonetheless. Emotions that, on any other night, he'd have dismissed and brushed aside.

He sighed and shook his head. The adrenalin rush following the encounter with O'Donoghue had, at least, served to drive the warm flush of alcohol from his bloodstream. The incident had also prompted him to leave his drink untouched on the counter when he'd walked away.

He stared down at the scuffed vinyl floor tiles, his view slowly moving up to absorb the stained white walls of the cubicle.

Sitting up straight on the toilet seat, he considered the rather poor depiction of an erect penis drawn in enormous scale on the back of the door. Beneath it, a rather shaky hand informed him that 'Seán O'Driscoll eats cock'. Worse still, he also, reportedly, 'likes it up the whole'.

Further down, an even more creatively challenged author, in a fit of overwhelming romanticism, had scribbled a short poem:

> The moon is out tonight
> Your eyes are bright
> My love is forever
> I'll hold you so tight.

Look out, Séamus Heaney! Your days are numbered.

Mos chewed on a thumbnail and was seriously considering giving up and leaving when he heard the door to the 'Mens' toilet swing open and slam into the wall behind it. Stiffening, he listened carefully as some heavy-footed individual staggered inside, shoes slapping clumsily on the wet floor.

There was a loud fart, the sound of a zipper, then a happy tinkle of piss hitting the metal coating of the urinal wall with a satisfying splatter.

For the umpteenth time that night, Mos stood up on the toilet bowl and peered carefully over the cubicle wall. Standing in front of the urinal, back towards him, was O'Donoghue, sighing in satisfaction as the pressure drained from his bladder.

Stepping back down onto the floor, Mos silently opened the cubicle door. He pulled an empty beer bottle from his pocket, holding its base in the palm of his hand as he eased up behind the unsuspecting journalist.

O'Donoghue never stood a chance. It all happened faster than he could possibly have reacted to, particularly given the quantity of alcohol he'd obviously consumed. The first he knew of the assault was a diabolically sharp pain in the left kidney as something jabbed into him from behind. Before he could cry out in pain or surprise, a hand grabbed the back of his head and smashed it directly into the wall above the urinal.

Writhing in pain, he collapsed into a puddle of his own urine.

Mos returned the beer bottle to his pocket and regarded his handiwork quietly. O'Donoghue, lying on his side, shivered violently and threw up. With one final kick to the groaning journalist, Mos turned and calmly left.

Chapter Two

West Cork, Early 1960s:

The sound of the motor vehicle was audible several minutes before it finally pulled into view. A big, fuck-off Mercedes designed for wide Continental motorways; it was having a hard time of it in the confines of the narrow boreen. Struggling in low gear, the grunt of its engine reverberated through the surrounding countryside as it painfully negotiated the overgrown track, avoiding protruding fuchsia, holly branches, an old stone ditch and the deep rut of tractor tyres carved into the sodden earth.

Sitting on an old milking stool at the eastern gable of the house called Carraig Dubh, Diarmuid O'Súilleabháin rolled a cigarette, tapped it on his knee and lit it as he watched the Mercedes make its ponderous approach. He was shaking his head in disbelief when it finally pulled to a halt at the end of the lane, impeded by a rusted iron gate that hung between two solid wooden posts.

The driver's door cracked open and a plump man in the uniform of a *Garda Síochána* emerged from the vehicle. Straightening up, he threw a quick glance towards the house then reached back into the car to withdraw a uniform cap that he placed fussily on his head. When it was fixed to his satisfaction, he opened the rear door with a painful creak of hinges and bent down as though to help someone else out.

Diarmuid sighed.

'*Lá binn, lá searbh!*' he muttered under his breath. '*Mallacht ort a chinneachain!*' One day good, one day bitter. A curse on you, oul destiny!

Turning his head, he spat into a clump of nettles flowering up at the side of the house. Beside him, a mongrel hound with grey hair around its muzzle sat up stiffly from where it had been lying. It glanced over at its master as though seeking a lead on how to respond to the visitors. Receiving no guidance, it growled and released a half-hearted bark.

'*Ah, dún do chlob, a mhadra!*' Shut your mouth, dog! 'You're bit feckin' late to be getting all fierce on me now.'

He looked up at the sky where stained, grey cumulus was blowing in from the sea, spawning across the heavens like some massive, airborne fungus. Portions of the cloudbank struck the summit of Cnoc Daod, the rocky edifice that dominated the landscape and squeezed the thin strip of farmland between its extensive base and the waters of Cuan Baoi.

Diarmuid turned on his stool and blew cigarette smoke out in the direction of An t-Oileán Mór. Focusing on the island's flat capped Roan

Inis rock and the bracing tang of salt in the fresh breeze up from the sea, he ignored the approaching clomp of heavy feet and the splash of muddy puddles. It was only when their shadows darkened the earth around him that he turned to acknowledge his visitors. Standing before him were the Garda sergeant and a fair-haired young boy of about seven or eight years of age.

'Hello, Diarmuid.'

'*Dia duit, a Phádraig,*' he answered.

'Don't be talking to me in that dead tongue, Diarmuid. English will do fine and it's well you know my name is Patrick.'

He smiled. It was not a particularly friendly smile.

'But you can call me Sergeant.'

Diarmuid shrugged.

The Garda took off his hat and wiped a band of sweat from his forehead. 'Lovely day. Might have a mild winter of it yet.'

'Yerra, 'tis grand.'

'Would you be wondering why I'm here at all, Diarmuid?'

'Why would I be wondering why you were here, Pádraig? Are ye not here to visit me? I know there's been no complaints.'

The Garda flinched, annoyed by the repeated gaelicisation of his name.

'That's true. There's been no complaint this time.' He pulled out a handkerchief, emptied a nostril full of wet snot into it and stuffed it back into his trouser pocket. 'I'm here because of the we'an.'

He angled his head towards the child who was standing quietly with his head down, staring fixedly at his shoes. There was a long silence and although Diarmuid had the impression that the Garda was awaiting some reaction, he was unsure what was expected of him.

'Say Hello to your nephew, Diarmuid.'

Diarmuid was surprised but loath to give the sergeant any satisfaction. He absorbed the statement beneath a veneer of indifference as he studied the boy with new interest. There was a lot of his brother Séamus in him all right, he realised. He had the same angular face and nose, the same fair-coloured hair. Apart from that he was like any other child of his age. A bit skinny and in need of a haircut, but his clothes were new and recently ironed.

'Is that right?' he said simply. 'Séamus' boy.'

'That's right,'

'Will Séamus not be a bit put out with you bringing his boy out here?'

'Ach, I wouldn't think so.'

He paused.

'You see, the thing is, Diarmuid, your brother Séamus is dead.'

This time Diarmuid was unable to hide his reaction for the news hit him like the kick from a horse's hoof. For several seconds, he stared at the policeman. Then his head filled with cotton wool and he felt himself slump back against the wall of the house.

The Garda made no move to approach or help him. The boy observed him with curiosity before quietly moving aside to where the dog was whining. Crouching down on one knee, he patted it on the head.

'When?' Diarmuid managed at last but he could hear his voice creaking with the effort.

'About a week ago. One of the neighbours called over to their place and found the door wide open. Séamus was lying at the bottom of the stairs with the bedroom cupboard on top of him. It was a big thing, thick bog oak that weighed a tonne. 'Twould have taken two or three strong men to lift but it's obvious he was trying to slide it down the stairs by himself. When he lost his footing, it fell and crushed him.'

Diarmuid tried to listen to what the Garda was saying but none of it seemed to be making any sense. It was as though he was listening to some garbled, unidentifiable tongue.

'I'm sorry for your troubles, Diarmuid.'

'No you're not,' he spat back.

'No, I'm not,' the sergeant admitted.

'You're the cause of most of my troubles, Pádraig. You and the rest of your bully boys in the *Gardaí*. Besides, you never even liked Séamus. You made his life a misery when he was a young fella.'

Diarmuid took a deep breath and left it out slowly. He was embarrassed, angry at himself for exposing such weakness in front of his old adversary yet, at the same time, surprised by the extent of the bitterness pouring up out of him. Some untapped well of despair had been lurking quietly beneath the surface all these years, he realised, a dormant spring of resentment to which he had been completely oblivious prior to the policeman's visit.

He continued to fume in silence as he pulled his thoughts together. The sergeant did not deign to respond, diverting his attention to the boy, who was down on his knees playing with the dog. Delighted with the attention, the dog had discarded any sense of loyalty and transferred all allegiance to the stranger. It rolled onto its back and wriggled happily as the boy tickled its stomach.

'Was the boy there?'

'He was. Never left his father. We think he was there alone with the body for three or four days. The neighbour said he was holding his father's hand when he found him.'

'Jesus Christ!' Diarmuid closed his eyes, an image of the child bent down over the body of his father forming, unbidden, in his mind. He shook his head to rid himself of the morbid scene. 'Did you ask him what happened?'

'We did. Ach, but he's soft in the head. Didn't understand a word we said to him, did you, son?'

They both glanced down to where the boy was absorbed in his play with the dog. He gave no indication of having heard what had just been said. There was something wrong, Diarmuid thought to himself, something unnatural about the way he just sat there obliviously as the two men discussed his father's death.

'Is it that he's deaf?'

'No. No, he's not deaf. He's just simple.'

'So why'd you bring him here?'

'His father is dead, Diarmuid. The nearest neighbour told us the mother disappeared years ago. They've no idea where she's got to or even where she came from in the first place. You're the closest living relation, in fact you're the only living relation that we're aware of.'

Realisation hit Diarmuid.

'God above! You want me to take the little fella in, is that it? That's fucking bollocks, Pádraig. I don't know how to take care of a child. And this one obviously needs care.'

'That's all well and good, Diarmuid, but if you don't take him in then he goes into state care and up for adoption. The boy needs a legal guardian. That's the law.'

'The law, the law! I don't give tuppence for the law!'

'Don't I know it well, Diarmuid.'

They stood in silence, their history of conflict and mutual dislike clouding the air between them.

'What's his name?'

'We don't know his name. He hasn't been able to tell us.'

'Well, what age is he?'

'We were hoping you could tell us. We don't know anything about him.'

'Sure, how would I know! I haven't seen Séamus in years. I didn't know he'd come back to Beara.'

He shook his head and turned away to conceal his despair.

'Jesus Christ, I didn't even know he had a son.'

'Well, he did. Although it's feckin' obvious he didn't bother fulfilling any of his responsibilities in that regard. Father Harrington and old Doctor Casey don't know anything about the child, and we couldn't find any paperwork on him – no birth certificate, nothing. Apparently, your brother didn't feel it was necessary to bother registering the birth.'

He scowled at Diarmuid.

'A serious offence.'

He grunted and shifted the waistline of his trousers to accommodate his girth more comfortably.

'It's fierce annoying. I'm doing me best to fill out the report, but I keep finding all these great big gaping holes where the facts should be.' He paused and studied the boy, thoughtfully sucking his teeth. 'Well, from the look of him I'd put him at about seven years old. What do you think?'

'Jesus, Pádraig. Does it actually matter?'

'We have to report all the facts, Diarmuid. In a case like this every statement has to have a confirmed origin, every piece of evidence has to have its own file and a number. We're not in the dark ages any more. It's the modern world. Everything in black and white, that's the future.'

Diarmuid rolled his eyes.

'Well, the future can feck off!'

Ignoring this outburst, the policeman unbuttoned his tunic pocket and pulled out a small notebook and a pencil. Licking the tip of the pencil, he placed the dampened nib on the paper, speaking the words out aloud as he wrote:

Age of unknown child found at the residence of Séamus O' Sullivan – seven years.

Holding it up in the light to compensate for his myopic vision, the Garda admired his handiwork. He clicked his tongue in satisfaction as he replaced the notebook and pencil, then from his side pocket withdrew a bulky envelope bearing the official stamp of the Department of Welfare. He handed them to Diarmuid.

'There you go! Them's the adoption consent papers. I'll leave the young fella with you and see how you go. If you don't want to keep him just sign these and drop them back at the station in town and we'll take care of the rest.' His smile was grim. 'Sure, you know where we are.'

Diarmuid's face remained expressionless and after a moment the sergeant shuffled impatiently.

'Well, I can't stay around here all day.'

'You're right, Pádraig. You'd better go.'

The Garda glared at him then turned and started back to his vehicle.

'*Slán abhaile.*' Safe home.

The sergeant didn't bother turning. 'Sorry Diarmuid. Don't understand that old rubbish.'

'*Gread leat mar sin, a phlicadh.*'

The policeman stiffened in mid-stride, threw an angry glance behind him then turned on his heel and continued on his way.

'You understood that, ye fecker!' muttered Diarmuid.

He watched the sergeant's waddling progress down the lane with a mixture of powerlessness and frustration, achieving only minor satisfaction at the sight of the plump policeman struggling to climb the flimsy gate. For a second it looked as though it might collapse beneath his bulk and crash to the ground. Unfortunately, it held, and any hopes of petty retribution were dashed as the policeman got into his car and started the engine.

It took the departing Mercedes several attempts to reverse back out the narrow track, navigating around the tight corner in a series of awkward, jerking movements.

'*Cén breall*' Diarmuid thought to himself. What a moron! What in God's name was he trying to prove, bringing such a cumbersome feckin' beast of a car into such a tiny road? It was surely a place of overwhelming egotism, Pádraig's modern world.

When the vehicle had finally disappeared, he breathed deeply and returned to his stool. Up on Cnoc Daod, the sunlight was playing along the hill's flanks, creating a myriad of patterns on the gigantic stone slabs.

You see, the thing is, Diarmuid, your brother Séamus is dead.

He felt empty suddenly, as though all substance, all those things that held him together inside had somehow been siphoned away. The policeman's words rattled around in his head like a stone in a tin can but he was unable to make sense of them, to absorb their truth and make it real.

He stood up. It was getting late and there was work to be done.

And then, of course, there was the child to take care of.

He turned to watch the boy, who was now chasing the dog around *An Párc Mór* - the wide field that spread around the front of the house. The dog was enjoying itself, barking, rolling on the ground, waiting for the boy to catch up and then sprinting away again before he could reach him. He was struck by how silent the boy was in his play. There were the usual sounds of physical exertion, the grunts and the exclamations, but there was no laughter, no expression of the normal carefree elation of child's play.

Diarmuid cursed and turned to spit into the nettles again.

'*Lá binn, lá searbh.*'

***

For the remainder of the afternoon Diarmuid attacked the farm chores with rigorous intensity, pushing himself beyond the point of fatigue to drive all thought of his brother from his mind. He didn't doubt that reality would sink in eventually. Deep down, he understood that he was simply putting off the inevitable, putting the death of his brother *ar an méar fhada* – on the long finger.

He paused and looked out to sea again.

He would face up to it eventually, of course. In the meantime, it was just enough to be able to put his head down and lose himself in his work. Later he could deal with the guilt, the recriminations.

He stood up and stretched. He was a tall man without an inch of fat and still remarkably sprightly for his sixty-plus years. Nevertheless, his back ached and he was sweating heavily from the effort of chopping the fallen ash trees into a suitable size for firewood. The boy and the dog, meanwhile, continued their games in the fields around the house. The dog had managed to find a small ball and there were plenty of rabbits to chase through the briars and the withered, rust-coloured fern.

Despite himself, Diarmuid found that he was growing irritated by the dog's behaviour. He scowled as he observed it running around and fetching the ball like some spoilt city pup instead of the hard-working old farm dog it was supposed to be. He knew he had no valid reason to feel betrayed by the animal's fickle acceptance of the youngster; nevertheless, he did.

Madra amaidach! Stupid dog!

When he'd cut and stacked the wood and milked the cows and completed everything else that needed completing, the sun was starting to sink behind the hills. Exhausted, he stopped to rest and pulled out the makings of another cigarette at a stone wall to the west of the house, one of the few spots still touched by the setting sun. Leaning against the wall, he rolled a fresh smoke and watched the sun begin its slow descent behind the girth of Cnoc Daod, momentarily losing himself in the deepening shadows of its rugged surface.'

After a while, he stood up again, ground the cigarette butt into the soil with his boot and walked around the yard looking for another chore to occupy his attention. Unable to find anything suitable in the yard, he turned his attention to the house.

The white-washed stone building was typical of most homes along the peninsula. Small but compact, it had two storeys, a grey slate roof, three north-facing windows on the top floor and two on the ground floor. A rectangular porch protruded from the front door, an extension onto the original building.

Diarmuid had lived in the house all his life, although it had originally been constructed by his father. He remembered it as a family home but now there was no family. His mother had died in the 1920s, his father ten years later. Now Séamus too was gone.

Over time, with the departure of his family, the house had lost its warmth, that intangible but perceptible sense of love and closeness that could soak into the walls of a building and make it something more. The memories and emotions had long since evaporated from those walls. The building was no longer a home but served a more straightforward function as a habitat, an austere residence in which he ate and slept and sheltered from the rain.

His brother Séamus had left the farm under trying circumstances, a year before his father had passed away. In his absence, and as the elder brother, ownership of the farm and the house had transferred to Diarmuid on the proviso that it would be shared with his brother should he ever return.

He hadn't.

Over the years, Diarmuid had made several structural improvements, including the porch, some updated plumbing and numerous repairs and replacements of the slate roof tiles. He'd also built a hay barn, and a stone milking shed that had cost him next to nothing apart from the investment of labour. In Beara, at least, there was no shortage of free stone.

He'd maintained the house to such exacting standards, in fact, that it currently required no major attention, certainly nothing that he could implement in the little time remaining before sunset.

As always, when he contemplated his home, his thoughts turned to his father. A true perfectionist, his father had spent a lot of time learning the requisite skills from renowned builders in the locality and had made sure he had all the necessary materials before putting their advice into practical application. The precision of his measurements was evident, not only in the exact alignment of the wooden rafters overhead but in the smooth straight lines of the walls. The resulting structure, firm and completely leak-proof, was testament to his craftsmanship and planning.

His father had also sought advice from the local *bean feasa* – the wise woman – to ensure it would be a lucky house. According to his father's version of events, the *bean feasa* had instructed him to remove his cap and throw it up into the air at the location where he'd intended to lay the foundations. If the cap landed there, she'd told him, it'd be an indication that the house did not impinge on any Sidhe path and would be safe from otherworldly intrusion. If the wind took his cap, however, he was warned to avoid it and lay the foundations where it eventually came to rest.

The cap had fallen straight to the ground.

His father's joke was that he'd made sure to follow these instructions on a windless day, demonstrating the practical form of 'spirituality' one acquired over many years of dealing with the competing values of evolution and tradition, of new ways and old ways. Knowing his father as he did, however, Diarmuid had no doubt that had some luckless squall taken the cap, he would also have changed his plans with respect to the location.

Such respect for traditional considerations had been typical of his father. He was a man whose upbringing had been steeped in the lore of older generations, of local knowledge garnered over hundreds of years through observation and subtle refinement. His father had also lived through some difficult times and the kind of hardships that people of his own generation knew of through the talk of the *Seandaoine*, the old people, but had never – thank God – experienced themselves. He had survived a childhood rife with disease and malnutrition and his own parents had survived *An Gorta Mór* – that great famine the old people still spoke of fearfully in whispers.

His father had done his best to pass on his language, his belief systems and his knowledge to his sons. In this regard, his efforts with Diarmuid had not been as successful as he might have hoped. Although they had spoken Gaelic effortlessly in the home and had enjoyed the stories and tales well enough, he'd never really placed much value in the instructions and learnings those tales contained. Although the younger Séamus had loved the stories, Diarmuid had always felt they were a little irrelevant, a little backward, but was too afraid of hurting his father's feelings by saying so outright. During a visit to the hospital in Cork as a child when he'd received treatment for tuberculosis, Diarmuid had been enchanted by the bright lights of the city and ever since they'd had a hold on him. From that time on, nothing at home had ever been as good as the city. Not the language, the stories, or the traditions.

Over the years, Diarmuid had come to re-evaluate and recognise the value of his father's teachings but by then, of course, the world had moved on. He'd often wondered how far Séamus would have been influenced by those instructions, for he'd taken to them with a lot more enthusiasm than Diarmuid. Now, of course, it was too late, and he would never have the chance to ask him. The last time he'd seen his brother had been at his father's funeral and even then they had barely spoken. Séamus had prepared the small gravestones that now marked both parents' graves. He'd selected a suitable flat rock down at the coast then carved the words of an old Gaelic poem into the gritty material and poured a glass of whiskey over the grave. Just as his father would have wanted.

Tradition had been fulfilled.

Diarmuid sighed.

And now it was upon him to ensure that tradition was followed once more. So that Séamus could rest in peace.

***

As soon as the sun sank behind the hill, night descended upon them like a murder of crows. They retreated inside and Diarmuid laid a fire to ward off the chill: dried twigs for kindling, built up with scraps of dusty turf from the shed to the rear of the house. Within minutes, it was burning fiercely and he was able to throw on some larger sods.

For dinner, Diarmuid prepared a rabbit caught in a wire snare he'd laid earlier that morning in An Páirc Beag – the small field to the west of the house. He was pleased with his catch. He'd come across the rabbit path a week earlier and his snare had delivered dinner twice since then.

Once he'd skinned it, he butchered the animal, diced the meat and fried it in a pan with onions and melted butter. When it had all sizzled to a deep golden brown, he tossed the contents into a pot with some herbs, carrots and spuds then brought it to the boil. Afterwards, he left it bubble at a low temperature while he washed the knives in a bucket of water. Soon, the rich aroma of rabbit stew began to waft through the tiny kitchen.

He returned to the living room while the stew simmered, settled into the rocking chair by the fireplace and poked absently at the embers with a fire iron. The young fella, he noticed, had taken up position in the far corner of the room, by the door. He seemed to have accepted the fact he was staying with Diarmuid. All the same. although he appeared content to sit there staring into space and fondling the dog's ears, Diarmuid could tell that the boy was alert and keeping a watch on him from the corner of his eye.

He studied the child for several minutes, struggling to associate his presence with the news of his brother's passing but unable to make it straight in his head. He was, he realised, at a loss as to what to do with the child. He had no experience with children and had no notion where to start. Rocking slowly in the chair, he lit his pipe with a twig from the fire and brooded in silence behind a cloud of tobacco smoke. The heat burned into his calves, relaxing the ache in his limbs.

He sighed.

He was tired. Too tired and too distressed to confront such issues effectively at the moment. It would be best, he decided, to simply ignore the child for the remainder of the night, to treat him as he would treat a foreign stranger to his house until he knew what to do with him. In the morning, when his head was clear, he would deal to it.

The decision gave him some respite. Although he acknowledged it for the temporary evasion it was, it served as a course of action – or inaction – for now. Pulling an old leather-bound book of poetry from the shelf behind him, he put on his reading glasses and started to read.

The turf burned low and even.

***

When the stew was ready, Diarmuid filled two bowls and placed them on the table in the sitting room, with half a loaf of soda bread, a knob of butter and a clay pitcher of cold spring water. The boy's nose twitched as he eyed the stew bowl hungrily, but he remained by the corner.

'Food,' said Diarmuid. He gestured towards the table. 'We're aiting now.' He picked up a fork and mimed eating from the pot.

Cautiously, the boy approached and sat at the table on the side furthest from Diarmuid. Picking up his spoon, he ate slowly and although he was obviously ravenous, he maintained a constant vigil on the older man's movements.

'So, is it true then? Are you my nephew?'

The boy glanced up and peered at him over the edge of his bowl, surprising Diarmuid, who'd expected him to shrink away as he'd done on every other occasion. This time, however, he returned Diarmuid's stare with an attentiveness that was as surprising as it was unsettling. Sitting there, he realised with a start that there was intelligence in those eyes, and it was not that the boy was simple, but that he simply had not been engaging.

He slumped back in his chair and, with a weary sigh, pushed the discovery to the back of his mind.

'Tomorrow,' he decided as he returned his attention to his meal. 'I'll deal to it tomorrow.'

***

After dinner, Diarmuid made up a bed by the fire – a straw-filled mattress covered with a sheet and a pair of blankets. The boy was obviously exhausted for he climbed into the bed compliantly and pulled the blankets around him before turning away to the wall. Within seconds of lying down, he was fast asleep.

Diarmuid extinguished the lanterns then climbed upstairs to the bedroom where he undressed and crawled into his own bed. The day had finally caught up with him; he could feel its weight tugging down on him as he lay there. He smiled grimly. He had, at least, achieved his objective. He was now so physically exhausted he was unable to experience the pain of his brother's demise.

Blowing out the candle, he pulled the night around him. Shortly before midnight he was fast asleep.

Chapter Three

Cork City, 2008

Stepping out of McCarthy's pub and onto the windswept street was like stepping into a darkened freezer. Mos stood on the pavement as his eyes adjusted to the shadowed surroundings. He shivered, assailed by the dramatic drop in temperature and a glacial wind that sliced through his overcoat.

Despite the cold, the worst of the weather appeared to have passed. The wind was easing, dropping from a force eight to an occasional militant gust. The rain, in a display of uncharacteristic restraint, had softened to a mist-like drizzle. Of the earlier thunder and lightning there was no sign. The storm, it seemed, had simply worn itself out.

A movement blossomed in the corner of his eye and he turned to find Ailbhe, the girl from the pub, crouched in the shelter of a nearby doorway. Resting on one knee, she had her back at an angle to him, oblivious to his presence. He watched as she rummaged through her backpack, finally withdrawing a flat hat and some kind of oversized black poncho that she proceeded to slip over her head and wrap around herself.

Christ! It's Mediterranean Fashion Week.

In down-town Cork.

Mos' lip curled in disapproval. The chic, flimsy covering might have worked on some glitzy Continental boulevard, but it was going to be hopelessly ineffectual against Irish rainfall.

He continued to watch as she stood up, slung the knapsack over her shoulder then pulled a cigarette and a lighter from her pocket. She made several attempts at lighting the cigarette, but the flint produced nothing more than a rasping click. Exasperated, she flung it into a nearby litter bin.

Mos chose that moment to step forward and hold out his own lighter, a battered Zippo that had seen better days. Startled by his sudden appearance, she recoiled, then relaxed as she recognised him, although her mouth tightened perceptibly. She accepted the Zippo and lit her cigarette. The lighter was returned with an exhalation of blue smoke but with no expression of gratitude.

'Not much baggage for a traveller,' commented Mos.

'I travel light.'

'Fair enough.'

Mos bent into the breeze and lit his own cigarette in the nook of his cupped palms. When he looked up she was still standing there, studying a crumpled tourist map of the city.

'Which way you headed?' he asked.

She looked at him coldly. 'The Western Road. I have a hostel there.'

'I'm headed that way. Why don't you walk with me?' He pulled up the collar of his coat and glanced at the sky. 'Who knows. We might be lucky and see a cab we can flag down.'

'No thanks.'

Her voice was polite but not particularly amicable.

'You wouldn't be much protection if we were attacked.'

She turned him a sudden and decidedly aggressive glare.

'Unless I offered you up as a potential sacrifice.'

Mos shrugged.

'I could get some help while you held them off.'

There was a flicker in her eyes and for a moment he imagined he saw the trace of a grin then, belatedly, recognised it as a grimace. He gestured towards the map.

'At least you won't get lost.'

She thought about it for several seconds.

'All right,' she conceded finally with a conspicuous absence of enthusiasm. 'You can show me the way ... but that's all you need to show me.'

Mos, not usually a person easily surprised, stared at her in surprise.

'What?'

She observed him with a dispassionate expression.

'I don't want you to have any unrealistic expectations.'

Mos laughed out loud, delighted by such outrageous bravado. He considered her as she stood there brazenly, exuding all the disdain of a Wall Street Banker at a hippy peace festival.

'Grand. I'll try to repress all expectations.'

Her mouth tightened again as she watched him deposit a beer bottle into the litter bin. 'Come on, then,' he called, as he started walking. 'It's this way.'

After some initial hesitation, she shook her head and followed. He paused, allowing her to catch up and march in step beside him. They continued for several hundred metres without speaking before she broke the silence.

'Your home is on the Western Road?'

He shook his head.

'I live by the university. My real home is in a place called Beara. Down in West Cork. You probably wouldn't know it.'

'Oh, I know it all right.'

Mos glanced sideways at her, taken aback by the bitterness in her response. She lunged ahead abruptly, increasing her pace with long strides that ate up the distance. and he was obliged to stretch his own step to catch up with her. He studied her closely as he drew alongside.

'So where do you live when you're not chasing the sun?'

'No particular place. I've stayed in Bucharest, off and on, for two years. I move around a lot for work.' She drew a kick at the sodden remnants of a fast-food container and sent it spiralling several feet ahead of them. 'It is my belief,' she declared, '…that the action of travelling overrides the importance of the actual destination.'

'I see. Well, that's all very fuckin' zen. What do you do to support this jet-setting lifestyle?'

'I work in the circus industry.'

Mos halted in mid-stride and stared at her.

'Fuck off! You work for a circus?'

Ailbhe too had drawn to a halt, frowning at his apparent scepticism.

'Yes.'

Her voice was brittle.

'Big tops and clowns and stuff?'

She shook her head angrily, drew herself upright.

'I was Ailbhe the Magnificent, Hellion of the High Wire, Titan of the Trapeze.'

Producing a glittery business card out of the air, she handed it to Mos. He looked down at the silver embossed calligraphy. The words repeated exactly what she'd just said except that here, 'Ailbhe' was spelt 'Ollva'. Suddenly, their earlier conversation made sense. When she'd introduced herself she had been using her stage name, a moniker that, due to his own background, he'd interpreted as 'Ailbhe'.

'You *was* Ailbhe the Magnificent?'

She gave him a haughty look.

'I stopped two weeks ago. At present I'm …' she yawned. '… between careers. I had to leave Bucharest in a rush.'

'What was the hurry?'

'A last-minute decision. I had to go to a funeral. That's the reason I'm in Ireland.'

'Oh, I'm sorry. Friend of yours?'

'No. My father.'

'Shit!'

'That's okay. We weren't very close.'

***

Despite the relatively early hour, the city was practically deserted. As they ambled through the lonely streets, they only encountered a single other hard-core pedestrian. Most of the population, it seemed, had sensibly decided to jettison their social arrangements and remain at home.

Naturally, because they were actively seeking a taxi, there wasn't a single one to be found. Like the pavements, the roads were bereft of traffic and had taken on a desolate, almost abandoned appearance. The few vehicles that did intermittently appear, sped by in a cloud of spray and disappeared back into the gloom without slowing.

Traversing the exposed length of Patrick's Bridge, they followed the curve of Patrick's Street down to the Grand Parade. By the time they reached the Washington Street intersection, the rain had started to fall again. Smattering at first, it surreptitiously grew to a light drizzle that abruptly exploded into a full-fledged downpour. Sheltering in the entrance to Saint Augustine's Church, they stared uneasily as curtains of rain swept down the street towards them, rippling in the orange gleam of streetlights like a parade of forlorn phantoms.

It soon became clear that the inundation was not going to ease and with no other viable alternative, they continued their journey. Exposed to the full force of the elements, they were thoroughly soaked within a minute. Cold and miserable, they took shelter once more at the first available refuge: the bright entrance of another pub. Momentarily dazzled by yellow light showering through the opaque glass panels and the muffled sound of laughter from within, they stood beneath the underhang of the illuminated doorway. Mos glanced at his companion, who nodded her head.

He pulled the door open and stepped inside.

The pub was markedly more upmarket than McCarthy's. The furniture and furnishings were new, the table surfaces well-polished and the bar taps gleaming in the glare of bright overhead lighting. A number of discreet speakers in the walls and ceiling, emitted soft, new-age music to the small crowd of well-heeled drinkers.

Despite the loud murmur of conversations, the pub was little more than half full, the patrons congregated mostly around the central bar. Mos selected a table immediately adjacent to a brick fireplace where a blazing coal fire sent waves of warm air into the room. Shedding their sodden outer layers, they placed them on the back of some chairs facing the flames. The rain had penetrated Ailbhe's poncho, soaking the jacket beneath and she removed this as well, hanging it over a second chair. Mos, noticeably drier due to the water-resistant material of his overcoat, left her and shouldered his way to the bar where he caught the barman's attention. A few minutes later, he rejoined Ailbhe by the fire with two pints of stout. Placing both glasses on the table, he slid one across towards her, drew up a seat and sat down.

'So', he said. 'Tell me about your Da.'

Ailbhe arched one eyebrow. 'Not much for the small talk, are you?'

'Best to get straight to the heart of things, I reckon.'

'There's not that much to tell. He's quite dead.'

'You said he was being buried in Beara.'

'That's right. Near Na hAoraí.'

She tapped the pint glass with the tip of her fingernail, producing a soft clicking noise that was barely audible above the chatter from the surrounding conversations.

'He returned to Ireland five years ago and resettled in Na hAoraí. He used to like it there because he could look across the bay at the Iveragh Peninsula without ever having to step foot on it.'

A somewhat reflective expression crossed her face.

'Or so I was told.'

'He was Irish?'

She nodded.

'His people were from the Iveragh Peninsula. He was desperate to leave as a child. He eventually got away when he was sixteen and ended up working on the Continent for several years. That's where he met my mother. And then …'

Her voice trailed off.

'And then …?' he prompted.

'And then, there was me.'

This statement was delivered with a brief, cynical smile.

'After that, he brought us back to live in Na hAoraí.'

'Us? *You* lived in Na hAoraí?'

Her gaze had swung away to take in the surrounding tables. It took a leisurely moment before her attention returned to settle on him. He could not tell if this was an affectation, done intentionally to provoke him, or simply a personal characteristic.

'We lived a few miles outside the village. Until I was six or seven. That was with my mother, mostly.'

Mos said nothing, imagining the kind of reception such a foreign-looking family would have received in rural, conservative, nineteen-sixties West Cork. It surely wouldn't have been easy.

'And yer Da?'

'He was usually away for work on the Continent.'

'Oh. A diplomat?'

For a moment she stared at him as though he'd spoken in a different language. Then she startled him by laughing out loud. It was a harsh, almost bitter laugh and she stopped suddenly as though she'd caught herself revealing something she shouldn't have.

'No, he wasn't. My father was the most undiplomatic person you could possibly meet. He was a ringmaster. That's how he met my mother. She was part of an Iranian acrobatic troupe touring around Europe in the early eighties. He was quite famous back then actually. He had his ringmaster duties, of course, but he also had a remarkably powerful voice. People would travel hundreds of miles to see him perform an act where he'd smash wine glasses by raising the pitch of his voice.'

'Uh-huh.'

Some trace of the scepticism he felt must have been evident in his voice for she leaned forward so abruptly that their faces were less than an inch apart.

'You don't believe me.'

Mos drew back, extending the distance between them. Her brown eyes, he noticed, had an unusually dark hue that gave her gaze an unsettling intensity.

'I've known you for less than an hour. So far you've given me a false name, you've almost got me involved in a bar-brawl, you've told me you're a circus performer and now you're claiming to have a ring-master father who breaks glasses by singing at them.'

He shrugged.

'Yerra, I dunno. Sure, maybe it's true.'

'You asked,' she said. 'I answered. Either it's true or it isn't.'

'Shit, girl, you're in Ireland now. Over here, it is *and* it isn't.'

A strange expression spread over her face and she stood up so quickly that for a moment, he thought he'd pushed her too far and that she'd decided to leave. Instead, she simply turned, pushed her chair two or three feet back from the table and pressed down on its arms as though testing its strength. In one swift movement, she rolled forwards onto the chair, taking her weight on the arms and raising both legs off the floor until they were stretched high and straight, vertical above her body.

Within the pub, all conversation ceased as seasoned drinkers stopped in mid-sip to stare at this unusual development. The soft, synthesised music in the background seemed to highlight the eerie silence as, arms straining, Ailbhe held her position for another ten seconds. Finally, with another seamless movement, she allowed her legs to drop to the floor and, at the last moment, flipped up backwards from the chair to land on her feet with the elegant poise of a professional gymnast.

The room burst into applause and for several minutes she was surrounded by people slapping her on the back and urging her to accept a drink. When the clamour finally settled and her newfound fans had drifted reluctantly back to neglected friends and discarded conversations, she returned to her seat, smirked smugly at Mos, and swallowed the contents of her beer glass with a single gulp.

'No comment?' she asked.

He returned her gaze.

'It's still raining,' he said.

***

'So, let's talk about you.'

Mos looked across the table, gave a cynical smile but said nothing.

'If I heard correctly earlier, you're some kind of historian or archaeologist.'

For a moment it looked as though he was going to remain silent. Then he shrugged, as though conceding some undefined point. 'From a professional perspective, I guess I'm both.'

'You don't look like an historian.'

'So, I'm told.'

'Shouldn't you have white hair or a beard or something? How do you explain that youthful composure to your colleagues?'

'Hallucinogenic drugs. Fetish sex.'

'Sex with history?'

'Plenty of sex in history. Otherwise, we wouldn't be here today.'

She smiled thinly at that.

'I see. Do you go and dig up ruins then?'

'Not really. I've done some but I usually just analyse the findings. These days, I mostly specialise in finding sites where the ruins have disappeared, places or structures that have slipped through the cracks of memory and recorded history.'

He lifted his glass and peered distractedly at it.

'Or which were never recorded in the first place.'

'How very mysterious. Is there some clever process for that then?'

He made a dismissive gesture, as though to say it was perfectly obvious.

'Research mostly. I do a lot of research. Ancient manuscripts, council land archives, old maps, reference books, topographical investigations, local stories. If I find a reference to anything interesting, I follow it up and search some more. Once I've identified a promising location, I'll carry out an initial site analysis. If it looks as though it has some historical potential, then I apply for funding or contact the real archaeologists who move in to do the excavation.'

'You make much money from that?'

'I make a living from that.'

She nodded but it seemed to him as though she was losing interest in the topic. She grew quiet and he watched her gaze drift across the room to a door with a sign marked 'beer garden'.

51

Lifting the knapsack up onto her knee, she pulled out a transparent plastic bag and held it discretely so that he could see the contents; a packet of rollies, some tobacco and a handful of grass.

'I'm bored with talk. Do you smoke?'

'Sure. I just don't inhale.'

She looked at him blankly.

'Bill Clinton's immortal line on cannabis. The equivalent of "I drank but I didn't swallow".'

'I ate but I didn't digest.'

He laughed but she shook her head. She had already tired of the game.

***

The beer garden consisted of a walled-in courtyard about thirty-six metres square. A raised balcony with a wide, sloping awning ran the length of three of the walls. The fourth had a poorly painted depiction of a beach scene that was strikingly out of place in the waterlogged enclosure. The centre of the courtyard was taken up by a bleak sea of concrete with a single break in its uniform, grey surface: a tiny island of mildewed grass, so small it looked as though someone had sneezed.

They stood beneath the awning by a wooden cask that had been converted into a rough table and stared out at the rainwater pooling around two sunken drains. Ailbhe sprinkled a mixture of tobacco and cannabis onto a narrow strip of cigarette paper, rolled it into an almost flawless cylinder and ran her tongue along the edge to seal it perfectly. She lit the joint, raised it to her lips and took a shallow toke before passing it to Mos. He'd just started to draw on it himself when she turned and unexpectedly addressed him.

'Why history?'

He exhaled slowly.

'What do you mean?'

'Why did you get into history? Why do you find it so interesting? It's all old stuff, isn't it? Things from long ago. Things that are done. Finished.'

He regarded her for several seconds, uncomprehending.

'History is never finished. Everything that we are, everything we say or do, is predicated by the genes or the actions of the people who preceded us.'

She grimaced. 'That's a depressing thought.'

'I wouldn't worry about it. We've just as much potential to fuck things up for our own descendants as they did.'

'Very reassuring.' She stared into her beer glass without speaking, swirling the residue of foam around the thick translucent base. She had a small scar, he realised. One he hadn't noticed earlier. A white, half-moon crescent on her cheek, just below her left eye.

'Don't take it personally, but studying history seems … an indulgence. I can't see how it could be a priority when we've got so many urgent issues to deal with in the present day.'

'Most people don't,' he conceded. 'But I think you'll find most of today's issues are a result of yesterday's actions. Studying history helps us to understand what happened back then. That's critical because if we don't, we'll never be able to resolve the impact those issues are having on us in the present. And we'll be doomed to repeat the same old mistakes that …'

He broke off as he felt the first buzz of the drug warming up the inside of his head. He handed the roach back to Ailbhe.

'The problem is that, as a society, we have a child's understanding of the passage of time. Most individuals see it as some kind of linear line with a defined past, a present and a future and no interaction between any of them.'

'Whereas there is,' she prompted wryly.

'Of course, there is. There isn't any line. All of humanity's actions – present, past and future – are intrinsically linked.'

He shrugged.

'But that's human nature. In some ways we haven't really evolved much since the apes came down from the trees and started scratching their arses on two legs rather than on all fours.'

He swirled the dregs of his stout, watching the black liquid merge with the brown-bubbled froth of the head.

'Our preoccupations are still dominated by the immediacy of our senses, the things that impact on us directly in the present as opposed to indirect impacts from the past or the future. The indirect impacts, of course, are the ones that are hardest to conceptualise. That's why we struggle to work strategically on future impacts like resource scarcity or climate change. As for impacts from the past, they're often hard to recognise even though they tend to dominate our lives.'

'Pleeeease,' she said with a sceptical drawl. 'That is such a cop-out!'

'What?' He stared at her.

'Believing that events of the past have such an impact on us. I'd like to think *I'm* responsible for my own actions, not my parents or my grandparents or some great unknown ancestor I've never even heard of.'

'Sure, you would. And you are to an extent. But past events have also impacted on you. You're just not aware of it.'

He leaned forwards onto the barrel. 'There's a sliding scale of historical impact. Some – usually the more recent events in the local area – affect you on a personal, immediate level. Others affect you at a more limited, more generic level. These are the events that tend to occur a much longer time ago or off in some distant region. Take the Russian Revolution or the Fall of Rome, for example. Both occurred several hundred years ago, and both were geographically distant from where you or your parents were born. Nevertheless, they've had an influence on you in that the first dictated current geo-politics in the world you live in and the second had a strong influence on what language you and I are speaking today.'

Ailbhe seemed to lose interest. She turned away and stared out at the dripping darkness for over a minute. As the silence stretched and intensified, she seemed to fade into the gloom as shadows from the surrounding walls peeled away and clustered about her.

'Wouldn't it be wonderful,' she said suddenly, 'to be able to start afresh? To start on a clean slate and …'

Intrigued, Mos observed her covertly and wondered where she was going to go with this fresh digression. Instead of continuing, however, she reached over and stubbed out the joint in a cheap plastic ashtray that already bore the scars and scorch marks of a thousand other cigarettes.

'Fuck it!' she declared. 'I think I need another drink.'

'Good idea.' He held out his empty glass. 'Your round.'

****

The conversation declined shortly after she returned with the second round of drinks. The joint had not mellowed them so much as accentuated the fatigue that weighed them both down. Even Ailbhe's obvious enjoyment of intellectual debate couldn't save them. She appeared to have hit some transparent wall – her engaging sense of argument had faded, her repartee dwindled to silence.

They made a desultory effort to pick up from their earlier discussion but neither really had their heart in it. Within a short space of time, a curtain of gloom settled down between them and the exchange dwindled into silence. The beer glasses, half-full mere moments before, were now, most definitely, half-empty.

It was Mos who suggested calling it a night, but he knew that it was a mutual intention, one that Ailbhe herself would probably have suggested a few moments later. Leaving the glasses on the table, they retrieved their coats and returned once more onto the unrelenting chill of the city streets.

Exposed to the full brunt of the wind and the rain, the walk from the pub to the university gates seemed to last an age whereas, in reality, it probably took less than fifteen minutes. Mos felt both exhaustion and relief when the university's high, cast-iron gates finally loomed into view.

'This is where we part ways,' he said. 'I live just up there.' He pointed towards his house.

Ailbhe stood, swaying wearily in the wind but saying nothing, a jaded – almost numbed – expression across her features. Since their earlier discussion in the beer garden, she'd retreated further into herself, barely responding to his attempts at conversation during the walk to the gates. Her shoulders were slumped, her fiery temperament completely doused by the unrelenting downpour.

Mos gestured vaguely towards the Western Road, barely visible through the driving rain. 'If you keep following the street in that direction, you'll reach your hostel in about five minutes.'

Rain ran slick down the side of her face, slipping inside the collar of the ridiculous poncho.

For an instant, some faint charitable impulse prompted him to invite her back to the house for a hot drink and some respite from the rain, but he immediately suppressed it. Despite his best intentions, such invitations, at such a time, had ramifications he just didn't have the energy or inclination to cope with. Right there and then, he wanted nothing more than to be alone, to crawl into the warm seclusion of his bed, pull the duvet up around him and hold the world at bay for a few blessed hours.

He stood in awkward silence, eager to get away but, at the same time, feeling guilty for abandoning her to make her own way back to her hostel. Fortunately, she saved him the embarrassment by taking the initiative.

'Thanks for the drink.'

Without another word, she turned and started to walk away, following the footpath towards the gloom on the Western Road.

A twinge of remorse rippled through his stomach.

'Hang on!'

She stopped and looked back over her shoulder at him.

He moved towards her, undoing the buttons of his coat. When he was standing in front of her he shuffled it from his shoulders and held it out.

She looked at the coat and then she looked at him.

'Take it. That wrap just isn't going to hack it in the Irish climate.'

She did not respond for a moment or two, just stood there with a blank expression on her face. He became conscious of the weight of the coat growing heavier in his hand as the rain pounded down upon him.

'Any time today would be good. I'm getting soaked here.'

Finally, she reached across and took it in both hands then wrapped it around her so that it hung over both shoulders. She gave a strained smile, as though at a loss to know how to respond to the unanticipated display of gallantry.

'Thank you,' she said stiffly.

He nodded but said nothing.

Turning away, he started up the rise of Donovan's Road. After several steps he paused, prompted by some undefined instinct to turn and look back. He caught a final glimpse of her just as she rounded the corner to the Western Road; a solitary figure in an oversized overcoat fading into a bleak curtain of cold, grey rain.

***

There was a comforting finality to the sound of the front door slamming shut behind him. Its solid echo followed Mos up the hall and into the living room, where he stripped out of his clothes and let them fall in a wet pile on the floor. Without a coat, the short walk from the university gates had been more than sufficient to get thoroughly drenched and he was shivering violently with the cold.

He turned up the central heating then switched on the lights, but the subdued illumination did little to improve the dreary interior. The room looked just as depressing as when he had left it earlier that evening.

He padded down the hall to the bathroom where he spent over twenty minutes in the shower with the water on full power and at high temperature. The continuous stream of hot water scraped the night away from him. When he emerged, the bathroom was clouded with steam but his skin was warm and he felt revived by the heat.

Retrieving a pair of track pants, a T-shirt and a woollen jumper from his bedroom, he dressed and returned to the kitchen. There, he put the kettle on and swallowed two paracetamols with a full glass of water. He smiled thinly at the irony that, now he was home, he no longer felt any sense of fatigue.

The living room had warmed up by the time he returned with a mug of hot chocolate. On a whim, he switched on the radio and tuned through several different channels but was unable to find anything that suited his mood. Switching it off again, he glanced half-heartedly through his own music collection but once again, found nothing there that he felt like listening to.

He settled into an armchair by the heater with the hot chocolate, sipping it as silence engulfed the room. The sweetness of the beverage did little to counteract the deep sense of dissatisfaction that had overtaken him. He'd had no real expectations for the evening and yet he couldn't shake the sense that it had terminated much more poorly than it should have – a subdued, disappointing, and rain-soaked anti-climax.

It came as a surprise when a mental image of Ailbhe formed in his head, and he winced at the pang of guilt it provoked. Hardly his finest hour, deserting her to her own devices on the stormy streets of Cork.

Ah, sod it! Sometimes there's only room in the life raft for one.

A strange one, though. Carting some serious baggage, he suspected, but undeniably attractive.

She drew the eye.

He'd noticed how people watched her when she passed, intrigued – as he had been – by the exotic features, the flamboyant dress sense and the assertive charisma she projected before her.

He mulled over that for a minute or two. It was true she'd conveyed the impression of haughty resilience but over the course of the night, when fatigue and rain had worn her down, the lofty eccentricity had given way to a frayed fragility that she'd been at pains to conceal.

The cell phone on the table beside the armchair suddenly pealed into life, scattering all Mos' thoughts to the shadowed corners of the room. He glanced at the display screen as he picked it up, surprised to discover that it was well past one in the morning.

'Hello?'

'Muiris. It's me.' Hegarty's unique, haughty intonation was instantly identifiable. 'Where have you been? I've been ringing all night.'

'Desmond,' he said. He was surprised at how deflated his own voice sounded.

'Muiris, forgive me for calling so late but you left without giving me an answer. Are you going to take up that offer?'

Mos felt his head spin in the aftermath of alcohol, regrets, cannabis, fatigue and strange accents and for a moment could barely make sense of where he was. The sensation faded, leaving him with a hazy recollection of Hegarty's proposal back in McCarthy's Bar.

'Can you remind me what that was about again?'

'Jesus Christ, Muiris. The meeting with the Opus Foundation.'

'Aaah! Right. They're the boys who want some kind of briefing on the *Fianaigecht.*'

'That's right.'

'Hmm.' He rubbed his chin in thought.

'They found an artefact, didn't they?'

'Yes, well they have but—'

'But all they'd actually want me to do would be to turn up, answer a few questions then sod off again.'

'Yes, that's pretty much it.'

'Oh, what the fuck!' he said. 'That doesn't seem too difficult. I'll probably regret this in the morning but, all right, I'll do it.'

There was an enormous exhalation of relief at the other end of the line.

'That's excellent, Muiris. Excellent. I'm sure you won't regret it.'

Mos unconsciously pictured Hegarty rubbing his hands together in glee.

'Not so fast. There are two conditions.'

'Oh.' Hegarty's voice suddenly lost all trace of warmth. 'What's that?'

'The first is payment in cash on completion of the briefing. The amount discussed in McCarthy's.'

'Okay.' Hegarty seemed relieved. 'Okay, I can organise that. And the second?'

'Stop fucking calling me.'

There was a brief silence at the other end of the line. When Hegarty's response finally came, his voice was strained.

'All right. But one last thing, though. Can you meet them tomorrow morning? Eleven o'clock.'

'That's hardly much notice.'

'They're working to a tight schedule, Muiris. They're not in Cork for long and they want the information as soon as possible.'

'Okay. I suppose for that kind of money I can afford to get up early.'

'Brilliant! Do you have a pen and a piece of paper handy?'

'Uh-huh.'

'Okay. It's in Shandon House. Fifth floor.'

Hegarty quickly reeled off an address in the centre of town. Mos automatically wrote it down although he already knew the building well.

'Right! The person to ask for is David Coffey. I've put together a brief synopsis of the *Fianaigecht* and sent it to him, so they have a basic idea of what it all entails. I'll fax you a copy of that once I've hung up. We can catch up tomorrow after you've had your little chat.'

The phone went quiet for several seconds.

'That's it then. Is there anything else?'

'Desmond, you are aware that I despise you, aren't you?'

The silence over the line stretched out for several seconds.

'Yes, Muiris,' he responded at last. 'Yes, I suppose I am. But to be honest I simply don't care. Sleep well.'

He hung up.

Mos replaced the mobile in its charger cradle. He sat and listened as the silence was obliterated by a fresh fusillade of hailstones pelting against the window.

Chapter Four

West Cork, Early 1960s

The grief struck Diarmuid on the following morning. Emerging from the murky sanctuary of slumber, he felt it there awaiting him; a black cloak to smother him with sinister thoughts for the coming day.

Séamus.

Despair lay across his chest like a cold weight and for the first time in his life he found himself lacking the will to rise from his bed. Motionless beneath the blankets, he watched the glow of daylight fill the room, listened as the early morning birdsong swelled and waned and the cattle in An Páirc Mór bellowed in complaint at the delay in milking. Still, he made no move.

In the end, it was the sound of the boy moving around downstairs that roused him. Struggling to his feet, he listlessly pulled on his clothes and stumbled down to the kitchen to prepare a late breakfast of tea, buttermilk, and stale soda bread. Tired and dispirited, he dropped the cutlery clumsily on the table and the metallic clatter was loud in the stillness of the room. As he blundered around the house, he noted that the boy had sensed his mood and was doing his best to keep out of the way. For some reason, this only served to irritate him more.

'Breakfast,' he grunted.

The boy remained where he was, staring at him with wide eyes.

'*Nach bhfuil ocras ortsa, mar sin?*' he growled, in his anger reverting to Irish. Aren't you hungry, then?

'*Tá.*' I am.

The response, although muted and hesitant, was so unexpected that Diarmuid could only stare, gobsmacked, at the youngster. The boy shifted nervously under the intense examination.

'*Is féidir leat caint!*' You can talk!

'*Is féidir.*' I can.

'*A Dhia na bheart! Cén fáth nár duirt tú rud eigean? Do bhí fhios agat go raibh an Gaeilge agam.*' Why didn't you say something? You heard I had the Gaelic.

'I don't know you,' he answered, still talking in Irish. 'And I didn't understand what you and the fat man were saying.'

Diarmuid continued to stare at him, all sense of his earlier despair obliterated by this new development. The boy edged anxiously towards the door.

'*Ná bí eagla ortsa,*' he managed at last. '*Ní gortfidh mé thú.*' Don't be afraid. I won't hurt you.

Great! The first thing normally uttered by those individuals with every intention of doing just that.

'Look,' he continued. 'I'll stay here on this side of the table. You stay there and we'll eat while we work this out. Afterwards we can talk. *Ceart go leor?* All right?'

The boy nodded and they both sat down and ate in silence, avoiding each other's eyes for several minutes. Shaken, Diarmuid dipped the soda bread in his tea to soften it and chewed intensely as he struggled to work out the ramifications of what he'd just learned. The child was a complete *gaelgoir* – a monolingual Irish speaker without a word of English. He considered this fact in subdued fascination. If this was the case, it was hardly a surprise that he'd not spoken with the *Gardaí* or the social workers. Apart from the trauma of trying to deal with his father's death, he wouldn't have understood a word they were saying. As they weren't in a Gaeltacht area, it wouldn't even have entered their heads to attempt communicating through Irish.

'For feck's sake!'

Diarmuid breathed deeply. He couldn't even begin to imagine what his brother had been thinking. To rear the boy through Irish, with a complete absence of English, he would have had to completely isolate him from every other person in the community. How in God's name would he have achieved that? And, more to the point, why? It just didn't make any sense.

Sighing, he pushed his plate away. Observing the movement, the boy reproduced it at the other side of the table.

'My name is Diarmuid O'Súilleabháin. I am your uncle. Your Daddy's brother,' he explained. 'Did he tell you that you had an uncle?'

The child nodded but said nothing.

Diarmuid raised his hand and gestured around the room.

'When your Da was a little boy like you, we lived in this house. He used to play with me here in this very room. He was smaller than me but he was a slippery little fecker, your Daddy. He bate me every time.'

The boy continued to regard him without expression. Nevertheless, Diarmuid thought, there'd been a sliver of interest at the mention of his father.

'Look at this! There's something I want you to see.'

He rose from the table and moved over to the wall by the fireplace. Crouching down, he pulled a wooden chest aside to reveal a number of words and a date engraved at knee level in the wall behind it.

Séamus O'Súilleabháin.

Mean-Fomhair, 1915.

'Your Da wrote that when he was a wee fella. No more than ten years old. But he got into fierce trouble. Our Dad – your granda – wasn't too happy when he saw what he'd gone and done. He gave Séam– your Da a fierce thrashing with an old fern root he pulled up from the front of the house.'

To his surprise, he found himself laughing at the memory.

'By God! Your Da had a sore arse. He couldn't sit for a week.'

The boy startled him then by rising from the table and coming over to join him. He too crouched down to examine the words cut into the stone. Diarmuid watched as he ran his fingers along the engraving.

'Séamus' son!' he thought. 'You poor cratur.' He bit his lower lip. Pain like a jellyfish sting seared his heart.

'What's your name, little man? I can't just keep referring to you as "you".'

'Demne.'

Diarmuid sucked air in through his teeth, but he kept his expression neutral.

'You mean Demne like with Fionn mac Cumhaill?'

The boy shook his head. It was clear he had no idea what Diarmuid was referring to.

The old man scratched his head in bewilderment. It did not make any sense for his brother to have named his son Demne. Locally, the tradition – although never rigorously adhered to – was to use the old naming pattern where the first son was named after the grandfather. As far as he was aware, this name had never previously been used by anyone in the family. In fact, that only time he'd ever come across it was in connection with the mythological hero. Demne, the childhood name of Fionn mac Cumhaill, was a bizarre choice, the equivalent of a Greek naming his son Hercules or an Italian calling his child Romulus. Then again, everything about this whole situation was bizarre.

He grunted.

'Well, Dem …' The name caught in his throat. 'Well, Demne …' he tried again. 'I …'

'Can I go home now?'

He stared at the boy.

'You can't go home yet, *a garsúr*. You'll have to stay here and put up with me for a while. You know.' He hesitated, unsure what to say next. 'Your Da … he's dead. There's no one back there and someone's got to take care of you.'

'You don't want me here.'

Although surprised and somewhat unsettled by the comment, Diarmuid was impressed by the boy's directness. He took a few seconds to think through his response for it was an astute observation and deserved a thoughtful and honest response.

'I'm a man used to living alone. The truth is I have no need of a nephew. I have my ways and I have my faults. You'll understand that yourself when you're older. Having another person here, particularly my brother's son, it complicates things.'

He paused and cleared his throat.

'All the same, we share blood so that puts a tie between us.'

He frowned and pursed his lips in thought.

'I'll tell you what! You'll stay with me for the next few days while I think on things. We'll try to get along and once we've done that, we'll throw the stones in the air and see where they fall. *An bhfuil margadh againn?*' Do we have a deal?

The boy considered his words in silence then grudgingly nodded his head.

Maybe it was the angle of the light or some subdued memory of his own but for just one instant, with that single gesture, the boy looked so much like Séamus that Diarmuid felt as though his heart had split right down the middle.

'Demne.'

His voice was hoarse with emotion.

'What happened, *a bhuachaill?* What happened to your father?'

The boy stared at his uncle and a look of almost complete incomprehension crossed his face. Suddenly, his eyes glazed, the colour drained from his face, and he folded like a punctured concertina, collapsing onto the floor in front of him.

The old man stared in horror at the pale, little figure lying on the ground like a discarded rag doll. Panic-stricken, he bent down, shook his shoulders, and slapped his face repeatedly but nothing he did could rouse the child. He placed his fingers over the boy's wrist but, despite several attempts, was unable to locate a pulse.

'*A Dhia na bheart!*'

Pulling the boy's shirt open, he laid his palm against his heart. There was no heartbeat.

In desperation, he grabbed a small mirror from the mantelpiece and held it above his lips. To his great relief, a tiny trace of vapour formed on its shining surface.

For two or three minutes he just stared helplessly at the child, struggling to work out whether he should attempt mouth-to-mouth resuscitation, run to the neighbours to send for a doctor or simply wait to see how his condition developed. On instinct, he tried checking the pulse again and this time, to his surprise, located it straight away; weak but regular and growing steadily stronger.

With a huge sigh of relief, Diarmuid allowed himself to fall back into a sitting position on the floor beside the boy, watching as his nephew's colour returned and his chest started moving again, his breathing finally getting deeper and settling into a regular rhythm.

Jesus Christ!

He was suddenly aware how fast his own heartbeat was beating, thumping rapidly as though in encouragement to his nephew. He raised both hands and found that they were trembling, his entire body shaking from the fright. The incident had shaken him badly. He'd truly thought his nephew was a goner.

Fetching a rug, he covered Demne and continued to sit with him. As time stretched on and the boy showed no signs of waking, he made the decision to carry him upstairs and placed him on his own bed. The boy was slight, as light as a feather in his arms.

Pulling a chair away from the wall, he sat by the bed.

And waited.

***

After a few minutes Demne finally stirred, snapping into consciousness with a startling suddenness. One minute he was lying comatose; the next, he was sitting up, his eyes scanning the room with confused awareness.

Diarmuid held out a cup of warm milk.

'Drink this.'

Demne accepted the cup. He drank greedily, gulping down the milk as though he had a great thirst on him.

'Are ye right?'

For a moment, the boy didn't seem to understand the question but then he gave a sharp nod.

'Do you remember who I am?'

'You're my uncle.'

He looked around at the unfamiliar room then down at the bed.

'Was I asleep?'

'You were, that,' Diarmuid replied with strained jocularity.

'Sound asleep. Far away in the land of Nod.'

Just then a loud bellow echoed up to the bedroom window from the field outside. Demne stared at the glass pane, an expression of bewilderment on his face.

'The cows want milking,' explained his uncle. 'But let's just rest aisy for a while.'

'I can help!' the boy declared. 'I'm fine,' he said, seeing his uncle's startled expression.

Diarmuid regarded him in bafflement as he swung his legs off the bed. By rights, the youngster should have been shaking like a leaf, physically debilitated from the trauma of such a near death experience. Instead, he

63

looked and acted as though he'd just woken from a refreshing afternoon nap, completely revitalised and fidgeting restlessly on the bed.

Did I really get it so wrong?

'All right, so,' he conceded at last. 'But if you feel even the slightest bit shaky you go back to bed. *Gealann tú?*' You promise?

'*Gealaim*,' agreed the boy.

Diarmuid kept a watchful eye on his nephew as he descended the stairs in front of him but despite his concerns, he exhibited no ill effects of any kind. In fact, Demne practically bounded down the steps, taking them two at a time and leaving the old man in his wake. The energy of youth, he reflected wearily. It was enough to make you feel your age.

With wry amusement he also noted that although Demne had no problems remembering his uncle or Carraig Dubh, he seemed to have conveniently forgotten the little detail of his fainting fit and the questions that had provoked it.

Diarmuid scratched his head as he followed the boy outside. Clearly the youngster was holding something back from him.

The four milk cows – Dubh, Donn, Bán, and Rua – were standing in An Páirc Mór. As soon as they saw him emerge from the house, they immediately commenced lowing and bellowing in discomfort at the pressure in their udders and crowded around the gate that gave access to the yard.

Diarmuid pushed the gate open and quickly moved aside as the animals brushed through, lumbering directly towards the milking shed. Behind them, the dog barked enthusiastically and nipped at their ankles as though claiming sole credit for driving them inside.

As they filed through the narrow door of the shed, the old man turned to Demne.

'Have you ever milked a cow, *a garsún?*'

Demne shook his head.

'Come in here with me then. I'll show you.'

They entered the small building to find each of the cows already lined up in the stalls. Diarmuid stuffed several handfuls of straw into the feed-dish at the front of each stall and they munched contentedly, waiting for him to get on with it. He patted the nearest cow on the flank.

'This,' he said, 'is Dubh.'

Demne and the cow looked at each other with mutual curiosity.

'Poor oul Dubh isn't feeling very comfortable because she's been waiting for me to come out and milk her. Cows have to be milked regularly otherwise, they get mastitis or dry up and we'd have no milk for the *tae*. Would you like to try it?'

He squeezed into the stall between the wall and the chewing animal and loosely secured its head with some rope, a process followed more through habit than precaution. A cow's temperament was directly influenced by the way the animal was treated as a calf and, unlike purchased cows where you'd never know how they were reared, he'd bought and raised all his cattle from calves. Dubh was a placid old thing, docile and well used to human handling and never providing anything but trouble-free milking.

He retrieved the little one-legged stool that had been lying on its side in the straw then showed the boy how to approach the cow, set the stool down and ease onto it, close enough to lean his head into her flank. While Demne tried this, he tied her tail to her off-side leg, got the metal pail and slid it down underneath her udder.

'Now, are your hands washed? Good. Now remember, she's a lady. Be gentle. Scratch her on the side and talk to her softly.

He watched with interest as Demne did as he was instructed. You could learn a lot about people by the way they milked a cow. The boy fumbled the pail as he sat on the milking stool.

'Easy now. Grip the two front teats. That's it. Now squeeze them. Gently. Start with your top fingers and squeeze down. There you go! You've got milk.'

There was a metallic rattle as the first spurt of milk hit the bottom of the pail. Diarmuid watched approvingly. The boy was a natural and had a good technique, holding the teat in his whole hand and expressing the milk with the fingers without pulling or stretching. He peered into the bucket. The milk was making a nice white foam in the bottom.

'Take your time. There are still the two back teats to milk. And hold the pail between your knees so you can rescue it if you need to.'

A shadow flitted across the floor of the milking shed. Diarmuid glanced up at the dark shape that appeared to fill the doorway.

'Well, Jaysus God Almighty! Is it only now you're doing the milking? The day's half-done!'

The gruff voice came from an elderly man in rough working clothes who was leaning heavily on a blackthorn stick. He was short, about a head lower than Diarmuid, and had a face that was creased from extended exposure to the wind and the rain.

'Hello, Dinny,' said Diarmuid. 'How are you?'

Dinny Murphy, his nearest neighbour and friend of over fifty years, brushed through the doorway with easy familiarity. He leaned against the inside wall and considered Diarmuid with an easy eye.

'Hello yourself, Diarmuid. Why didn't you leave your milk up the road? I was ...'

The words hung on his lip as he noticed Demne, who had been concealed from sight by Dubh's broad flank.

'Oh Hello, *a garsún*! And who might you be?'

'He's my nephew, Dinny. Leave him be. He's very shy and scared of strangers.'

'Sure, aren't I scared of strangers, meself! You gave me an awful scare there, young fella.'

Demne returned his stare with a blank expression. When it became obvious that no reply was forthcoming, Dinny turned a curious glance towards Diarmuid.

'I didn't know you had a nephew, Diarmuid.'

'Sure, I didn't know it myself. Will you have a sup of d'oul *tae*, Dinny?'

'Ah no, I won't. I'm only here to borrow that file of yours for a few hours. I have to sharpen up the axe for the firewood tomorrow.'

'Ah, sure, go on.'

'Yerra, I'm grand.'

Leaving the boy to complete the task he'd been assigned, the men returned to the house, working through the time-honoured Irish ritual of offering and refusing tea. Their exchange was an extension of the usual convention, mutually developed over more than two decades. Every Saturday afternoon for the last fifteen years, Dinny, fleeing a household saturated by the female hormones of his wife and four unmarried daughters, turned up at Diarmuid's to borrow an object or return something he'd previously borrowed. For two hours or so, they would then argue over tea and discuss the world's troubles at length before Dinny finally departed to return to the pleasures of domestic bliss.

When the habitual routine had been played through to their mutual satisfaction, Diarmuid made the tea and they sat themselves down by the heat of the fire. Both men pulled identical pipes with a black stem and a walnut bowl from their pockets. Lighting them up was a complex process that involved tapping the pipe on the hearth to remove the carbonized remains of the previous smoke, refilling the bowl with some deep brown, rich-smelling tobacco, then lighting it carefully with a burning splinter of wood. Once the tobacco had taken hold, both men puffed on them contentedly.

'Isn't it a strange world, Diarmuid, where a man doesn't know how he has a nephew?'

Diarmuid frowned. His neighbour was teasing him and although it was a normal, even essential, part of their habitual interaction, this time the subject matter was not one he could take lightly.

'I was serious, Dinny. I didn't know.'

The other man considered him as he sipped from his teacup.

'I see. Would he be your brother's then?'

'He would. You know I don't have any other siblings apart from Séamus.'

'Mmmm.'

Dinny put his cup aside on the hearth, puffed on his pipe and regarded Diarmuid through a cloud of blue smoke. 'Diarmuid, I'm not the type to sink my snout into another man's business but … Well, 'tis a long time since you've mentioned Séamus' name. It's not on me to ask but I know there was a major falling out between you two.'

When the older man made no response, he regarded him with a worried expression.

'Is everything all right, Diarmuid?'

'Séamus is dead, Dinny.'

'Oh, sweet Jaysus! God bless him and save him, the poor cratur.'

Diarmuid repeated everything that the policeman had told him and followed that up with the developments around the breakfast table earlier that morning. By the time he'd finished, both men's pipes had gone cold.

'Jaysus, Diarmuid. That's a dreadful tale. What are you going to do? Will you take the young fella in?'

Diarmuid shook his head. 'I don't know. I really don't know.' He pulled a fresh splinter from the fire, reignited his pipe then passed it to Dinny. 'It's little enough I know about children. I was behind the door when that sort of knowledge was being handed out.'

'What about the boy's mother?'

'Pádraig says that nobody knows who she is.'

'I find that a biteen hard to believe, Diarmuid. The father, sure enough. It certainly wouldn't be the first time to see that kind of carry on. But it'd be a rare thing to find a child not knowing the womb he came out of.'

Diarmuid chewed irritably on the stem of his pipe then his eyes lit up with excitement.

'You and Margaret! You've got four fine children, Dinny. You'd know all about rearing. What do you think I should do?'

Dinny shook his head doubtfully.

'I've always worked to the principle of *'mol an óige is tiocfaidh sí'*. Praise youth and it will bloom. That seems to have stood me in good stead over the years. To be honest, I shouldn't be advising you at all. It's far from all this quare stuff I was raised. I'd only be setting you wrong if I told you what to do. All I'd say, Diarmuid, is to do what's right. Do what feels right to you.'

'That's the problem, Dinny! I don't know what's right. My head is telling me he's blood and I should take responsibility, but then I look at him and see Séamus in his eyes and it's all too much.'

Diarmuid looked at his friend and his eyes were heavy with shame.

'I know, I know! It's a terrible thing to say … but my heart says get rid of him.'

Dinny puffed gently on the stem of his pipe and exhaled the smoke with a sigh.

'Well, Diarmuid. At the end of the day, you're the only one that can make that decision. If you don't want the boy here, it's best not to have him here at all. Kids are fierce clever at sensing that straight off.'

You don't want me here.

Diarmuid ground his teeth together grimly as he remembered the boy's words. He'd sensed it, sure enough.

For the next few minutes, the men smoked and sipped tea in silence. It was, Diarmuid reflected, the most subdued visit he'd had in many a year. His foot tapped an anxious jig against the stone of the hearth.

'I want to know.'

Dinny's brow furrowed up in consternation.

'What do you want to know?'

'Everything. I want to know everything.'

He paused at the look of incomprehension on his neighbour's face.

'I want to know why Séamus is dead.'

'I thought it was an accident. Didn't Pádraig say …?'

'Yerra, Pádraig's a feckin' eejit. He wouldn't know his head from his arse because of all the shit flowing out of it. I want to know what happened. I only have half the story and it's an unbelievable one at that. Why in God's name would any man attempt to drag a big bastard of a cupboard that's three times his weight down the stairs without any help?' He glared at Dinny. 'It doesn't make any sense. And what's worse, I think the boy saw something.'

Dinny's face reflected his surprise. 'What do you mean? What did he see?'

'I'm not sure. I just have this feeling he saw something but he's too scared to tell me.'

'I don't know, Diarmuid.' Dinny shook his head doubtfully.

'Well, what about all the other quare stuff, then? Why was Séamus raising his boy without any English? How was it that he was able to live in Beara all these years without me ever learning about it? Who's the boy's mother and where did she disappear to. I want to know …'

He stopped suddenly, hands shaking, and voice choked with emotion.

'I want to know where the poor man is buried. *A Dhia na Bheart*, Dinny! I didn't even ask that copper where he was buried. Poor Séamus is lying in some far ground away from his own people.'

He shuddered and looked down at his trembling palms.

'I've got to find his grave and make things right.'

His neighbour regarded him in alarm. In all their many years as neighbours and friends, he'd never seen the old man so upset.

'Diarmuid, you've been my good friend these many years. It hurts me to see you tormented like this but I've got to go away home now. Get your thoughts together and if you need to know these things then also know that I'll help you.'

He stood up, emptied the cinders from his pipe with a quick blow against the fireplace and placed it in his shirt pocket.

'I'll come with the car after mass tomorrow and we'll head over to Na hAoraí and locate your brother's grave. We'll find out where he was living and then we'll ask his neighbours what happened. Once you know these things, your heart'll be more at ease for that decision. Will you shake my hand on that?'

He held out his hand and after a second or two Diarmuid reached across and shook it.

'You're a good friend, Dinny Murphy.'

'Sure, don't I know it? But I still need to borrow that file – and it'd be the wise man that checks the boy milking his cattle.'

***

Demne, as it turned out, had done an excellent job with the milking. By the time the old man returned to the shed there were two full pails of milk standing in the corner and he was perched on the stool with Rua, milking into a third pail.

Diarmuid helped the boy finish the job then poured the foamy white liquid into the dairy churn. He placed the metal container onto the small wheelbarrow he'd constructed specially to carry it out onto the road. He had an old agreement going back several years with Dinny, Pat Harrington and Seán O'Shea, the other farmers who shared the road leading down to the sea. As the only vehicle owners, Dinny and Seán took it in turns to pick up their neighbours' churns twice daily for transport up to the intersection with the main Cork Road. This was the point where all the local milk was collected and separated by the milk truck for delivery to the creamery in Baile Chaisleáin Bhéarra.

When they were finished, Diarmuid gestured to Demne to follow him indoors for an early lunch of bread, butter and potatoes. After the meal, he cleared the table and rummaged through the cupboards to retrieve a new packet of crayons and some brown wrapping paper for the boy.

'Here you go. A good workman deserves good wages. That was meant to be a birthday present for one of Dinny's daughters last year, but I had to get the vet in for Dubh that day and never got around to it. I've been meaning to, but—' He shrugged.

Demne was delighted with the unexpected reward and immediately spread the paper out on the table. He opened the packet of crayons with a child's exaggerated care, sniffing each individual crayon as he withdrew it from the box and laid it down next to the others. The dog sat beneath the table, the ball in its mouth. It whined hopefully then, sensing that the boy was preoccupied, reluctantly released it and settled down to sleep.

Diarmuid busied himself around the house for the next half-hour with the washing up, some paperwork and a creaking step on the stairs that needed fixing. When he'd finished, he came around behind the boy and peered over his shoulder to examine what he'd drawn. It was a simple picture with clearly defined lines and extensive use of colours that depicted a valley with a small castle-shaped building surrounded by high hills on either side. The sun was sinking in the distance and there were two matchstick figures – a man and a dog – standing beside a solitary tree located off to the right of the house.

'That's a lovely picture. Is that a castle?'

'No. That's home.'

'Your home? You live in a castle?'

The boy nodded. Diarmuid managed to hide his incredulity, neatly slotting it away at the back of his head for later consideration.

'I see. Well, you're a great drawer. Did you learn that at school?'

Demne shook his head.

'Daddy taught me drawing,' he said simply. 'And geography and sums. And reading and writing.'

Diarmuid nodded to himself. A foolish line of inquiry. If he'd been to school, he would have spoken English.

'Did you have many friends back home? Anyone you played with?'

'An Gruagach.'

'*An Gruagach*?' Diarmuid wondered. Literally, the phrase meant 'the hairy man' or 'the hairy one'. He was just about to dismiss it as nonsense when his eyes fell on the matchstick dog in the picture.

'Was An Gruagach your dog?'

'My goat.'

The boy spoke with a sad voice.

'He died. Daddy killed him. I buried him in the small field.'

Diarmuid nodded in sympathy.

'Sometimes, Demne, people have to do things that seem cruel or thoughtless when you don't understand the reasons behind it. Your Dada must have had a good reason to put your goat down. The poor animal was probably in pain.'

He scratched his chin in reflection.

'Was that how you learned to milk?'

The boy inclined his head once in confirmation.

Diarmuid mulled that over thoughtfully.

'Did your Mammy teach you how to milk *An Gruagach*?'

Demne stopped drawing and looked up at him with wary eyes.

'Your Mammy' he pressed. 'What did you say your Mammy's name was?'

The boy gave him a dubious look and Diarmuid squirmed, suddenly embarrassed for trying to fool the child like that.

'Mammy,' he said at last.

Diarmuid turned away, a sudden weariness heavy on his shoulders. 'Of course! That was fierce stupid of me.'

The boy nodded as though in complete agreement then turned back to his paper and crayons.

Diarmuid had the bizarre feeling that he'd been dismissed. He bit his tongue, tempted to probe some more but decided not to pursue the matter further. He still had a definite sense that the boy was not being completely open with him, but he couldn't be sure and after his reaction to the questioning earlier that morning he was loath to chance it again. Demne might have been hiding something but there was no doubt in Diarmuid's mind that the boy had been severely traumatised. Instinctively, he knew that if he pushed too far, the shutters would come down and no amount of coddling or persuasion would ever get him to speak again.

***

Diarmuid watched the afternoon sky as he stood outside and smoked a cigarette. It was a relatively mild afternoon but grey cloud in the distance offshore threatened rain and an early nightfall. Dinny had had it right with his comment on the lateness of the hour. After his own tardy rising, Demne's fainting fit and his neighbour's visit, the day was, indeed, half done.

He tossed the butt onto the ground. He was finding it increasingly difficult to think straight for his routine and his natural equilibrium had been shaken, not only by the news of his brother's death but by the presence of an unwelcome nephew.

He sighed. He was being unfair. The child was odd but he could hardly be blamed for having himself thrust into the existence of a relative he knew only by name. If anything, he was managing remarkably well given the horrific circumstances behind his arrival to Carraig Dubh – and he'd done his best to help and keep out of the way.

Diarmuid's lip twitched in irritation.

Nevertheless, his presence was an unpleasant reminder, an unremitting headache that he could temporarily overlook but could not ignore on a permanent basis.

Returning inside to the porch, he retrieved a coat and called to the boy, who was still drawing pictures.

'*Téann liom*! Come on! We're going across the fields. It's about time you got a measure of the place.'

He whistled at the dog as he left the house, clearing the dry-stone wall
that bordered the yard then cutting west across An Páirc Mór. Delighted at
the prospect of a walk, the dog took off, running ahead of them and
barking with excitement.

'Will ya go aisy, ye mad eejit!'

At the far end of the meadow, they passed through a gap in the ditch.
Here, a narrow path wove through a copse of ash and beech trees where a
pair of crows sat on a high branch observing them solemnly.

After ten minutes or so, the path brought them to a large stone wall so
overgrown with fuchsia and willow and brambles that only patches of the
original stonework were visible. Walking parallel to the wall, they eventually
reached a breach that allowed them to emerge onto the large field known as
Párc an Cnoic.

The field in which they found themselves was spread in a wide curve
across the crest of a low hill and offered a panoramic view of Cuan Baoi.
Behind them, the imposing mass of Cnoc Daod loomed as substantial as
ever, distant white spots of houses dotting the grey rock and patchy green
paddocks of the lower slopes.

Diarmuid stopped to take in the view, absorbing the familiar contours
of the countryside. Over the years, he had developed a habit of pausing
here, both to admire the view and to reflect on the passing of time. It was
at such times too, that he felt closest to his father, grasping a clearer
understanding of the physical and emotional connections a man could have
with the land that sustained him and his family.

He led Demne to a small section cordoned off from Párc An Cnoic by a
low fence constructed from the remnants of an old stone wall, some
barbed wire, and thick clumps of blackthorn pulled together to form a
barrier. The interior – a flat patch of grass – had a single ash tree at its
centre. Lying beneath the tree, with a view over the bay, were two
weathered gravestones.

Clambering over the wall, Diarmuid approached the graves and stood to
one side with his head bowed. Closing his eyes, he made a silent prayer to
his parents. He wasn't a religious man by any stretch of the imagination,
but it felt right to stand there and remember his parents, to acknowledge
their memory and the kindness of the two lives that had brought his own to
this point and time.

He released a soft sigh. It was good that their graves were so close, that
he could visit them often and keep them in his thoughts. By all rights, of
course, they shouldn't have been there at all. The law was very clear that all
burials were supposed to take place in one of the local graveyards.

Then again, there were legal responsibilities and there were other, more
important, personal responsibilities, and the two did not always align. His
father, with typical Gaelic disregard for authority, had always tended more

strongly to the influence of the latter. For this reason, he'd instructed his sons to bury him on the land he loved, just as he himself had buried his wife several years earlier. The day before the funeral Diarmuid, Séamus and Dinny had laid his body to rest under the shade of the oak tree, beside his wife. There'd been an official ceremony with a coffin, elegies and a reception back at the house for the neighbours and friends but the only thing put to rest in the cemetery that day was a hundred pounds of rock.

Diarmuid opened his eyes. The boy was standing beside him, observing him with an expression of detached curiosity.

'*Cad tá tú á dheanamh?*' What are you doing?

'I'm praying. What do you think I'm doing?'

'*Tá daoine faoi fhód.*' There's people buried here.

Diarmuid stared at the child, unsure what exactly he was trying to say. He'd used the Irish expression '*faoi fhód*' meaning 'buried' or, literally, 'under the sod.' He didn't appear to quite understand the relevance but, at the same time, neither did he appear to be asking a question.

'They're your grandparents. It's your grandfather's grave. And your grandmother's.'

He regarded the child again. Demne appeared completely confused. Was he being intentionally obtuse? It was hard to imagine but the only logical assumption was that he really had no idea what a grave was. The old man shifted uncomfortably. Whoever did end up with the child on their hands certainly had their work cut out for them.

He approached the ditch and bent down, brushing some dead ferns aside to retrieve a long object wrapped in sackcloth. The outer layer pulled away to reveal a slasher, with a blade worn from many years of sharpening and a battered-looking handle. Diarmuid knew that the rugged appearance was cosmetic. The blade was still sharp and unrusted and the implement worked as well as the day his father had bought it from the store in Baile Chaisleáin Bhéarra. Hefting it in both hands, he gave it a few experimental swings then started to hack away at the branches of the nearby blackthorn bushes, cutting off large boughs to plug the growing gaps in the makeshift wall. Given time, those openings would grow and unless they were closed off, the cattle would get in and damage the gravestones.

To his surprise, Demne started to work beside him, collecting the blackthorn limbs and arranging them without instruction to fill the holes in the fence. They worked in silence together for a time. Tiring, Diarmuid stopped to catch his breath and peer up at the sky. The clouds seemed to have changed their mind, holding off with the rain – there was even a trace of evening sunshine.

Settling back into the physical routine of swinging and slicing, the old man relaxed and started to croon to himself, veering off into a sustained *laoidh* for several seconds until he became aware of Demne watching.

Diarmuid stopped and leaned on the handle of the slasher.

'I'm practising. Not as good as some. But not as bad as others.'

From his expression, Demne had no idea what he was talking about.

'It's a *laoidh*, a kind of poem. Back in the old days – the way-old days – the people used to chant their poems instead of reciting them or reading them the way they do today. He cleared his throat. 'Listen to this.'

Standing up straight, Diarmuid released a deep chant. Welling up from the depths of his stomach, the words emanated from his mouth in a resonant but oddly plaintive drone.

Scél lem duíb
Dordaid dam
Snigid gaim
Ro-faíth sam

Gàeth ard uar
ísel grian
gair a rith
ruirthech rían

Here's a song
stags give tongue
winter snows
summer goes

high cold blow
sun is low
brief his day
seas give spray

He paused to catch his breath and looked at his nephew. The echo of the chant remained in the soft, windless air, hanging like some intangible aural memory several seconds after he'd finished it.

'What did you think?'

The boy fidgeted, unsure how to respond to the question. 'I didn't understand all of it,' he said at last.

'That's because it's in old Irish. We don't speak the same Irish they spoke back in the olden days, though it's still similar enough to make out some of the words. That particular poem is one of the old nature poems. They say it was written by your namesake, Fionn mac Cumhaill. It has a bit of an edge to it, doesn't it? Like Japanese haiku.'

The boy stared at him blankly.

'Never mind,' he shrugged. 'Sometimes I talk too much. Or maybe I simply don't explain things well enough. Let's get back to the house. It's getting late.'

Chapter Five

Dublin City, 2008

Dr Casper consumed his sandwich in small, precise bites. A simple ham, cheese and tomato combo, the complete absence of flavour was both perplexing and annoying, particularly given its outrageous price. Nevertheless, he required sustenance. Pathetic though this offering was, it would suffice until something more substantial could be obtained.

He grimaced in vexation as he ran his finger along the edge of the bread where the sandwich had been sliced in half. It was a ragged cut, one that looked to have been made with a blunt saw as opposed to a sharp knife. How, he wondered, could anyone go so wrong with a simple sandwich?

Although not one to linger on negative experiences, the poor quality of the sandwich seemed an apt metaphor for his Irish experiences. The balding, overweight figure behind the counter at the sandwich shop had clearly struggled with the initial instructions concerning his preference for spreading the butter, inserting the fillings in equal amounts and slicing it finely in four perfectly formed triangles. When Casper had completed the order, he'd simply stood there staring at him for several seconds before braying, 'Ye want wha'?'

The situation had descended into farce when he'd attempted to leave the squalid little bread shop. The rickety wooden door that had operated so effectively on his arrival suddenly took it upon itself to wedge solidly in the ancient doorway.

Despite his best efforts, Casper had been unable to budge it. After his third attempt, he'd slowly turned with muted fury to regard the sandwich maker. Wisely, the latter had decided to address the issue personally.

Scurrying around the counter, he'd delivered a sharp kick to the bottom of the door while simultaneously pulling it inwards in one smooth motion. On this occasion, it opened effortlessly. The sweating proprietor had then issued grovelling apologies.

'Sorry 'bout tha', mister. There's a bit of a knack to d'oul door.'

Casper dabbed his lips with a paper napkin and brushed the memory from his mind. Placing the remnants of the sandwich in a paper bag, he returned his attention to the detached house and its tree-strewn front garden. This view and the street scene visible through the windscreen had been artfully reproduced in two pencil sketches that lay on the passenger seat beside a thick tome on the architecture of Ancient Mesopotamia.

He frowned.

It had not been his intention to be sitting in this quiet suburban street. On his arrival at Dublin airport that morning, he'd sought nothing more than a good hotel room, a refreshing shower and a decent breakfast. Shortly after picking up the rental car and exiting onto the M5 motorway, however, a young woman in a green Toyota Corolla had rudely cut in front of him, forcing him to brake in order to avoid a collision. Outraged, he'd pressed heavily on the car horn. The response, predictably, had been 'the finger', that lewd gesticulation so beloved by the Irish.

Glaring at the Corolla, he'd caught a brief glance of the driver.

And felt compelled to follow.

Dropping behind the speeding Corolla, he'd pursued the vehicle at a discreet distance for almost twenty minutes, following when it finally left the motorway and entered a leafy residential housing estate. It proceeded through a labyrinth of identical, well-maintained streets before pulling into the kerb in front of one of those standard, semi-detached monstrosities so beloved by the Irish since the initial brash mewlings of their Celtic Tiger.

As Casper drove past, he caught another glimpse of the woman swaddled in a heavy brown overcoat with the collars turned up. He was unable to get a clear look at her. In the rear-view mirror, he saw her leave the car and pass through the front gate of the nearest residence. Continuing to the end of the street, he initiated a careful U-turn then retraced his route and parked several metres from the Corolla, on the opposite side of the road.

He studied the house and the surrounding residences for several minutes, noting the lack of motor or pedestrian traffic. His watch, an expensive Swiss model, informed him that it was twenty-five minutes past nine. That made sense, then. This area looked to be a relatively upmarket residential area, inhabited by professional career people who were, no doubt, off earning a crust for the day.

He had commenced his initial sketch at this point, but the drawing had been abruptly forestalled when the front door of the house opened and the woman emerged once more. Although wearing the same coat, this time her features were even more obscured by a thick scarf and a woollen hat pulled down over her forehead.

Slamming the door behind her, she hurried down the garden path towards the gate and out onto the sidewalk without a glance in his direction. After a full minute of fussing around with the Corolla's tangled safety belt and vociferously revving the engine, she finally managed to pull the vehicle away from the kerb and departed in a cloud of black exhaust fumes.

For one of the few times in his life Casper had wavered, swamped by a wave of indecision as he struggled to choose between following the car or remaining where he was. Powerless, he watched impotently as the decision was taken from his hands, the Corolla rapidly taking a corner at the end of the street and disappearing from sight. Even had he wished to do so, it was now unlikely that he would have been able to catch up with her.

Disturbed by such uncharacteristic prevarication, Casper had gritted his teeth and fumed. By then, however, his stomach was gurgling with hunger and, grateful for the distraction, he'd decided to drive to the nearest shops to purchase his unappealing sandwich.

Twenty minutes had passed since his return. He'd utilised that time to observe the windows of the house for any sign of occupation and to complete a second sketch.

Several droplets appeared on the windscreen, and he peered up through the tinted glass. Overhead, the sky was a grey-blue bruise, swollen and bulging with the threat of rain. Mercifully, the clouds appeared content to withhold their burdens for the time being, at least.

Dublin.

He sighed.

Ireland.

He exhaled slowly. He disliked this country.

Immensely.

Miserable weather, miserable people.

Casper's dislike of things Irish had originally manifested itself during his first visit to Dublin some seven years earlier. After less than a day of interaction with its inhabitants, he'd come to the conclusion that the Irish were a slovenly lot with a penchant for drunken exaggeration and hyperbole. This initial conclusion had been confirmed and reinforced on two subsequent visits.

In many respects, he felt, it was a miracle the country ran at all. In a practical sense, the people living here appeared to be completely detached from reality. Nothing in the country ever seemed to work the way it should. When people spoke, they never seemed to say what they actually meant. And the profanity! To this day, after thirty years of international travel, he had yet to encounter a more foul-mouthed lot. A uniform spread of vulgarity, its boorishness seemed to permeate every level of society, from the plebeian dregs of the inner city right through to the upper echelons of business and politics. In effect, it was as though the nation was composed entirely of outpatients from a specialist Tourette's syndrome clinic.

Casper took a deep breath.

Time to get to work.

Placing a thick pair of spectacles on his nose, he examined himself briefly in the rear-view mirror before crowning this new appearance with a soft felt hat. He stepped out of the car, crossed the street at an unhurried pace and paused briefly at the letter box as though to check for mail. With a leisurely air, he entered the garden through the small wooden gate, taking care to close it behind him. Dressed in his suit and holding a briefcase, he was confident that any casual observer would automatically assume he was a member of the household or a frequent visitor.

Ignoring the front door, he proceeded around to the rear of the house. The back garden consisted of a square patch of grass surrounded on three sides by a high hedge that obscured all view of the surrounding houses. The grassed section was bare apart from a revolving clothesline that held four tea towels, flapping in the breeze. It sloped up at a gentle angle to a narrow concrete patio that gave access to the house via a wide sliding door.

He peered through the door into a modern, well-furnished kitchen, then knocked firmly on the thick glass pane. He waited and knocked several more times until he was satisfied that the house was deserted. Opening his briefcase, he removed a hammer, a thick roll of insulation tape and a pair of leather gloves. He pulled on the gloves and removed two damp tea towels from the clothesline. These he wrapped tightly into a ball that he wedged against the glass panel of a small window beside the sliding door. Securing the cloth ball firmly, he attached it with several strips of insulation tape, which he also used to cover the remaining glass. When he had completed this task, he leaned forward and struck the ball softly three times with the hammer. On the third blow, there was a muffled crack, then the tea towels and taped up glass fell quietly inside onto the kitchen floor.

Casper inserted his hand carefully to avoid the jagged slivers still attached to the window frame and, by stretching, was able to reach the internal lock of the sliding door. It flipped into the 'open' position with an audible click. Withdrawing his arm, he slid the door back and slipped inside, closing it behind him.

He stood in silence to get his bearings and scanned the room's various entranceways. Satisfied, he was just about to proceed further into the house when a strange tinkling sound stopped him in his tracks. His eyes flickered towards the wide, arched entrance to the lounge but even as they did, a dark shape suddenly lurched up out of the corner of his eye and landed on the table beside him. He staggered back in alarm even as his startled senses began to make sense of what he was seeing. It was a cat! A damn cat!

Heart pounding, he struggled to regain his composure as he examined the animal. It was a healthy-looking specimen, relatively young – not much more than a kitten really. It had a sleek black coat broken only by two white socks on its lower front paws. Around its neck was a leather collar with a little bell and a metal nameplate with the name 'Noodles' stamped on it and outlined in red. The cat purred and rubbed its head against his hip. On impulse, he reached down, and it leapt into his arms.

He strolled through the lower level of the house with the cat snuggled contentedly against his chest, touching nothing but observing everything in detail as he sought to get a sense of the house and its occupants. The building was relatively modern, constructed in the last twenty years or so with quality materials and chattels. It was, he assumed, a rental property. He doubted the true owners would have allowed such an asset to be so haphazardly maintained. The evidence to hand suggested it was the habitat of a number of young females – probably three – a mixture of students or recently employed young women, possibly in their first professional employment. Unusually for this particular age group, there were no pictures or photographs spread about to give some indication of what they might look like. Frustrated, Casper's lips formed a thin, unhappy line.

The lounge, the largest of the downstairs rooms, contained an assortment of mismatched, new and second-hand furniture including a scuffed white sofa, a table and chairs and several beanbags strewn around the floor in no apparent order. The room was dominated by a home entertainment system set within a metal frame in one corner, next to a window that looked out onto the front lawn. The centrepiece of this array was a widescreen television, connected to a DVD player and other electronic equipment via a tangled mess of coiled black wires.

The mantelpiece above the gas-powered fireplace had been put to use as a shelf to hold a burgeoning collection of DVDs: a mediocre selection of chick-flicks and a 'Do it Yourself Yoga' series, proof positive that this was a female domain. Two old black and white classics – *The Third Man* and *It's a Wonderful Life* – had, he suspected, been placed there to display the owner's knowledge of recognised cultural masterpieces rather than out of any true artistic appreciation.

Further along the wall, a wooden bookcase struggled to contain the heavy university texts, reference books, paperbacks and self-help guides with unappealing titles such as 'Love Your Food, Like Your Body!' crammed into its upper shelves. Casper bent down, using one finger to flick though the contents of the lower shelf: cheap atlases, dictionaries, and even a set of old encyclopaedias.

Straightening up, he did a quick visual stocktake of the lounge, taking in the posters of various concerts (appropriated, no doubt, from the venues), a wine rack with a surprisingly good collection of French Bordeaux and a fully laden clotheshorse in the centre of the room. He examined the damp assortment of female clothing without emotion before moving on towards the doorway leading into the hall.

A cheap plastic table beside the door held a wicker basket overflowing with bank statements, electricity bills, overdue notices. There was also a cheap Japanese stereo system and an untidy clutter of CDs and USB drives.

The cat purred again as Casper stroked its head.

'What do you think, Noodles? A little music?'

He sorted through the CDs but none of the artists on the covers – feminine-looking boy bands or pouting young women with large breasts –

were familiar. Locating a single classical album, he removed the disc from its case with one hand and inserted it into the CD player. A moment later, the introductory chords of a Violin Concerto swelled around the room.

Casper hummed along to the music as he strolled smoothly back to the kitchen, avoiding the clotheshorse with a graceful movement so as not to disturb the cat. As they approached the fridge, however, it let out a hopeful meow and raised two bright, green eyes towards him.

'Hungry, are we? Oh, very well. Let's see what we have here.'

He released the cat onto the kitchen table and opened the fridge, surprised to discover that as well as the usual staples, the shelves were also stocked with an array of quality foods: full cream milk, smoked salmon, a selection of Danish cheeses, two bottles of French Chardonnay.

Retrieving a bowl from one of the cupboards, he poured some milk into it and placed it on the table. The cat greedily started to lap it up.

'Now, what else do we have?'

He peered a little further amongst the heavily laden shelves, before selecting a bulky item tightly wrapped in silver foil. The crinkling material unfolded easily to expose a large portion of cooked New Zealand lamb.

'Goodness me! They certainly haven't been depriving themselves, have they Noodles?'

He placed the meat on the kitchen table, removed a plastic chopping board and large kitchen knife from one of the drawers then sliced off a segment of meat, popped it in his mouth and chewed it thoughtfully.

Attracted by the scent of meat, the cat left the milk and started sniffing around the silver foil, nuzzling the package with its nose.

'Very well. I suppose you deserve some, Noodles.'

The cat nudged closer and he sliced off another sliver of meat then fed it to her. It was nibbling the meat delicately when the kitchen knife came down again, cutting through its back and erupting out of the stomach with such force the animal was impaled on the table. It convulsed ferociously, spilling its entrails even further for a second or two before going completely still.

Ignoring the cat's final agitated movements, Casper proceeded into the hall. Here, he squeezed past a mountain bike and two cardboard boxes of books to mount the staircase to the upstairs level.

The upper storey of the house consisted of three separate bedrooms and a bathroom. Two of the bedrooms were quite large, one with its own en suite. The sink in the main bathroom contained several items of make-up, some cheap jewellery, and stained glasses holding three toothbrushes and a half-used tube of toothpaste. The cabinet above the basin held an impressive variety of creams, powders, perfumes, soaps and sanitary items.

Once again, he carried out an initial inspection, passing through the various rooms, examining and observing until he was certain he'd identified that occupied by the young woman from the Corolla. In this respect, he was aided by an enlarged photograph on one of the walls that featured the individual in question holding hands with a skinny, goatee-wearing youth.

Casper stood in front of the picture and stared, studying the girl's features with grim intensity.

It wasn't her.

With a furious expression, he ripped the picture from the wall and stowed it in the inner pocket of his suit jacket. Leaning back against the wall, he exhaled deeply and made a fresh assessment of the room.

Of the three he had examined, the one in which he now stood was the second largest. It contained a queen-sized bed, a chair and study table holding a laptop computer and numerous piles of books, handwritten notes, and assorted A4 pages. Beside the table, a wire rubbish bin was filled to the brim with balls of crumpled paper.

The built-in wardrobe was narrow and bulged with an excessive selection of coats, blouses and dresses, but also contained a wet suit and a fancy-dress nurse's costume. The space at the bottom of the wardrobe was similarly crammed with cardboard boxes of bric-a-brac and a metal shoe-rack crushed beneath a mountain of mismatched shoes and leather boots.

Casper shuddered and closed the door.

The surface of the bedside cupboard supported a cheap lamp, a box of tissues, and a discarded romantic novel. The internal drawers contained little more than a range of neatly folded pullovers, tee-shirts, underwear, socks, and handkerchiefs. Further investigation yielded a collection of photographs, personal letters and a diary.

The computer proved ridiculously easy to hack into. Once he'd switched it on and obtained the initial access screen, it only took three attempts to work out the password. His first endeavour – 'password' – was, admittedly, a little too obvious but he was a more hopeful with his second effort: 'Noodles'. For the third attempt, he entered the name of the boyfriend (obtained from the diary) and the happy chime of Microsoft welcomed his entry to the operating system.

He spent half an hour searching through the computer files, mostly within the email system and the 'My Photos' folder. In the latter, he discovered a sub-folder marked 'personal' which contained several risqué photographs of the young woman scantily clad in suggestive poses. He grimaced as he scanned through them. It seemed so typical of this new generation. They were a vain lot.

When he had completed his examination of the laptop, Casper sat on the bed for over a minute, struggling to contain the fury that had been building up inside him. He calmed himself with the knowledge that a variety of potential options lay open to him, some feasible within the parameters of his current schedule, others less so. He looked at his watch.

According to his estimates, his timetable allowed approximately twenty minutes to draw a line underneath this particular situation.

With a final, decisive nod, he stood and withdrew a Stanley knife from his inside jacket pocket.

He had work to do.

He was methodical in his destruction, wherever possible maximising the damage for minimum effort. He made an exception where there was an explicit point to be made. The girl's clothes, for example, he removed from the wardrobe and drawers and systematically cut to ribbons. The knife sliced through them easily – even the wetsuit – and soon there was a pile of rags as high as the bed lying on the floor beside it.

Once he'd finished with the clothes, Casper started on the rest of the room, steadily moving through and demolishing anything he considered to be of personal value. He started with the computer, emailing the details of the girl's bank account (obtained from bank statements in the wicker basket downstairs) to a Nigerian address he had memorised for such occasions. He also added a short note thanking them for the opportunity to invest in their business and hoping it would be mutually profitable.

Several of the most revealing 'personal' photos, he attached to an email to various internet porn sites. He then entered the woman's social networking page, uploaded the same photos and forwarded a link to three hundred of her closest 'friends'.

The diary and letters he kept, stuffing them into a pocket for later.

When the destruction of the bedroom was completed to his satisfaction, he proceeded to the two upstairs bathrooms and firmly affixed the plugs inside the sink plugholes with a mixture of sealant and superglue. When he was certain they could not be removed, he turned on the taps.

Downstairs, he focussed his efforts primarily on the living room. The DVD player and the television he smashed quietly, but expertly, with the screwdriver. He collapsed the clotheshorse onto a pile on the floor and poured the contents of the Bordeaux bottles all over it. Some of the items, he knew, would almost certainly belong to other occupants of the house but, given the time constraints, such collateral damage was unavoidable.

Sweating from his labours, he paused to take a breath then glanced at his watch, surprised to discover that he was almost out of time.

He did one final visual sweep of the room, noting several potential areas of significant destruction before brushing such temptations from his mind. It was frustrating, but the sad fact was his time was up. It would have to do.

He left himself out through the front door of the house after carefully checking to make sure that nobody was watching the building. His face was blank as he closed the door of the house behind him. The sound of running water was loud on the stairs.

Chapter Six

Cork City, 2008

The noise of the phone resonated throughout the house, stirring the silence with all the delicacy of a heavy foot in a muddy puddle. It continued to ring for a full minute and when it finally rang out, its echo lingered in the air like a shrill afterthought. Twenty seconds later it started again.

'Ah, fer feck's sake!'

Cursing profusely, Mos emerged from beneath the duvet and roughly grasped the offending object.

'Fuck off, whoever you are!'

'It's eight o'clock, Mos.'

The voice was feminine with a soft West Cork accent and, in Mos' ill-tempered opinion, inappropriately bouncy for that time of the morning. It was also completely indifferent to the cantankerous nature of his greeting.

'Wake up, you cranky oul bollix!'

Mos sighed and wearily rubbed his eyes.

'Good morning, Bróna. How pleasant to hear from you.'

'Good morning, Mos. Late night, was it?'

He grunted in the affirmative.

'Ah, that's nice. It's good to know you can occasionally drag yourself out of that reclusive existence.'

'What reclusive existence?'

'Please, Mos. If the human race was composed of social butterflies, you'd be a moth.'

'Oh, feck off.'

'Ah,' she sympathised. 'The pathetic protests of the social derelict. He never goes out, he never maintains contact and, you know, for the life of me I can't even remember the last time he ever had a girlfriend.'

Her voice took on a playful quality.

'Would you like me to suss out some of my friends down here, Mos?'

'Very kind of you, Bróna but no thanks. Too close. Much too close.'

'Well, why don't you pick up some floozy when you're off working up in Dublin or Sligo or wherever.'

'Too far. Too far away.'

'Oh well, have it your own way then. If you ask me, though, you'll end up one of those sad losers who walk around in trench coats, masturbating in cinemas.'

There was a startled silence. Mos cleared his throat.

'So, why are you ringing me again, Bróna?'

'Yerra, nothing really. Just for a chat, ye know. Actually, no! Hang on! There was something. Some fella came around to the house the other day.'

'Ah, unlike me then, you're not socially derelict. Good for you.'

'Very funny, Mos. Unfortunately, it wasn't me he was interested in. He was asking about you.'

Mos suddenly went very quiet.

'Asking about me?'

'Yeah. Said he was an historian, but he seemed a bit young, so I figured he was lying. After all, I thought you had to have two-thousand-year-old dust coming out your arsehole to be an historian.'

'That's a desirable character trait, Bróna. Not a qualification.'

'Whatever! Anyway, he said you were an old friend, and he was trying to look you up, so then I just *knew* he was lying. Cos I know you don't have any friends.'

A surprisingly hearty burst of laughter erupted from the speaker. Mos rubbed his eyes as he waited for her amusement to subside.

'What did he look like?'

'Tall. Late forties, about six-foot, short brown hair. Actually, he didn't look particularly healthy. His skin had a nasty-looking sheen to it. Oh! He had a Dublin accent. D4, by the sound of it.'

'Great. I'm being investigated by an ailing, up-market Jackeen.'

'Looks like. Naturally, I told him I hadn't seen you around for a few years, but he didn't seem to believe me. When he left, he headed west the road towards your place, so I rang Ciarán. He drove over and found yer man poking around the house. He told him to get the feck off out of it or he'd call the cops.'

'Good man, Ciarán.'

'Yeah. Brothers are great like that. Apparently, the Jackeen left fast enough. We haven't seen him since. Ciarán got the registration number of the car he was driving – a blue Subaru. Do you want it?'

'Sure.' Mos fumbled around until he located a pen then wrote the number on the palm of his hand. 'I suppose I'd better go down and check the house.'

'Ciarán didn't notice anything amiss. I don't think he had time to break in or anything like that.'

'Ah, sure, I've been meaning to head down for a while.'

'Grand. Call in when you can. Don't get me wrong. The undiluted thrill of being your unofficial housekeeper will never fade, but it'd be nice to see ya a bit more often.'

'Right, so.'

There was a momentary silence.

'Mos?'

'Yeah?'

'Listen, I'm sorry about that crack. You know! About you having no friends.'

'Ah, you're grand. No biggie.'

'It doesn't have to be like that, Mos.'

'No, Bróna. I'm afraid it does.'

***

After he had hung up, Mos remained in bed for several minutes working through the ramifications of Bróna's call. The thought of some stranger poking around Carraig Dubh concerned him. Most of his acquaintances, although aware that he hailed from West Cork, were unlikely to know from which part. He was certain that none of them knew where the family home was located.

He scratched the stubble on his chin as he considered the implication. Clearly, somebody had been doing some digging in relation to him or, possibly, the land itself. Given the recent surge in housing along any types of coastal land, the likelihood of some developer sniffing around for a deal was certainly a possibility. The individual in question had, however, stated – probably untruthfully – that he was an old colleague, which was a concern. The title of Carraig Dubh was held through a private trust that was managed through a small, family-run solicitor's office in Cork, and his name on the official trust deed was the only formal link between the land and himself. If the stranger had known this, he knew a lot more than most people.

Mos rolled out of bed, wrapped himself in the duvet and shuffled over to the window to draw the curtains. Subdued, grey daylight seeped into the room. Gloomy and overcast again. But at least it wasn't raining.

That's it, Mos. Positive thoughts. Positive thoughts.

After a quick shave, he dressed in his most formal working clothes: a dark suit, sensible black shoes and a freshly ironed blue shirt. In the kitchen, he sliced an apple and added it to a bowl of muesli. He ate breakfast standing by the window.

When he'd finished eating, he brewed up a coffee on an ancient Italian espresso machine purchased on the Continent several years earlier. It was an old, unfashionable model but one he'd never regretted buying for it produced a consistently good cup of coffee.

After a second cup, he rinsed it in cold water, deposited it in the drying rack and, then made his way upstairs.

The layout of the upper level had been significantly altered since the house's original construction. Most of the interior walls had been replaced with a series of supportive pillars so that where once it had comprised four bedrooms and a bathroom, it was now almost entirely open plan. The only element of the original layout that remained was the walled-off bathroom and a small storage room.

The most significant portion of the upstairs floor – the working area where Mos spent the majority of his time – was centred about three separate tables. The first and largest, a long slab of oak supported by four thick metal legs, was situated in the middle of the floor. Several maps – some ancient, some modern – were spread across it. A complicated angle arm with a magnifying lens was bolted onto one end.

A second, narrower table had been pushed up against the wall and was cluttered with papers, folios, periodicals, loose A4 papers, photographs, journals, oddments, curios and electronic equipment. The last table, a simple office bench, held three laptop computers and was piled high with stacks of files that resembled giant paper sandwiches.

The area also contained several filing cabinets, crates and an antique grandfather clock with an imposing face decorated with ancient Irish symbols. A set of floor-to-ceiling bookshelves ran the length of two walls, crammed with a vast assortment of reference books in several different languages. The remaining wall had a whiteboard squeezed between two double-glazed windows that looked down over the spartan front garden. Beneath the board was a wide metal box with various wires emerging from it and connecting into the wall space behind. Sealed with a formidable lock, this unit contained the hardware that supported an internal computer system, a network wired throughout the house. Bróna, a talented IT technician and security software developer, had established the infrastructure for him several years earlier and continued to maintain it as required through a secure off-site connection, accessed from her own place in West Cork.

Mos pulled a face when he noticed a red light blinking anxiously on the fax machine. Hegarty's fax – five sheets of A4 paper – was lying in the in-tray. Old technology these days, of course, but still useful for a line of work where much of the ancient documentation was still years from being scanned or digitised.

He pulled the papers from the tray, stapled them together then slipped into one of the leather office chairs to read. Scrawled across the first page was a note in Hegarty's heavy hand.

Good morning, Muiris. I trust you slept well.

Attached is a copy of the background material on the Fianaigecht I sent to David Coffey, yesterday. It's an old article I came across in a journal years ago. I realise it's a very simplistic summation, but I felt it'd be useful as a basic introduction. At the moment, their knowledge of the Fenian narratives is quite limited. I'll leave it to you to rectify any omissions or factual errors.

Talk to you soon.

Professor Desmond Hegarty

Mos flipped to the next page, which held the title of the article in question.

"A Summary of the Fenian Stoires from the Past to the Present Day."

He frowned then for he'd recognised the title. It was not, as Hegarty seemed to be suggesting, an article from one of the peer-reviewed academic journals, but a piece written for an out-of-print amateur history magazine called *The Celtic Historian*. The publication had lasted for little more than a year as it struggled to find a viable market within the limited Celtic Revisionist and Wicca audience. Despised as lowbrow by the academics and overly technical by the Celtic Revisionists, it had folded and gone out of circulation shortly before the millennium.

Mos' lip curled in jaded cynicism. Providing a client with such a half-baked summary of the source material – a kind of 'Rough Guide to the Fenian Stories' – was astonishingly poor practice and yet, at the same time, typical of Hegarty. Although a competent historian and philologist, Hegarty was also an exceptionally lazy one. Preoccupied with games of academic power play, he lacked the passion for scholarly investigation needed to carry him through the dreary hours of research and to garner meaningful insights for his chosen field of expertise. Unable or unwilling to commit to such endeavours, he was reliant on the acquisition of academic deductions from other sources to maintain a semblance of professional credibility. In most cases – as Mos' personal experience had aptly demonstrated – these sources tended to be the work of other people, which he subsequently passed off as his own.

Such machinations had come back to haunt him over the years, of course. In recent times, Hegarty had become something of a pariah in academic circles and even his own post-graduate students knew better than to share their work too closely (whilst doing their utmost to seek alternative academic oversight). The most dramatic consequence of his declining reputation, however, had been his exclusion from the evaluation of the Fadden Psalter. An early medieval manuscript discovered in July 2006, it was a subject that was clearly within his area of expertise. Nevertheless, those in authority, aware of his reputation for plagiarism, had pointedly excluded him from the process.

The slight had been a major blow to Hegarty's credibility within the sector and a severe blow to his ego. Although Mos felt no misplaced sense of sympathy for the man, the event did go some way to explaining his desperation to be involved with the Opus Foundation project. Any association with a newly discovered early medieval artefact, no matter how minor, would go a long way to restoring his reputation on the international academic circuit, even if not within his homeland itself.

Shaking his head, Mos began to read.

Fionn mac Cumhaill, the most important figure of Irish mythology, and his company the Fianna, are the subject of several thousand narratives collected in written and oral form across Ireland, Scotland and the Isle of Man. This collection of tales is known collectively as the Fianaigecht.

Because of its wide-spread origins, the Fianaigecht has no clearly defined beginning. Nevertheless, in the most well-known narratives, the saga commences with the death of Fionn's father, Cumhal.

In these versions, Cumhal, an important leader of the Clann Baoiscne sept, is slain during the battle of Cnucha (Castlerock), against the Clann Morna. During this battle, Cumhal receives a mortal blow from Aodh mac Morna. Before he dies, he finds the strength to lash out at his killer and succeeds in blinding him in one eye. From that time on, Aodh mac Morna is known as Goll, or 'One-eye', mac Morna.

Muirne, Cumhal's pregnant wife, learns of the death of her husband and the defeat of Clann Baoiscne with despair and flees into the forest to escape the vengeance of the Clann Morna. Shortly after going into hiding, she gives birth to Cumhal's son and names him Demne.

Unable to care for the child under such trying conditions, Muirne places the baby under the protection of Bodhmhall and Liath Luachra, two caregivers who accept the responsibility of raising him in secret within the forest of Sliabh Bladhma (Slieve Bloom in county Laois). Over the following years, Demne's caregivers raise him and train him to become a skilled hunter and fighter. He grows into a young boy with long blond hair from which he derives his more common appellation, Fionn, meaning 'fair-haired'.

When he comes of age, Fionn bids Bodhmhall and Liath Luachra farewell and strikes out in search of his father's brother, a warrior by the name of Crimall. After much wandering, and many adventures, he eventually locates the old warrior living in an isolated part of Connacht with his remaining servants. Despite his advanced years, Crimall is an enthusiastic host and regales his nephew with tales of his glory days in the Fianna. Inspired by these stories and encouraged by his uncle, Fionn resolves to join the Fianna and reclaim his father's position as Rígfénnid, leader of the Fianna.

Pleased with his nephew's decision, Crimall enlightens him on some of the challenges facing him on such a quest. He explains that, according to custom, new recruits to the Fianna must first pass a series of physical and intellectual tests that include:

> *(a) escaping through a forest from nine warriors without breaking a twig underfoot;*

> *(b) leaping a branch at head height and slipping under a branch as low as their knees; and*

> *(c) reciting by heart twelve books of poetry and legends.*

Although sufficiently skilled from his childhood training to tackle the rigours of the physical tests, Fionn lacks the necessary experience of poetry to pass the intellectual test. On his uncle's advice, therefore, he travels to the banks of the river Boyne to study under a renowned ollamh – senior druid – by the name of Finnegas.

A respected teacher of the power of words, Finnegas is also a seer of some repute who has foreseen a day when he would catch the Salmon of Knowledge, a great fish living in a pool on the Boyne River. The ollamh has spent many years fishing its waters and waiting for this prophecy to come true as, according to legend, the Salmon of Knowledge contains all the 'fios' or wisdom of the world, and this knowledge will be transferred to the first person who tastes its flesh.

Several months after Fionn's arrival, Finnegas finally fulfils his own prophecy. Hooking the Salmon on his fishing line, he battles with the great fish for many hours before eventually wrestling it out of the water and onto the bank. Too exhausted to cook the fish, he instructs Fionn on how to prepare it for his dinner and explicitly warns him not to eat or taste any of it.

Following his teacher's instructions, Fionn builds a fire and places the Salmon on a spit to rotate over the flames. When the blazing heat causes a large blister to form on its skin, Fionn breaks it using the tip of his thumb but the juice of the Salmon bursts out and scalds him. Without thinking, Fionn sticks his thumb into his mouth to cool it down but in doing so tastes the fish's juice and, instantaneously, receives the Salmon's knowledge.

When Finnegas returns to the fireside that evening and sees the light of knowledge in Fionn's eyes, he immediately comprehends the ironic hand that fate has dealt him. Acknowledging that there is no longer anything else he can possibly teach the boy, the ollamh sends him on his way. From that day forward, whenever Fionn requires information, he obtains it by simply placing his thumb in his mouth and drawing it up.

After several further adventures, Fionn makes his way to Tara, arriving in time for the festival of Samhain. There he enters the assembly area where the Fianna warriors are gathered, identifies himself to the Ard Rí — the high king — Cormac Mac Airt and pledges his service to him. Goll mac Morna, Rígfénnid of the Fianna since the death of Fionn's father, is none too pleased to see the return of his old rival's son but is prevented from doing him harm due to restrictions on fighting during the festival.

When the evening's feast is over, the Ard Rí stands to ask the assembled warriors if any of them are brave enough to protect Tara from Aillén Mac Midna, an evil spirit that has blighted the settlement during Samhain for several years. Equipped with a gift for playing magical music that lulls the inhabitants to sleep, Aillén Mac Midna has been haunting the city during the festival, setting fires after all the inhabitants have been rendered unconscious.

Fionn, naturally, volunteers and manages to defeat the spirit using a magical spear (gifted to him by an old friend of his father) that prevents the magic music from affecting him. When the Ard Rí rises on the following morning to find his fortress intact, he immediately offers Fionn the leadership of the Fianna and grants him land at the hill of Almhuin to build a fortress of his own. Goll mac Morna expresses his anger at the situation but is given the choice of accepting Fionn's leadership or leaving Ireland. Under some duress, he reluctantly swears allegiance to his new leader.

A golden age follows Fionn's uptake of the Rígfénnid role. Under his leadership the Fianna fight many successful battles and take part in many fantastic adventures. Like King Arthur, Robin Hood and other literary heroes, Fionn gathers a group of intrepid warriors about him. These include his son Oisín, an accomplished poet and fighter; his grandson Oscar, the most renowned warrior within the Fianna; Goll mac Morna; and Goll's braggart brother Conán Maol. The group also includes the handsome warrior Diarmaid Ua Duibhne and Caoilte Mac Ronáin, a great warrior renowned for his running ability.

After many years and many successful adventures, however, the golden comradeship begins to tarnish. Fionn's popularity with the people causes friction with the Ard Rí. Clann Morna, who have never completely relinquished their desire for the position of Rífheinnid, also grow restless from time to time, their dissatisfaction occasionally erupting into outright battle with Clann Baoiscne. In an attempt to improve relations with the Ard Rí, Fionn asks for the hand of his daughter Gráinne. Repulsed and disgusted by the older warrior, however, Gráinne drugs the company during the wedding feast and places the handsome Diarmaid Ua Duibhne under a magical obligation to elope with her. Incensed by her *rejection and his comrade's apparent treachery, Fionn assembles a hunting party and pursues Diarmaid and Gráinne across the whole of Ireland.*

For pragmatic political reasons the two are finally forgiven but, the insult posed by their elopement is never forgotten. Some years later, when Diarmaid is grievously injured during a boar hunt at Beann Ghulban, Fionn refuses to use his skills to help his old comrade, who subsequently dies from his wounds. Shortly afterwards, during a feast at Almhuin, the rivalry between Clann Baoiscne and Clann Morna flares up again. Goll and Fionn argue over tributes and the men of Clann Morna leave the Fianna refusing to accept his leadership any longer. War breaks out between the two septs once more.

Several skirmishes take place over the following months but in the end Clann Baoiscne gains the upper hand. Pursuing Clann Morna relentlessly back to the river Shannon, they trap Goll Mac Morna in an isolated cave and put him to the sword.

Battle-weary and exhausted, the remaining Fianna return to Tara to discover that Cormac Mac Airt has died and that the kingship has been taken by his son Cairbre. No love is lost between the new Ard Rí and the leader of the Fianna, and no one is surprised when a short time later, Cairbre orders the Fianna to disband. Infuriated by this command and the affront to his personal authority, Fionn declares war against Cairbre. Many of the Fianna, however, refuse to take arms against the appointed Ard Rí. Others go so far as to join Cairbre's force and take up arms against their old leader. When Fionn eventually musters his supporters at the hill of Gabhra, he discovers that the size of his fian has significantly diminished.

The subsequent Battle of Gabhra is bloody and violent and many warriors on both sides are killed. Of Fionn's forces, only Fionn, Oisín, Caoilte and a handful of soldiers survive the slaughter. Oscar, their mightiest warrior, succeeds in slaying Cairbre but dies shortly afterwards as a result of his own wounds.

Broken and disillusioned, the Fianna retreat to Loch Léin and spend the remainder of their days hunting around its lonely shores. During one of these hunting expeditions, the Fianna warriors encounter a beautiful woman who has ridden across the waves on a white horse to find them. This magnificent and glamorous newcomer, Niamh, explains that she comes from Tír na nÓg (the Land of Youth) and convinces Oisín and Caoilte to accompany her back to her homeland. There, they live in happiness and luxury for hundreds of years, although for them it seems as though only several years have passed.

Eventually, the two men grow homesick and return to Ireland only to discover that everyone they ever knew is long dead and that all trace of Fionn and the Fianna has disappeared over the centuries. Dismounting from their magic steed, the two warriors are transformed into withered old men as soon as they touch their native soil and time catches up with them. Assisted by some passing monks, they are brought to meet St Patrick and recount all their great adventures to him before being baptised and passing away.

Muiris regarded the last page then, on an obscure whim, picked up a pen and wrote:

This is, of course, a complete load of shite!

He grinned cynically as he regarded the words, for his comment was merited. The author had done his best, but the summary was based on an English interpretation of Irish culture which was flawed at best. It was also notoriously difficult to succinctly summarise the entire *Fianaigecht* in any meaningful or accurate manner for the breadth and variation of the tales was simply too extensive.

Something about Fionn mac Cumhaill had touched a deep chord within Ireland's early population. Their fascination with the character and their demand for new tales had prompted professional storytellers and raconteurs to continually expand on the existing storylines. As a result, the original narratives had evolved in scope and geography, spreading from their oral origins in the Leinster region to encompass a significant body of oral and literary forms throughout Ireland and Scotland.

This development had a significant impact on the integrity of the original narratives. Exposed to the rigours of artistic license, variants to the story emerged. The location of events was switched to suit the locality; new characters were introduced; and in more extreme variants the tales ended differently.

Given the number of regional variations to the Fenian tales it was probably true to say that the complete breadth of the Fenian adventures had never been successfully collated (although one attempt – the *Dunaire Finn* – had made a credible effort). It was probably just as true to say, however, that because the stories were continuing to evolve in contemporary versions, it never would.

And, sure, there's nothing wrong with that!

Mos tossed the document onto the table and glanced up at the grandfather clock. Only nine o'clock. Still, plenty of time before his meeting.

He briefly considered a stroll but then decided instead to catch up on some outstanding paperwork. Some weeks earlier, he'd been commissioned to write an article on the Uí Néill sept for a European journal but hadn't found the time to complete it. Already more than a week overdue, the delay was preying on his mind, and he knew it was only a matter of time before they started chasing him up on it.

Gathering a number of reference books, he moved to the table in the centre of the room and pushed a large map aside to make a space for his papers. Using a blank sheet, he mapped the structure of the article out with a series of headings and titles to break it down into manageable sections. When he'd completed the plotting process, he slowly began to fill in each section.

He immersed himself completely in the subject, surfacing only once to verify a reference from one of his books. Years of intensive analysis and report-writing meant that he'd developed an impressive discipline for cerebral concentration, and he wrote fixedly for over forty minutes before raising his eyes.

He stood up, stretched and glanced once more at the clock. His thoughts turned to his appointment with the Opus Foundation, and he suddenly realised he had no idea what to expect from the meeting. The lack of any preliminary communication with the client – apart from Hegarty's vague instructions – meant that he was not only unclear on which aspects of the *Fianaigecht* they wished to discuss but didn't know which materials he could collate in preparation.

Irritated at these fresh misgivings, he paced vigorously around the room as though attempting to physically work the unease from his system.

The decision to meet with the Opus Foundation, he reasoned, had been made during a moment of weakness but the fact of the matter was that, apart from the article he was working on, he had no other compelling projects lined up. More importantly, the meeting purportedly had the potential to grant him access to a new source of information relating to the *Fianaigecht*.

He took a deep breath.

What the hell! If this mysterious artefact actually exists, it'll be worth it just to have a look at it before the beardies get their hands on it.

In this respect, at least, Mos harboured no illusions. Academic research and findings were jealously guarded and for some, the prestige associated with a new discovery was often more important than the discovery itself. Operating as he did, an independent on the fringe of the mainstream, more 'reputable' institutions – those very entities the Opus Foundation was at pains to avoid – he was used to carrying out the critical, but low-profile, research and analysis, then being firmly pushed to the background when the findings were made public.

This had never really bothered Mos. Although his professional reputation held some (minor) importance to him, he had no real interest in an academic career or the associated politics, egos and patch protection that went with it. He'd spent a significant proportion of his life avoiding the limelight, focussing his professional and personal efforts solely on the recovery of past truths that added to the great body of human knowledge.

He realised, of course, that many of his colleagues within the sector did not quite understand his motivations. Ignorant or, more likely, sceptical of what they probably saw as haughty and condescending aspirations, the Irish historical/archaeological academic fraternity had never entirely trusted him and considered him something of an eccentric. Despite this, he knew that he'd more than vindicated his worth over the years, producing a body of work and research leading to more historical insights and findings than his contemporaries could hope to match.

Over time, his high success rate meant that as a professional he could not be completely ignored. Some institutions, because of his proven expertise, were happy to contract him for their own research or archaeological programmes, particularly given that he rarely took credit for the findings. Because of his obvious usefulness, therefore, even if he was never really accepted, he was tolerated.

Mos brushed such thoughts aside as he looked out the window to Donovan's Road. The street was relatively quiet for a Monday morning. The cloud had cleared a little, filtering a watery sunlight that fell like a weak shower over the city. Further up the road, a neighbour's dog was barking furiously at a pair of crows perched in the lofty sanctuary of a tree. One of the birds cawed dismissively at the canine's outrage and released a solitary patch of white excrement that exploded onto the roof of a blue Subaru parked beneath. The incident was greeted with much amusement by a group of passing students. Wrapped in heavy coats and scarves, they laughed at the crows as they hurried by and Mos grinned, experiencing a subtle rebellious empathy with them. If he'd been down there himself, he'd probably have …

He stopped.

A blue Subaru?

His eyes returned to the vehicle. Yes. There it was. A blue Subaru.

He stiffened.

Nah! It couldn't be

He glanced down at the palm of his hand, annoyed to discover that the number Bróna had given him was practically indecipherable following his shower and an hour of writing and typing. He cursed as he realised that he'd forgotten to transfer it to paper.

Holding his hand up to the light, he found that he could just distinguish the first three letters: 'C', 'Y' and 'G'. He peered out through the window, squinting to make out the Subaru's registration plate. Although partially obscured by an overhanging branch, the first three letters were easily legible against the plate's white background.

'C', 'Y' and 'G'

Shite!

He pulled back from the window, suddenly conscious of the fact that he was visible to anyone seated inside the vehicle. The upper level of the house had no curtains and he'd raised all the blinds to get the best of the natural light.

Crouching, he moved to another window and edged his head around the frame. The Subaru was still in sight, parked benignly against the kerb. It appeared to be a relatively new car. The exterior was fresh and polished, although a small mud spatter streaked the bottom of the driver's door and, of course, there was the crow's recent deposit. The stylishly tinted windows, however, prevented him from making out whether the car was occupied.

After several minutes, the lack of any activity made Mos wonder whether he was overreacting. He chewed anxiously on his lower lip. He'd never really taken much notice of the cars parked in the street before and, for all he knew, the Subaru could belong to one of his neighbours.

Well, only one way to find out!

Pulling back from the window, he rushed downstairs and hurried outside. Leaving the house, he followed the street around the corner to Donovan's Road and quickly approached the Subaru.

Up close, there wasn't really that much else to see apart from the birdshit on the roof which, admittedly, closely resembled the physical profile of the current *Taoiseach*, Ireland's political leader. Mos tried to peer inside, but the window tinting made it impossible and reflected his own irritation back at him. He went through the motion of knocking on the driver's window but was not too surprised when no response was forthcoming. The car was obviously unoccupied.

He straightened up and looked around, scrutinising the surrounding buildings and passers-by for any kind of reaction to his presence by the vehicle. Life on the street, however, continued its usual routine, the passing students and cars ignoring him as though he wasn't there.

I'm getting paranoid in me old age.

Amused at his melodramatic reaction to a perfectly innocent vehicle, Mos shook his head and started back to the house. He was ambling back around the corner when the soft cough of an engine made him stop. Turning, he stared through the fence to see the Subaru pulling smoothly out from the kerb.

'Oh, ye sly fuckin' bastard!'

He rushed back towards the car but by the time he got back onto the street, it was already accelerating up Donovan's Road. He ran uphill, pursuing it, but it drew away from him effortlessly. At the intersection with College Road, it halted briefly before turning the corner and driving out of sight.

By the time he got to the top of the road, he was panting heavily. He stood at the intersection, glaring around in a mixture of fury and frustration and cursing between laboured breaths.

The Subaru had disappeared.

Chapter Seven

West Cork, Early 1960s

Pádraig was washing his car at the front of the house when Dinny's Volkswagen roared into the driveway. The rusty vehicle screeched to a halt just in front of the stationary Mercedes and remained there, rattling and shuddering. When Dinny finally switched off the engine, it seemed to slump onto the tarmac surface like an exhausted beast.

The two men got out of the car. Diarmuid stretched and stamped as he worked the stiffness out of his legs. 'Old age,' he thought. 'Stiff in all the wrong feckin' places.'

His lips compressed as he gazed up at Pádraig's house, an ostentatious palace done up in a mock Mexican hacienda style. Since the building's erection five years earlier, he'd always considered it a visual monstrosity, an incongruous eyesore on the rain-swept coastline. Driven by a pretentiousness that he shared with his hefty Dubliner wife, Pádraig's pride in his home surpassed the pride he had in his car. He was oblivious, or perhaps simply indifferent, to the fact that it had made him a local laughingstock, that he was now commonly referred to as 'Paddy the Mad House'.

Despite his disapproval, Diarmuid had to concede that the building appeared to be well constructed and offered an excellent view of the harbour and an t-Oileán Mór. He'd never been inside – and most likely never would – but word from those who had seemed to indicate that it contained had all the latest mod cons and luxuries as well.

Pádraig had stopped washing the Mercedes when they arrived and was observing them with open curiosity. Out of uniform, he cut a noticeably less imposing figure and resembled an overweight merchant rather than a guardian of the peace.

'Well, well. If it isn't Dinny and Diarmuid, the demon drivers of Beara.' He beamed in satisfaction at the cleverness of his unintentional alliteration.

'Hello, Pádraig. You missed a bit.'

Diarmuid pointed to a tiny smudge on the bonnet of the Mercedes. Pádraig gave him a sour look but scrubbed the indicated spot just to be on the safe side.

'The name's Patrick.'

He dropped the sponge into the bucket of soapy water before depositing a glance of contempt on Dinny's car.

'When are you going to get rid of that crock, Dinny?'

'Sure, it's a grand car. What's wrong with it?'

'It's a rusty bucket of bolts, is what's wrong with it. It can't be safe at all, so it can't.'

He considered the vehicle once more then spoke in his most authoritative voice.

'I'll have to ask you to remove it from the road by the end of the month, Dinny.'

Ignoring Dinny's look of indignation, he directed his attention to Diarmuid. 'Where's the young fella then, Diarmuid? Or have you decided to keep him after all?'

Diarmuid pretended to admire the view for a moment, making him wait for his answer.

'I have not,' he said at last. 'He's back at Dinny's place with Margaret and the kids and he's grand there for the moment.'

It took an effort to keep the tightness from his voice. That very morning, just before three o'clock, a horrific scream from his nephew had ripped him from his sleep. Stumbling downstairs, shreds of a lacerated dream crashing to the floor behind him, he'd found the child backed up against the corner of the room, squirming against the stone walls as though trying to force his way through. Although Demne's eyes had been wide open, he'd been oblivious to his uncle's presence. Pupils dilated and darting about the room in unfocussed terror, the boy had clearly been reacting to things that existed only in his head.

Subduing his own growing sense of dread, Diarmuid had approached the boy and cautiously put a hand on his shoulder. Demne had reacted violently to the touch, releasing an animal growl and drawing on some final reservoir of energy to beat the old man's hand away.

'Aisy on, boy. Aisy on!'

He had eventually succeeded in calming Demne sufficiently to guide him back to his cot. There'd been no rational persuasion, no convincing. He'd essentially worn the boy down, waiting until he was so exhausted that he could no longer remain upright and had no energy left to fight him off. Collapsing onto the mattress, his body had taken on the corpse-like stillness that had terrified Diarmuid the day before and, once more, he found himself feverishly searching for a pulse. Although a faint beat had finally reappeared a few minutes later. Diarmuid's lingering disquiet at the boy's apparent death-like state remained.

He regarded the policeman with bleary eyes.

'You didn't tell me about the nightmares, Pádraig,' he said.

The policeman offered an apathetic shrug.

'What's to tell? The social welfare people said he had a few bad dreams. He's only a young fella. He'll grow out of it.'

Diarmuid struggled to contain his anger. He should have known the policeman would wash his hands of any responsibility that did not affect him personally. Behind the Garda, Dinny's eyes flashed in warning. He'd made a point of cautioning his friend on the way into town, reminding him that it'd be pointless incurring Pádraig's enmity until they had all the facts.

Diarmuid forced himself to swallow the bitterness but it was a foul little pill to choke down. The Garda, meanwhile, absorbed in a fresh monologue, was droning on oblivious to the fact that the old man's fists had tightened, the knuckles showing white.

'But that's the new generation for you. If you ask me…'

'I'm not here to ask you about that. I'm here to ask where Séamus is buried.'

Pádraig's eyes widened. He was startled both by the question and the brutal tone of the interruption.

'Over in Na hAoraí, of course. At the Gortnabulliga cemetery.'

Without another word, Diarmuid turned and walked back to the car.

***

'Pádraig was a bit put out with you walking away on him like that.'

Dinny's eyes were focussed on the road as the vehicle struggled up the steep incline outside of town, gears haemorrhaging on another laborious corner. Diarmuid did not doubt, however, that his friend would be gauging his reaction from the corner of his eyes.

'The fecker'd have been even more put out of I'd stayed and smacked him in the puss.'

He took a deep breath and released it slowly.

'Jaysus, did you hear the shite out of him? *Cén ráméis!*

Dinny pursed his lips, doing his best to conceal his own resentment. He hadn't been impressed by the directive to remove his car from the road.

'It's many the time a man's own mouth broke his nose. And Pádraig'd certainly be the man to prove that, so he would. He hasn't changed a bit, you know. He was an awful gobshite when he was a youngster as well. Always trying to let you know how important he is.'

He gave a sour smile.

'Perhaps it was best that you walked away, all told.'

The village of Na hAoraí came into view some twenty minutes later, a scattered clutter of houses on a low hill overlooking Bá na Cuaillí and Kilcatherine point. Less than quarter of a mile from the first few houses, Dinny turned the steering wheel of the Volkswagen sharply to the left, bringing it down onto the road to Na hAilichí and the Gortnabulliga cemetery.

They located Séamus' resting place without too much difficulty. Situated off to one side of the graveyard, a respectable distance from the plots of the local families, it was the only fresh grave in sight. Diarmuid stared down at the recently turned earth, struggling to accept the reality of his brother's body lying just a few feet beneath. A few solitary blades of grass were already pushing up through the soil as nature, indifferent to his sensitivities, rushed on with its own agenda. There was no headstone, of course. No flowers or memorials. That was the family's responsibility.

Poor Séamus. The oul family haven't been much use to you, have they?

Diarmuid pulled a hip-flask from his pocket, unscrewed the cap and took a deep swig. The whiskey burned a coarse trail down his throat as he upended the container and poured several drops onto the grave. The liquid quickly seeped into the earth and disappeared.

'*Slán agus beannacht, a Shéamus. Tá an bhrón orm, a dheartháir.* Rest in peace and I hope you forgive me.'

He made to pass the vessel across to Dinny then paused in mid-action. Dinny, who'd been reaching out expectantly, glared at him in exasperation.

'Should I even be sharing this with you? What with you being the driver and all?'

'Will you just pass the feckin' thing here, ye eejit. Sure, it'll help me focus.'

The hardy farmer grasped the flask, took a deep swallow then repeated Diarmuid's action of pouring some onto the grave. They finished the flask in this manner, sharing it between themselves and Séamus. When it was empty, Diarmuid stared thoughtfully at the grave.

'Don't even be thinking it, Diarmuid.'

'What?'

'Of trying to move him. I haven't a notion of helping you.'

Diarmuid said nothing.

'Everyone'd know straight off who did it. And you'd have that fat eejit Pádraig after you. He'd love that.' Dinny sniffed and tapped the toe of his boot into the soft earth. 'Besides, you need to think of Séamus. Right or wrong, it was his choice to come and live over here and, sure, maybe he would've wanted to end up lying in this piece of earth. You can't make that decision for him.'

Diarmuid furiously ground his teeth together. He looked around at the sea and the cold grey hills then released a deep sigh. He knew his friend was making sense, though he was damned if he'd admit it.

'All right, all right! You've made your point. Let's go.'

With one final glance at Séamus' grave, they left the cemetery.

Out by the car, Dinny was in the process of opening the driver's door when a tall, spare figure in a black coat appeared from around a bend in the road. Head bowed down over the heavy bicycle he was pushing, he appeared to be absorbed in some private contemplation and completely oblivious to the two men observing him. It was only when he was almost upon them that he raised his head to stare at them in surprise.

Diarmuid considered the newcomer closely.

'Jaysus, Mary and Joseph. Tadhg Mac Carthy. Is that you?'

The man with the bicycle squinted back short-sightedly at Diarmuid. He was an elderly individual, frail and somewhat sickly looking. His forehead had receded so far back over his skull that he was almost completely bald apart from two white clumps of hair behind his ears.

'Diarmuid O'Súilleabháin? As I live and breathe!'

The bike fell into the ditch as he lunged forward with surprising alacrity to take Diarmuid's hand. The two men shook firmly, then each stepped back as though to assess the physical toll the years had taken on the other.

'You're looking old, Diarmuid. I hardly recognised you.'

'You've put on a few years yourself, Tadhg. For a moment there I …' Diarmuid stopped in mid-sentence and stared open-mouthed at the clerical collar that had been half-obscured beneath a thick scarf knotted loosely around his old friend's neck.

The other man gave an easy gesture of acknowledgement.

'That's right, Diarmuid. I've taken up the cloth.'

He smiled but it was a tired expression.

'I know. 'Tis hard to believe after the bad times we saw, Diarmuid.'

He sighed then, breathing the cold autumn air in deeply as though to cleanse himself of the memories. When he realised that the two men were watching him, he forced a lopsided grin.

'Then again, that's probably why I decided to do it in the first place.'

Diarmuid continued to stare at the clerical collar. Tadhg Mac Carthy, a prize-winning hurling player and road bowler from one of the neighbouring townlands, had always been something of a hero for him when he was young. As a teenager, and even into his early twenties, he had always been awed by his friend's easy manner and the confident way he handled himself with the people who invariably congregated around him. A handsome man with a charming gift for the gab, Tadhg was one of those people who had the knack for making people feel at ease and many of the younger lads had looked up to him. During the Troubles it had been Tadhg's decision to join the Volunteers that had inspired Diarmuid, Séamus and several of their contemporaries to sign up as well.

Tadhg's overall competence and innate sense of military strategy had made him a natural warrior. Mere weeks after joining the local brigade, he'd been promoted to a position of responsibility and participated in two direct actions against Crown forces, one of which had resulted in the successful removal of a despised member of the Black and Tans. Several months later, after organising a successful raid for weapons on the Dúnmaonmhuí police barracks, he'd been shoulder-tapped by Michael Collins himself and transferred to Dublin to become a key member of the infamous 'Squad'.

Tadhg had spent the remainder of the fight for independence in the capital, carrying out assignments that involved a significant degree of danger and bloodshed. Although he'd never discussed his experiences with Diarmuid it was clear that they had taken a heavy toll on him. On the few occasions that Diarmuid had seen him back in West Cork prior to the negotiation of the Treaty, he'd seemed a changed man, for he'd lost his easy affability and became withdrawn in the presence of unfamiliar company.

He'd departed the country for America shortly after the establishment of the Free State, avoiding the self-destructive mayhem and the bitter reprisals of the subsequent civil war. Twelve years later, Diarmuid had encountered him on a street in Cork, back home on a rare visit. Fresh off the boat, he had lost a lot of hair since the last time the two had met but, conversely, seemed to have recovered the characteristic sense of humour that had always made him such a favourite. He'd been in a mood for serious celebration when he'd bumped into his old friend and they'd spent a wild time sampling the stock of every pub in town, drinking to their exploits and the friends they'd lost in the fighting.

That night had been almost fifteen years ago but the extreme nature of the celebration still remained fresh in Diarmuid's memory. He recalled the utter vivaciousness of his friend that night, the fierce joy of singing, the insatiable hunger for porter and women. It was almost impossible to reconcile that memory with the withered figure in the clerical collar standing before him now.

'Bad times, indeed, Tadhg,' he murmured.

Dinny, who'd been too young to join the Volunteers and knew of Tadhg by reputation only, had been watching the two men silently. 'Are you the new parish priest now, Father?' he asked. 'I thought Father…'

'No, no. He's away in Boston for his cousin's funeral. I'm only filling in until he gets back on Tuesday. I'm up in Offaly now, meself, but I couldn't resist the chance to come back when it presented itself.'

'Ah.' Dinny nodded in understanding. The three men stared at one another for a moment and the conversation softly ran aground. The priest clapped his hands together in an effort to dissipate the stillness.

'So, what brings ye lads over here, Diarmuid?'

'We came over to say goodbye to my brother Séamus.' Diarmuid jerked his head back over his shoulder in the direction of the cemetery. 'Buried last week.'

The priest's eyes widened.

'That was Séamus? Oh, sweet Lord have mercy on us! I'm terribly sorry, Diarmuid. I had no idea.' He shook his head as though bewildered by the injustice of the world. 'I heard all about it – the accident – the day after I arrived. A terrible story. Apparently, there was a young boy…' He glanced curiously at Diarmuid.

'Your nephew?'

Diarmuid suddenly felt dull and exhausted. He nodded curtly and looked down at his feet, overwhelmed by an unexpected sense of devastation. To his relief, Dinny chose that moment to speak up again.

'Ah, that'd be Demne. He's a lovely *buachaillín*.'

Diarmuid took a deep breath and sniffed before raising his eyes. 'Tadhg, we're heading back into the village. Would you be on for a drop in Séamus' memory?'

'Of course, I would,' answered the priest.

***

Three miles into the mountains, the road disappeared. One moment, the car had been edging slowly along a rough track; the next, the trail simply petered out, its faint contours absorbed without trace into the surrounding countryside.

Dinny pulled the car to a halt and switched off the engine. Diarmuid stared out at the surrounding countryside, assessing the land with a farmer's eye. It was a grim spot, typical of much of the high hill country with stretches of burnt-brown, boggy terrain weaving between enormous peaks of rugged granite. Interspersed amongst this were a few faded patches of green, clumps of boggy pasture fit only for sheep and goats.

There were no trees, of course. Not much good for anything, this land.

Dinny, he noticed, was saying nothing, diplomatically refraining from asking the obvious question. What the devil had Séamus been doing out in such a desolate spot?

'What do we do now?' he said instead.

Diarmuid peered ahead towards the north. Before it'd disappeared, the trail had been leading them towards a low ridge that stretched between two rocky outcrops. Although he could not be sure, he suspected there was a pass somewhere along the ridge. It seemed the most logical option, at least. They were surrounded by steep hills and the other passable routes seemed to lead into constricting, dead-end gullies.

He grunted.

With regret, he realised that it'd probably have been a lot feckin' easier if he'd asked Demne for directions before leaving Carraig Dubh. After the events of the previous night, however, he'd been loath to trouble the boy with any mention of his father or his old home.

'Well, we can't drive any further. That's for sure. Let's leave the car here and head for that ridge. If we can't see the house from there, we'll have to go back the road and ask directions.'

Dinny remained silent but there was a dubious expression on his face. Diarmuid could guess what he was thinking. The last ramshackle building they'd passed – more than two miles back the tortuously twisted route – had looked more like a derelict shed than a house. Apart from the difficulty of backing onto solid ground to turn the car, it would take time to retrace their path, find someone to give them the proper directions and then start off again on the correct route.

He blew his cheeks out in frustration.

Things had not seemed anywhere near as complicated back at the pub in Na hAoraí. When they'd finally left the warmth of the bar and hit the road, his mood had been surprisingly optimistic, his spirits lightened by the company and the chat. Despite his initial reservations, he'd had a satisfyingly intimate conversation with Tadhg, although he'd diplomatically avoided the topic of religion or his old friend's astonishing adoption of the ecclesiastical life. Instead, the talk had focussed on happier days, old times and old friends; some alive, some dead, some departed overseas and never heard of again.

The only low point in the conversation had occurred when the old priest had unexpectedly asked Diarmuid if he'd been close to his brother in the last few years. Taken by surprise, Diarmuid had found himself unable to answer the question and, confounded, stared mutely into his glass. Realising belatedly that he'd stomped his *cábóg* deep in some unanticipated shit pile, the priest had quickly backtracked, changing the subject with impressive adroitness as he offered to organise a headstone for Séamus through his cousin, a stonemason in Baile Chaisleáin Bhéarra. He'd also promised to call around to Carraig Dubh and drop the stone off personally before he left for Offaly.

The barman, an overweight man with disturbingly hairy eyebrows, had proven a useful source of information. He'd been familiar with Séamus by sight despite never having exchanged more than a few words with him. Neverthless, as the central gathering point for all village gossip, he'd heard all the rumours and was more than happy to pass them along.

According to the publican, Séamus had been something of a recluse and had kept very much to himself. Diarmuid had been surprised to learn that Séamus had been living in the hills up the coast for several years. He'd rarely ventured into the village and even then, only to collect some mail or the occasional pile of groceries. No one, the barman included, seemed to have any idea that he'd originally hailed from the other side of the peninsula and Diarmuid made a point of keeping this to himself.

Such lack of social interaction within such a closeted community had, of course, fed into the local gossip mill and resulted in several interesting theories being spun about Séamus. Some claimed that he'd been in trouble with the law and was lying low in Beara. Others seemed to suggest he was the illegitimate offspring of some rich American businessman. This latter claim had garnered some credibility from an associated rumour that he was living in 'Daingean an Poncán', or 'The Yank's Fortress', a folly constructed by an eccentric American millionaire on the site of his mother's birthplace almost two decades earlier. Since the millionaire's death, the building was now (another rumour claimed) rented out for a pittance by a trust in the States.

No one had known anything of a boy until Séamus' body had been discovered by one of the local mountain men.

The only rumour the publican deemed to have any degree of substance was that Séamus lived in Daingean an Poncán. Although he wasn't sure of the exact location of the 'castle', he had heard that it was somewhere up in an isolated area known as Glonnyhust, inland of Dhá Dhromend. He hadn't seemed to think locating it would be a particularly onerous task. Even if it was isolated, he'd reasoned, there was bound to be someone they could ask for directions before they went astray.

Diarmuid sighed as he stared around the inhospitable landscape. The barman – it seemed – had been overly optimistic. He had obviously been unaware how deserted the area really was. Steep, unsheltered highland, it was a bleak and hostile country that was not conducive to habitation or agriculture. Back in the old days there would have been more people there, of course; back before *An Gorta Mór* when subsistence farmers scratched a living from any scrap of dirt they could get their hands on. Since the famine and the subsequent waves of emigration, the population of the peninsula was still significantly less than it had been prior to the 1860s, particularly in areas of such marginal land.

'All right, so. Let's go.'

Leaving the car, they struck off towards the ridge. Initially, it wasn't a particularly difficult climb although they were repeatedly obliged to retrace their steps to avoid boggy ground. To their surprise, after several minutes of walking, the trail reappeared beneath their feet as suddenly as it had disappeared from beneath the car. Its return improved Dinny's humour immediately.

'Fairy road,' he laughed. 'You never know when you're on it, you never know when you're off it – and if you follow it you'll never know where it takes you.'

The track, little more than a worn line of trampled earth, led them higher towards the ridge where the incline began to steepen. The bog land dwindled away, gradually displaced by a landscape of rocky expanses, riven by fissures and littered with broken fragments and boulders. Rounding a tight bend by a particularly large outcrop, they were surprised to encounter a skeletal individual with a worn, paper-thin overcoat and a shotgun cocked over one arm, looking down over the hills. It was obvious the figure was as startled by their sudden appearance as they were by his. He observed their approach through narrowed eyes, clearly torn between a desire to be left alone and curiosity as to what they were doing out there in the middle of nowhere.

Diarmuid pushed his cap back and wiped the sweat from his brow. 'Hello,' he said.

The mountain man nodded but no flicker of emotion crossed his face.

''Tis a soft day.'

''Tis.' The stranger contributed nothing further.

Diarmuid nodded at the gun. 'Rabbits?' he queried.

The question apparently touched an area of some sensitivity. The man's eyebrows furrowed up and his grip on the shotgun tightened.

'Rabbits, me arse. There's something been after the sheep. I've lost three ewes the past month.'

'We saw a wild dog back the road,' said Dinny. He gestured back in the direction they'd come. 'Back that ways a spell.'

The man scowled then spat on the ground. 'This wasn't any type of dog.'

Unsure how to respond, Dinny fell back on the regional default expression.

'Is that so?'

The man grunted, more in irritation than acknowledgement.

Diarmuid considered the stranger carefully. 'We're looking for Séamus O'Súilleabháin's place. Would we be going the right way for that at all?'

The mountain man regarded them dubiously and remained silent for so long that Diarmuid ran out of patience.

'Are we going —'

'Over the hill.' He pointed uphill at a gap in the rocks above them. He studied Diarmuid with sudden interest. 'You've got his face.'

'My brother.' Diarmuid paused. Normal behaviour at this point would have been for the other man to offer some form of condolence. Instead, he just stood there staring at him.

Diarmuid took a deep breath. 'Would you have known him at all?'

The man sniffed and wiped his nose with the sleeve of his coat.

'I would not. He was a mad fecker.'

With that, he tucked the gun up under his arm and stalked off downhill.

Gobsmacked, Diarmuid and Dinny stared at the back of the departing figure. Although no strangers to hill country themselves they were still surprised at how quickly he disappeared from sight, swallowed abruptly into the uneven landscape of rocky fissures and crevices.

'Jaysus,' Dinny muttered under his breath beside him. 'He was a quare yoke.'

'Out here in the open with that thin coat on him.' Diarmuid shivered. 'They breed them tough hereabouts.' He shook his head and turned to face the ridge. 'Come on, so,' he said. 'Let's go.'

The ridge was higher than it looked for it took another twenty minutes of steep, uphill effort to achieve the narrow rocky flat of its crest. They halted, catching their breath as they looked down into a valley that had been hidden from sight. Three hundred yards east of where they were standing, the precipitous walls on either side of the valley converged to a blunt, boulder-strewn apex. There, a shimmering cataract flowed down in silver rivulets over an ancient rock fall and welled in a deep black pool around its base. A stream issued from the still waters, running parallel to the base of the opposite ridge. The valley floor was a large meadow of thick, green grass, with a number of buildings clustered close to a raised mound near the rock fall.

'Janey Macks! Will you look at that?'

'Daingean an Poncán, indeed.'

The largest and most prominent of the buildings was a square, three-storey edifice that had obviously been built to somebody's warped interpretation of what an ancient Irish castle might have looked like. Constructed almost entirely from local stone, the pseudo-keep had a number of arrow slits that would have served no practicable application given that most Irish castles were built in an era when gunpowder had become commonplace. Adding insult to the injury of historical inaccuracy, the upper level was bordered with highly ornate imitation battlements and had turrets that would have looked more appropriate on a Bavarian palace projecting vertically from each corner. From their elevated position they could also make out a small extension constructed from the same stone facing them on the southern side of the building, and a withered flagpole set into a solid encasement in the roof's surface.

Situated on the mound, close to the building, were three smaller stone outbuildings. Off to the left, Diarmuid was surprised to see an enormous oak tree, the final component of Demne's drawing. His picture, it appeared, had a foundation of substance after all.

'What sort of quare, feckin' eejit would build a monstrosity like that!'

Dinny was still staring at the castle, affronted by the sight of such an alien intrusion in this isolated spot.

Diarmuid slapped him on the back.

'Yerra, you know some of them Yanks. They come back expecting land and a castle of their own because their parents told them they were the descendants of kings.' He shook his head as he stared at the mockery of a defensive structure. 'Mind you, the eejit that constructed this must have been away with the fairies.'

A rough path that repeatedly twisted back on itself to reduce the gradient led them down the side of the ridge. When they reached the bottom they walked towards the buildings, dubiously keeping an eye on the walls of fractured, grey rock that loomed on either side.

'Jaysus. Doesn't it feel a bit like a fortress, Diarmuid?'

Diarmuid snorted. 'More like a feckin' prison.'

He was surprised to realise that he'd automatically spoken in a whisper, as though some subconscious instinct was alerting him of danger. After a lifetime of living beside the broad expanse of Cuan Baoi, the presence of the surrounding cliffs had a disquieting effect on him and something about the muted stillness and the absence of birdsong disturbed him. As they made their way through the ankle-high pasture, the noise of their feet brushing through the grass was oddly amplified, resonating back at them from the blank rock walls.

Unsettled, he drew to a halt and looked at the narrowing enclosure of rock that surrounded them. A sudden shiver rattled down his spine.

'What's wrong?'

Dinny was looking back at him in surprise. Embarrassed, Diarmuid shook the sensation off.

'Nothing. Let's go on.'

Dinny, however, had bent down to wrench a handful of grass from the earth.

'D'you know, Diarmuid, this looks like it would've been one of those old booley spots where they'd bring the cattle for summer grazing. It drains well and there'd be grand pasture here for cattle in summer. And there's great protection from the prevailing wind.'

Diarmuid considered his surroundings with more attention. Dinny had it right, he realised. The sides of the valley acted as a natural barrier and its encompassing shelter prevented the passage of even the merest breeze. He relaxed, comforted by this rational explanation for the eerie stillness around them.

While Dinny continued to examine the grass, he turned his gaze towards the wider, western end of the valley. The meadow appeared to broaden considerably as it spread away from them. Less than quarter of a mile from where they were standing, it dipped sharply and disappeared from sight. In the middle distance, he could see some of the lower coastal land. Beyond that, the grey waters of the Atlantic, framed to one side by the even darker grey of the Iveragh Peninsula.

Dinny stood up and brushed his hands against his trousers.

'Well, there's been no cattle here for a long while. That's for sure.'

Diarmuid didn't bother with a response. Anyone could tell the site had never operated as a working farm although, given the quality of the pasture, Dinny's observation that it was an old booley site was probably accurate. It was possible, he mused, that if they looked hard enough they'd find remnants of the original huts used by the cattle herders. In this remote location, they'd probably have remained undisturbed for generations.

That thought made him wonder briefly at the efforts his brother had gone to in order to live in such isolation. Séamus, he reasoned, must have had a good reason to set up out here in the middle of nowhere, although he was damned if he could figure out what it was. Or, for that matter, how he'd supported himself in the meantime.

He turned his head and spat onto the grass as he looked towards the distant structures. With a bit of luck, maybe they'd provide some of the answers he was seeking.

As they drew closer to the buildings, some initial evidence of neglect and disrepair began to manifest. A dense tangle of briars had invaded one of the outbuildings and was aggressively protruding through a broken window. The roof on a second structure had partially collapsed and rusted barbed wire and a pile of sodden coal were visible through the empty doorway.

Large segments of stone were missing from the battlements of the keep. The outer layer of the lower walls was patched and crumbling and, in places, had been half-heartedly and ineffectively repaired with concrete. The earth immediately adjacent was almost entirely overgrown with weeds and nettles.

Despite his grief, Diarmuid couldn't entirely suppress a sense of disappointment. His father had raised his sons to appreciate the benefits of hard work and organisation and would have been turning in his grave to see such poor management of a property. He knew for a fact that his brother had been a competent handyman yet, for all intents and purposes, it looked as though he'd just given up on the place, slowly allowing the maintenance of the site to slip away to the point where it was no longer salvageable.

The entrance to the keep was through the little extension they'd spied from the ridge. The building was made up to resemble some kind of gatehouse and was accessed by five wide stone steps leading up to a wide, arched doorway. As they considered the two wooded doors, each bearing an enormous, rusted iron knocker, Dinny sucked air in through his teeth to create a low whistling sound. 'Should we go in?' he asked.

Instead of answering, Diarmuid placed both palms against one of the panelled doors and pushed, surprised when it swung smoothly inwards.

Within, the gatehouse was a square chamber with a high, triangular ceiling supported by thick wooden rafters. It was poorly illuminated, the only daylight coming in from the doorway and a small glassed opening high in the western wall. Once his eyes had adjusted to the gloom, Diarmuid was able to make out a single fireplace below the window, a rough table and two chairs. There was also a long beam lying on the floor by the doorway.

This, he assumed, would no doubt have been inserted in the metal brackets on the inside panels of the doors, to bar them securely from the inside.

Approaching the fireplace, he stirred the contents of the fire grate with his foot – a few charred pieces of coal and cold ashes. Beside it, a coal bucket empty except for a thick layer of soot.

A narrow doorway in the northern wall provided access to the keep itself. On entering, Diarmuid found himself in a dark hallway with a doorway in each wall, including the one through which he had just passed. The door to his left was ajar and through the opening he could see a basic bathroom containing a toilet and a sink with rusted taps. A door to his right opened into a small room that was bare apart from some dusty furniture pushed up against the far wall and a number of carpets rolled up into long, dusty cylinders like giant, discarded cigarettes. The tip of one of these partially obscured some broken floorboards and a narrow cavity in the floor. Curious, Diarmuid crouched down to peer inside but was unable to see beyond the dark shadow where a shallow hole turned inwards at a sharp angle.

Brushing the dust from his trouser legs, he returned to the central hall to find Dinny examining a boot with long laces that had four wheels attached to its sole.

'What in God's name is that?'

'It's a skate. A rolling skate.'

'What do they do, then?'

'You roll on them. You can go fast with them on flat ground.'

'What would you want to do that for? Anyway, sure, wouldn't you get stuck in the mud?'

Dinny's brow creased into a number of thin horizontal lines. 'I'm not sure,' he admitted. 'Margaret tells me they've been all the rage with the kids for the last year or two.'

Diarmuid rolled his eyes and proceeded through the narrow doorway. With Dinny in tow, he followed the curving corridor for several metres until it opened onto a wide room with a high roof.

His immediate impression was of having stumbled into some long-lost medieval banqueting hall. Three of the walls were adorned with shields bearing colourful coats-of-arms. The fourth was taken up by an enormous – albeit empty – fireplace. Overhead, a circular, metal chandelier encrusted with blackened stumps of candles hung listlessly from a vine-like cable, which was fastened to a stanchion in the far wall.

A long wooden table in the centre of the room, set with cutlery and plates for two, still held the rotting remains of a long-abandoned meal. A grey rat sitting brazenly on one of the plates regarded them with cold intensity as it gnawed on some unrecognisable item of vegetable matter.

'Go on! Get on out of it you little fecker!'

Diarmuid stamped furiously on the floor. The rodent leapt from the table, shot along the wall and disappeared through a hole in the skirting.

'Sweet Jesus, Mary and Joseph!'

Startled by the intensity of the exclamation, Diarmuid turned to find Dinny blessing himself and staring, wide-eyed, at the bottom of a stairway leading up to the second floor. He followed his neighbour's gaze to where a wide bloodstain had congealed and dried into the floorboards just below the first step.

It took him several seconds before his mind could actually come to grips with what he was seeing. As he stood there, staring fixedly at the discoloured surface, he was vaguely aware of his friend's voice murmuring in the background but couldn't seem to hear what he was saying. Inexorably, he found his eyes drawn along the dark trail of red streaks leading from the stain to the far wall, where a heavy wooden cupboard was lying on its back.

He was seized abruptly by a sudden nausea but, to his relief, it passed almost immediately. Dinny's hand, resting on his shoulder, steered him gently out of sight of the stairs and he allowed himself to be guided towards the table. He sank onto a coarse wooden bench, breathing raggedly as though he'd run a marathon and oddly aware that, although his body was sweating, he felt surprisingly cold.

It took a while for the shock to wear off but after a time he found he was able to think clearly again. Although physically drained, he managed to nod at Dinny, who was watching him anxiously.

'I'm so sorry, Diarmuid. I'm so stupid. I just didn't think of ...'

'It's all right, Dinny. It's all right. It was just the shock. Don't worry.'

With a deep breath, he straightened up and got to his feet.

'*Téann liom. Tá obair againn a dhéanamh.*' Come on. We've got work to do.

He turned around to confront the stairs with fresh resolve, although he averted his eyes from the tarnished floorboards as he stepped over the bloodstain and mounted the rough wooden stairway. He could feel Dinny's eyes on his back as he climbed – two steps at a time – and knew that his friend was concerned by his apparent lack of emotion, but it wasn't something he was up to dealing with at present.

The second floor consisted of four rooms – an office, a library and two bedrooms – and another, smaller spiral staircase that led up to a hatchway in the roof. Bizarrely, although all of the rooms had a wide doorway, none of them had an actual door.

The office was a snug space with a single window overlooking the rock fall and the pool. A wide desk occupied a significant portion of the floor space but there was also a hard-backed chair, a filing cabinet, and a small, lockable wooden cabinet, the security of which was undermined by the fact that the key was in the lock and its door was wide open. The interior was bare apart from some dust and a fingernail-sized scrap of paper.

Numerous papers lay scattered about the room. Many of those on the floor bore the imprint of heavy boots. The drawers of the desk had been forced open and their contents – mostly items of stationery – had been removed and dumped in a small pile on top.

'Burglars!' exclaimed Dinny. 'The feckers have ransacked the place.'

Diarmuid shook his head. 'It was probably Pádraig and his Garda cronies. He said they'd taken all the official looking papers.' He gestured at the remaining documents strewn about the floor. 'He probably left these because they're in Irish. In his mind, he'd automatically assume they were worthless.'

Dinny grinned, suddenly looking a lot younger than his fifty-five years. 'Can you imagine that fat *amadán* coming all the way up here? I'll bet he sweated a week's worth of lard just climbing over the far ridge.'

He was still smiling as he turned to examine a number of framed certificates and photographs that lined the wall.

'I didn't know Séamus was a university man.'

'What?'

Dinny pointed to a black and white photo of a bearded man in a graduation gown shaking hands with some anaemic individual wearing a suit and tie. In the background, Diarmuid recognised the quadrangle from University College Cork, but it took him a moment to realise that the man in the gown was Séamus.

'Holy Jaysus. I didn't recognise him with the big *féasóg*. He was clean-shaven when I last saw him.'

'Was Séamus an important fella then, do you think?'

'I don't know, Dinny. I honestly don't know.'

Diarmuid gathered up the scattered papers and piled them loosely on the desk alongside the contents of the drawers. Plucking a sheet at random from the collection, he glanced at it briefly before putting it aside again.

'Yerra, I suppose there'll be time enough for reading later. Is there anything to put them in, at all?'

Dinny wordlessly retrieved a canvas bag that was lying on the floor behind the desk.

Diarmuid looked at it dubiously. 'I suppose it'll do.'

They stuffed fistfuls of papers deep into the sack and followed them with the photographs from the wall. Diarmuid surveyed the room for a moment and contemplated adding some more, then thought better of it and left to explore the rest of the building.

His parents' wedding photograph sitting on a chest of drawers in the first bedroom was sufficient confirmation for Diarmuid that this was where his brother had been sleeping. Only one copy of the picture had ever existed at Carraig Dubh and Séamus had taken it with him the day he'd left for good.

His joy at the recovery of the family heirloom, however, was tempered not only by the circumstances but by the overwhelming disorder, the *ruaile buaile,* throughout the room. Diarmuid looked around in silent disapproval. The windows were unwashed, the curtains filthy, the iron-framed bed unmade and the sheets looked as though they hadn't been changed in months. Discarded pieces of paper, dirty plates and other bric-a-brac were strewn all over the floor. The most striking feature was the mound of clothing and wooden hangers deposited by the wall, where the floorboards had a faded discoloration in the shape of a rectangle. With a sinking sensation in his stomach, he realised that this was where the wardrobe at the bottom of the stairs had been located.

He considered the untidy pile in silence for several seconds and frowned. To his eyes, it looked as though someone in a hurry had dumped the contents of the wardrobe in an effort to reduce its weight before moving it.

He bit down on the skin on the inside of his check. Unfolding the top of the canvas sack, he placed the framed photograph of his parents inside, wrapping it in one of his brother's old shirts so that it wouldn't be damaged.

The second bedroom contained a single bed with some rough blankets, a table with an enamel washbasin and a wooden box that held a variety of children's clothes. Beside it, a second, smaller box contained a number of hand-carved wooden toys. He recognised Séamus' signature style.

'Look at this, Dinny.'

Diarmuid fished out two objects and held them up so that his friend could see them clearly. They were *buaircíní* – pinecones – and four matches had been cleverly inserted on the underside of each. Hand-carved heads had been fastened to the tops with thin slips of wire and the resulting objects bore a remarkable resemblance to a pair of cows.

He rubbed the surface of the *buaircíní,* enjoying the rough sensation of the grain against the skin of his fingertips. 'Just like the ones we used to make when we were we'ans. Mind you, Seámus' were always better. He had the hands for wood, he did.'

He began to stuff the clothes and the toys inside the sack. Removing several crayon drawings from the wall, he folded them up and added them to the growing load.

'The young fella might feel better with his own clothes and toys.'

Dinny nodded in assent. 'Well, you may as well add these, so. I found some more in the landing.' He threw in two rolling skates like the one that he'd shown to his friend earlier.

The library wasn't a room so much as a triangular space between the two bedrooms. It had no doorway as such and contained little more than three heavily laden bookshelves and a table weighed down by a grimy assortment of history books and Irish language tomes. After a brief glance, Diarmuid decided against adding anything further to the sack. It was already growing cumbersome and, of the titles he'd seen so far, none struck him as being of any particular interest to a child.

'Sure, we can always come back for more,' Dinny suggested cheerfully.

Diarmuid said nothing. He had no intention of ever coming back this way again if he could possibly help it.

Emerging from the library, Diarmuid peered up to the ceiling where a square hatch with a transparent cover provided some welcome natural light. A rickety spiral staircase ascended to the hatch. With a wry glance at his friend, he shrugged and placed a foot on the lowest rung.

To his relief, the staircase was considerably more solid than it appeared. When he reached the top and tested the hatch, he found that it lifted easily, rolling backwards on a set of fixed hinges until it lay flat on the rooftop.

Diarmuid emerged from the stairway into winter sunshine and onto a surface that was sealed with bitumen, badly weathered and cracked in several places. Picking his way between the breaks, he approached the battlements and leaned cautiously against the crumbling merlons. The valley rolled out below him, a long, V-shaped carpet of green that stretched towards the sea. He inhaled deeply but was unable to smell any trace of it. The air around the *Daingean* hung silent and heavy, too far from the coast and with insufficient wind to drag the salty tang up to the mountain.

The remains of several discarded cigarette butts littered the roof surface around his feet, and he had a sudden mental image of his brother standing where he was now, drawing the smoke into his lungs as his eyes took in the same view. His knees creaked as he crouched to pluck one from where it had wedged beneath a loose chip of bitumen and held it up to his nostrils. Despite the butt's exposure to the elements, he could just discern the stale scent of tobacco that smelled remarkably similar to the brand he smoked himself.

The sound of a shoe scraping against the bitumen alerted Diarmuid to Dinny's arrival. His friend took up an unobtrusive position beside him and both men contemplated the landscape without speaking. Finally, Diarmuid turned to confront his neighbour.

'This is mad, Dinny. What the devil was Séamus doing away out here. This is no place to raise a child.'

'Yerra, sure, it's not too bad. It's nice and quiet. I like that.'

'That's just because you live in a house full of shrieking women. You'd think an empty desert was nice.'

He scowled and cast a glance up at the surrounding ridges.

'I dunno. I think there's something forlorn about this place. Can't you feel it?'

'I can't say that I do. Maybe it's because of what happened here. You've associated the place with black thoughts.'

'I don't think so. The place is haunted sure enough. It's tainted.'

'Well, if it is, it's only recently tainted. There were people up here doing the booley for centuries. They wouldn't have come if it was haunted.'

'So why don't the locals know about the booley?'

'Well, I suppose they must have done, but with the famine and the emigration I think the memory was lost. All the old people died, all the young people moved away and there was no one left to remember.'

Diarmuid grunted in acknowledgement, unable to find fault with the old farmer's reasoning.

Dinny cast an anxious eye at the sky. 'All the same, maybe we should start thinking about heading back to the car. I really don't want to be driving on that road in the dark.'

'Fair enough. I don't think we can do any more here.'

Flinging the desiccated cigarette butt out over the battlements, Diarmuid took one last look around then followed his friend down into the stairway.

***

The intensity of the sunlight had changed perceptibly by the time they left the house. Weak and watery, it had already started its inexorable fade to grey as they commenced their climb back up the ridge trail.

Both men were sweating heavily by the time they reached the summit. Pausing to recover his breath, Diarmuid removed his cap and wiped the perspiration from his brow. Casting a long glance back down the route they had taken, he found that the hills were now preventing the sunlight from penetrating the valley and the Daingean below was already shrouded in shadow.

He sighed. The events of the last few days weighed heavily on him as the sun sank away, and the world seemed a small, senseless and brutal place.

'Jesus, Mary and Joseph, I'm getting too long in the tooth to be traipsing up and down these feckin' hills.'

Dinny silently put a hand on his shoulder.

'Come on now, *Dadó*. Buck up man.'

Diarmuid released a coarse laugh at that. Grandad, indeed! There was only eleven years' difference between them, but it was an old joke they'd been trading on for more than a decade.

''Tis the old dog for the hard road. No need to be cheeky now, ye young pup.'

Dinny chortled in response and seemed about to push the joke further when he suddenly stiffened and stared across to the far side of the valley.

'What the devil is that?'

'What's what?'

'Up there on the ridge.'

Dinny raised a hand, shielding his eyes from the glare of the sun, which now hung just above the opposite ridgeline.

'Is that someone over there, do you think?'

Diarmuid followed the length of Dinny's finger to the indicated spot. At first, he was unable to see anything through the dazzling effect of the sunset before them. After a moment, he caught sight of some movement up on the far summit and an indistinct shape that could have been a man silhouetted against the brightness. Despite the great distance, he suddenly had the distinct impression that he was being observed and although he could not have said why, the sensation made him feel distinctly uncomfortable.

He glanced nervously towards Dinny's car, a distressingly small white speck in the distance, down in the valley on the other side of the ridge.

Unlike Diarmuid, Dinny appeared to experience no disquiet. He stared across the valley with open curiosity.

'Would it be a neighbour, do you think?'

Although he was feeling increasingly uneasy, Diarmuid fought the sensation down and forced himself to answer calmly.

'I don't know. But we should really be going.'

Dinny grunted in acknowledgement.

'Well, whoever it is, I think he's seen us.'

Diarmuid squinted into the sunlight once again. It might have been nothing more than cloud shadow moving across the surface of the rock but the blur on the summit appeared to be shifting rapidly, disappearing then reappearing moments later beside a large outcrop, several metres further down the ridge.

'Jaysus, will you look at that! Christ, he's a fast fecker.'

'Jesus, Dinny. Nobody could move that fast.'

Dinny said nothing but continued to peer into the dazzling sunlight as the indistinct smudge moved down the side of the ridge. 'Do you know,' he said, and this time there was a trace of anxiety in his voice. 'I have an awful feeling that whoever or whatever it is, it's coming over here to us.'

'Well, then let's get the feck out of here, so. I don't want to be dealing with any more strange fellas out in the wilderness with no one around to help us.'

This time, his friend displayed no inclination to delay. Possibly some instinct of his own had finally kicked in or perhaps it was simply that he'd noticed Diarmuid's obvious apprehension. Whatever the reason, Dinny was quick to match his pace downhill towards the car.

They made good progress on the downward slope, but Diarmuid could not help wishing he was thirty years younger. Back in the day, he'd have slipped down the slope as nimble as a mountain goat. Now he was all stiff limbs, fragile ankles and gristle.

The two men found themselves unconsciously caught up in a growing sense of panic, increasing their pace almost with each stride. Three quarters of the way down the trail, Dinny stumbled and would have fallen if Diarmuid hadn't grasped him by the arm.

'Slow it down,' he hissed. 'Let's get a grip on ourselves.'

He watched as Dinny regained his balance, struck by the fear in his friend's eyes.

'Are ye all right?'

'I am, I am.'

Dinny nodded eagerly as though impatient to be away again.

'I'm grand. Let's go. Keep going.' His voice was tight with tension and his eyes darted off down the valley to where the car still seemed despairingly far away.

'Right, so. Let's just take it easy. Only ten minutes down to the boggy patch, across that and we're there.' Diarmuid did his best to sound reassuring but suspected his voice sounded just as strained as Dinny's had.

Continuing their descent, he became so focussed on the placement of his feet and the need to move as quickly as possible that he lost all sense of time. It was only when Dinny shouted in relief that he looked up and became aware of their proximity to the Volkswagon.

'Thank God for that!'

Rushing for the driver's door, Dinny heaved it open, slid into the seat and started patting his pockets for the keys. Fighting for breath, Diarmuid leaned against the car and threw a fearful glance back over his shoulder. At that precise moment, an indistinct figure appeared over the top of the ridge they had just descended.

His body already tingling from the combined effects of adrenaline and exhaustion, Diarmuid felt a physical lurch of dread at the sight of the apparition. Before he could pull his thoughts together, however, the car engine roared into life beside him, wrenching his attention from the ridge.

'Are you feckin' getting in or what?'

Dinny pushed the passenger door open, but he was already reversing the vehicle as his friend clambered inside, lining it up to follow the faint track leading out of the mountains.

The engine revved with an angry snarl and the car jerked forward. Slamming his own door shut, Diarmuid turned to stare back at the ridge. The sun had now completely sunk behind the hills and murky fingers of dusk were already smoothing over the cracks in the brittle landscape, softening them beneath a mantle of deeper grey. The figure on top of the ridge, still as indistinct as when it had first appeared, did not appear to have moved.

'Well?' snapped Dinny.

'What?' Diarmuid gawped in confusion.

'Did you see anything? Anything back up there?'

Diarmuid bit his tongue. 'Nuttin',' he said quickly. 'Nary a bit.'

'Well, thank fuck for that!'

Dinny withdrew into silence, focussed solely on negotiating the faint trail that was growing even fainter in the gloaming. Ignoring his fear that Dinny was driving too quickly for the state of the track, Diarmuid willed him to drive even faster. Within a few minutes, they curved around a low hill and the ridge fell out of sight behind them.

With a great sigh of relief, Dinny relaxed back in his seat and eased his foot off the accelerator. He turned towards the passenger seat.

'Diarmuid,' he said. 'You know you are my friend.'

'I do.' Diarmuid regarded his old companion with subdued amusement. 'Yes.'

'So, please don't take this the wrong way.'

'All right.'

'I'm never, ever taking you back to that feckin' valley again.'

With that, Dinny turned back to the road and pressed his foot down. The vehicle jerked forward and began the long road back to civilisation.

Chapter Eight

Cork City, 2008

It was well after ten thirty when Mos entered The Beach, a glitzy cafe in one of Cork's pedestrian inner-city streets. Despite the hour, the coffee shop was practically deserted, with the exception of two teenage waitresses absorbed in a detailed conversation on the merits of a new facial cream. Their discussion continued unabated as Mos stood at the counter waiting for his presence to be acknowledged.

I must be showing my age. This is the first time the staff have been too fucking cool to serve me.

One of the girls, a strawberry blonde with a face scatter-blasted by raw, red pimples, eventually deigned to notice him. She shouted loudly above the noise of the coffee grinder going hell for leather on the workbench beside her.

'What'll it be?'

'Espresso.'

'Wha'?'

'Espresso.'

'Grand, so! Grab a seat and we'll be right there.'

He glanced around the empty room.

'Right, I'll see if I can find somewhere to squeeze in.'

Leaving the frowning waitress, he opted for a window seat that offered an unrestricted view of the street outside and sat scrutinising the faces of the passing pedestrians. Although he was aware that he was probably overreacting to his earlier experience with the Subaru, he figured a certain healthy paranoia could never go too far astray.

Not that I have any fucking idea what I'm looking for. I didn't get a look at the driver and whoever it was, they're hardly likely to drive it down here.

He absently massaged the tension in his neck, cursing when his fingers touched the tender spot at the base of his skull.

'Do you want me to wipe tha'?'

Startled, he looked up to discover the red-haired waitress gazing at him with an expression of abject boredom. She stood with one hand holding a white saucer on which a cup of coffee was precariously balanced. The other clutched a teacloth with disturbingly large stains of a sticky, red substance. It looked as though it had recently been used to mop up a murder scene.

'Huh?'

'Do you want me to wipe tha'?'

They both regarded the debris left on the table surface by a previous occupant: a creamy clutter of dried crumbs, spilt milk and some oily substance that vaguely resembled butter.

'Whatcha going to do? Rub it in?'

'Wha'?' The waitress stared at him in incomprehension.

Mos sighed.

'Never mind. You've got it just the way I like it.'

'Ah, right so.'

With a shrug, she deposited the cup on the table and floated apathetically back towards the counter. Mos watched as she resumed her post beside the cash machine. Her colleague had disappeared through a door at the rear of the counter and, temporarily bereft of company, she took up her earlier position, contemplating the empty space in front of her eyes with an air of resignation.

Mos took a deep breath and shook his head. It was the classic story of inner-city development over the last decade. An old, family-run establishment purchased by new owners with pretentions of grandeur, delusions of cool and a degree in social marketing. Despite their best efforts, an undercurrent of weariness always lingered beneath the flamboyant veneer. The premises seemed to exude some inbuilt subliminal message that no matter how much money was poured into the exterior decor, underneath it would always remain the same old, bog-standard greasy spoon.

Mos picked up his coffee and swirled, dubiously examining the dark liquid. Despite evolutionary leaps in coffee-brewing over the previous decade, some coffee shops just couldn't relinquish certain long-held traditions of a tea-drinking nation. Such places stubbornly insisted on serving up coffee that either originated from a powdered packet or was boiled to a shit-coloured tar, which was subsequently drowned beneath a deluge of milk and sugar.

He took a tentative sip and found, as expected, that the coffee had the consistency and flavour of boiled dog turds. He sighed.

Nothing like crap service to put you in your place!

He mechanically stirred the steaming liquid with a plastic teaspoon as he studied the grey bulk of Shandon House. Situated across the street from the cafe, it consisted of four storeys of smooth, locally quarried Cork stone, to which an additional three floors had been added in 2003. This extension had been carried out to the minimum standards of quality and design and had used the cheapest of materials and immigrant workers available. As a result, it had also been plagued with structural problems ever since construction had been completed. Less than six years later, it was already showing signs of wear and tear more commonly associated with buildings ten times its age.

As a result, much of the building's floor space was empty and the owners struggled to attract or retain even short-term occupancy. It now to specialised as a transitory working space for small business start-ups and office hire for the occasional workshop or meeting.

Although Mos himself had attended meetings there on at least two previous occasions, he could not recall the interior in any detail. For the most part, those visits had been short affairs, brief engagements with clients passing through the city. The only impression of any depth that he could recall was one of indifference.

He sniffed and looked at his watch. It was 11:00.

In am imeacht! Time to go!

Leaving the coffee untouched, Mos stood and left the cafe. The two waitresses, engrossed in a fresh conversation about an attractive male soap opera star, did not see him go.

Six strides took him across the street to the low steps leading up to the entrance of Shandon House.

The internal lobby was a wide space with marble floor tiles. The surrounding walls featured unremarkable white panelling with some high curved arches and poorly reproduced Roman columns. Three lifts faced the entranceway and, as though on cue, one of them opened with a high-pitched chime as he approached.

Stepping inside, he noted that the nameplate for the fifth floor – his destination – was blank. His index finger hovered as he was caught by a sudden and inexplicable sense of disquiet.

Getting skittish in your old age, Mos. Just press the feckin' button.

Unable to put his finger on the niggling unease he was feeling, he put it instead on the button for the fifth floor.

With a depressing sense of finality, the twin doors closed.

***

The lift doors opened to a broad semi-circle of matte-patterned carpet enclosed by a curved grey wall. Three bland reproductions of pastel-coloured landscapes and two equally spaced sets of double doors failed to lend interest to the colourless surface. A compact wooden counter facing the lifts sat like an island on the carpet. To its left was a spartan waiting area comprised of a minimalist sofa, two chairs and a low coffee table. To its right, a white sign with bright red letters loudly instructed all comers to *'Please approach reception'*.

The extreme physicality of the figure who sat behind the reception desk contrasted jarringly with the sanitised business environment. An enormous, broad-shouldered individual with a military-style haircut, he was wearing a striped business suit that stretched over a well-muscled body. This adherence to corporate dress code was fundamentally undermined by the intimidating burn mark that stretched down the left side of the man's face, from his eye to the curve of his chin.

The receptionist greeted Mos with a cold stare as he approached the counter.

'Good morning! I have an appointment with a Mr David Coffey.'

The scarred man did not respond at first, but merely considered him with an indifferent expression. He sniffed, turned to consult a computer screen behind the counter and began to type. Mos could not help but notice how laboriously he used the keyboard, painstakingly tapping each key with the index finger of his right hand.

'Mr O'Sullivan, is it?'

A Dublin accent. Inner-city but certainly not D4. Then again, that was hardly surprising. He didn't look like your typical D4 resident.

'No. Mr O'Súilleabháin.'

'Sure, but that's "O'Sullivan" in English, isn't it?'

'No, it's "O'Súilleabháin" in English. The same way "Picasso" is "Picasso" in English or "De Niro" is "De Niro".'

The scar tissue stretched as subcutaneous muscle tightened into a frown. The receptionist regarded Mos with sour hostility but refrained from further comment. An offhanded gesture indicated the double doors directly behind him.

'They're in the board room. Go on through.'

He turned away, picked up a newspaper and started to read.

Well, aren't you the conceited little prick!

Mos stared at him for two or three seconds but said nothing. Circling the counter, he advanced to the doorway and ran a curt rap of knuckles along one of the panels before pushing it open and stepping inside.

The room was bigger and brighter than he'd expected, primarily due to an enormous window that took up one entire wall and offered a heady view over the chaotic rooftops of the surrounding buildings. A generous expanse of carpet separated the window from its other key feature, a long, rectangular table enclosed by twelve leather-coated seats.

Two men were standing by the window, conversing softly. Both glanced in his direction as the door opened behind him.

'Muiris!' Hegarty crossed the room, hand outstretched. 'Good to see you.'

Mos managed to conceal his displeasure at his ex-colleague's presence. He accepted the academic's proffered limb for appearance's sake and shook hands without enthusiasm.

'Muiris, I'd like you to meet Dr David Coffey, an old friend of mine from Oxford.'

The man who stepped forward was tall, with a slim build and a wide forehead crowned with a full head of curly black hair. Although Hegarty had mentioned that Coffey was in his forties, his fresh, baby-faced demeanour gave him a much more youthful air. A waft of some delicate aftershave preceded him as he reached forward to take Mos' hand, but the subsequent handshake was firm.

'A pleasure to meet you, Mr O'Súilleabháin.'

An American twang took Mos by surprise. He'd assumed, given the reference to Oxford, that Coffey would be English. Unlike the Dubliner at reception, however, he had made the effort of pronouncing Mos' name correctly. Hegarty had evidently alerted him of Mos' prickliness in that regard.

'We're very grateful to you for agreeing to meet us at such short notice.'

Mos shrugged. 'I'm being well compensated.'

'Nevertheless …' Coffey beamed enthusiastically and shuffled, transferring his weight from one leg to another in a series of jerky movements that gave him the excited air of an over-eager puppy. It was difficult not to respond in kind to his infectious smile. Nevertheless, Mos managed it.

'Has Desmond explained why we asked you here today?'

'I understand you want a background briefing on the *Fianagecht*.'

'That's right. I—'

'Without involving any of the universities or the national historical institutions.'

'Ah!' For the briefest of moments, Coffey appeared embarrassed. He glanced away, with an accusing flicker of his eyes to Hegarty. The rotund academic appeared suddenly absorbed in the task of removing a loose thread from the lapel of his suit.

'I see.' Coffey sighed deeply and brushed the incident aside with a brusque sweep of one hand. 'I suppose it's not too important at this point, but Desmond's been a little more forthright than he should have. To be honest, Mr O'Súilleabháin, you weren't invited here because of your institutional independence, although I'd be lying if I denied it was a consideration. You're here primarily because you're an experienced historian and archaeologist and Desmond says you have an unsurpassed knowledge of the *Fianagecht*.'

He paused to glance, once again, at Desmond.

'A "Gaelic Indiana Jones". I believe that's the expression he used to describe you.'

Bemused, Mos turned to stare at Hegarty, who was now busily engaged in cleaning a spot of dirt from his shoe.

'I'm sure that was meant more in terms of your academic success,' Coffey was quick to reassure him. 'As opposed to any hazardous fieldwork techniques, of course.'

'I wouldn't underestimate the hazards of Irish archaeological fieldwork, Dr Coffey. I caught a bad cold last year. I also remember one particularly precarious site where I had to climb up a steep hill.' Mos grew quiet, as though recalling some traumatic event. 'I could have seriously injured myself if I'd happened to fall.'

It was evident that Coffey was not entirely sure if his guest was being serious or not. In response, he played it safe with a vague nod and quickly turned to Hegarty, who had remained uncharacteristically subdued throughout the entire exchange.

'Thanks for all your help, Desmond. Mr O'Súilleabháin and I can probably take it from here. I'll contact you later to finalise the contractual details.'

Hegarty nodded. 'Of course. Of course, David. Sure, you know where to contact me.'

Coffey escorted him to the door. Glancing back at Mos, Hegarty quickly held his hand up to the side of his face, little finger down by his lips, thumb stretched up to his ear, and discreetly mouthed the words 'Call me'.

Just as discreetly, Mos raised his own hand, bunched up his fist and raised his middle finger. He was rewarded with an expression of outrage on Hegarty's face just before the door closed on him.

Oblivious to the muted display of antagonism taking place behind his back, Coffey clapped his hands together.

'Before we start, can I offer you a coffee, tea …?'

'I'm grand, thanks.'

Coffey gestured towards a small glass drinks cabinet lined with a selection of spirits and numerous glasses.

'It may be a little early, but …' He coughed delicately. 'Do you drink, Mr O'Súilleabháin?'

'Only to excess, Mr Coffey.'

For a few seconds, Coffey watched him uncertainly, then his lips curled up in relief as he realised his guest was joking. 'Oh. Oh, I see. Maybe we'll just pass on the refreshments in that case.' He directed Mos towards the table. 'Let's make ourselves comfortable and get down to business instead.'

The American took a seat at one end of the table, in front of a laptop and several other items of electronic equipment. He gestured for Mos to position himself in the adjacent chair. A microphone and a tray with two glasses and a crystal decanter of water occupied the space between them.

Mos sat and placed his satchel on the ground. He glanced down to the far end of the table, where a webcam on a raised mount had its lens trained directly on them. A sickly green light on the outer casing flashed intermittently.

Coffey pressed a button on the laptop and a screen slid down the wall they were facing with a muted electronic whine. Mos regarded him with a curious expression.

'Bear with me, Mr O'Súilleabháin. I'll just take care of this and then I'll explain.'

Mos nodded and watched as the blond man worked through several adjustments on the laptop. A projector protruding from the ceiling above them hummed loudly and flared into life, casting a rectangle of soft white light onto the screen. A digital image of a decimal clock appeared for several seconds and was replaced by a view of an empty office. The camera transmitting the scene was angled to capture a wide mahogany desk and a leather chair with large armrests. There were several framed certificates and photographs on the wall behind the chair but these were too indistinct for Mos to be able to make out any detail. Beside the desk, a window overlooked a city street dominated by office buildings and heavy traffic. The scene blurred momentarily as the webcam focussed in on the empty armchair and Coffey swivelled in his seat to face him.

'Thanks for being patient, Mr O'Súilleabháin. I've just been establishing a connection with our head office in London.'

He gestured at the screen.

'That's Reverend Quinn's office. He'll be joining us in a moment or two.'

'Reverend Quinn?'

'The Chairman of the Opus Foundation.' He turned back to the computer to tap on the keyboard once more. 'My boss.'

Mos heard the sound of a squeaking door and realised it was coming from a set of speakers embedded in the wall on either side of the screen. Moments later a quiet voice floated hollowly into the boardroom, as clear as though the speaker was standing beside them.

'Coffey. Are you there?'

The speaker – a man – was American. His voice was hoarser than Coffey's, like that of a heavy smoker, and had a strong northern inflection.

'I'm here, Reverend.'

'Is the connection secure?'

'Yes, Reverend. The transmission's encrypted and secure. And Mr O'Súilleabháin's here with me.'

The view onscreen was obscured as someone moved in front of the camera. Mos caught a quick glimpse of a broad back then the screen blurred as the webcam attempted to compensate for the changing focus. When it finally cleared, a man dressed in a simple black cassock had settled into the chair and was staring at them. Mos realised he must have a similar communications set-up at his end.

Reverend Quinn was older than his compatriot. In his mid-sixties, Mos estimated. Although he appeared to have a full head of hair, it was white and had been cut short, close to the scalp. He had an oval face with sharp eyes, high, arched eyebrows and a prominent patrician nose.

A strong face, this one.

'Good morning, Mr O'Súilleabháin.'

Like Coffey, he pronounced Mos' name correctly.

'Hello,' Mos responded in a cautious tone.

'I must apologise for not being with you in person. Regrettably, circumstances beyond my control mean I have to leave international travel to trustworthy lieutenants like Mr Coffey here.'

He directed his attention to the younger man.

'How are you, David? Enjoying your stay on the Emerald Isle?'

'Very much so, Reverend, thank you for asking.'

The old man smiled with almost paternal affection before returning his gaze to Mos.

'From my name, Mr O'Súilleabháin, you've probably already guessed that I've a strong element of Irish heritage myself.'

'Is that so?'

'Yes. My grandparents were actually born in Galway. They emigrated to the States during the Second World War but maintained strong connections with the "oul sod". I try to get back there myself and visit when I can manage it.'

'I see.'

'Forgive me. I'm rambling on. One of the downsides of age, I'm afraid. Invariably, whatever wisdom one tends to pick up over the years is offset by the inevitable onset of senility.'

He released a hearty chuckle that reverberated through the speakers.

'Anyway, I'm sure you're a busy man. Would you prefer to get down to business?'

'That'd be nice.'

'Very well, then. Let's get straight to it. What do you know about the Opus Foundation?'

Mos stared, startled by the man's almost instantaneous shift in tone from genial small talk to professional directness. Despite the fact that he hadn't moved in any physical sense, Quinn gave the impression of having sat up straight and now exuded an air of determined authority that hadn't been there seconds earlier.

He made the cleric wait for his answer, taking a deep breath and releasing it slowly before he responded.

'Not much. To be honest, I'd never heard of you until Desmond contacted me.'

'Yes, well there's a reason for that.'

The Reverend scratched his chin thoughtfully.

'Perhaps it's best if I give you a little background on our organisation. Then we can discuss what we need you to do. Does that work for you?'

Mos nodded.

'Excellent.'

A flicker of a smile sealed the Reverend's evident satisfaction like juice in a snap-seared steak.

'Essentially, the Opus Foundation is a private, altruistic organisation that specialises in the recovery, restoration and conservation of cultural antiquities. I assume Professor Hegarty's already told you this.'

Mos confirmed this with a nod.

'The Foundation was established back around 1979, which means that we've been operating in one form or another for almost thirty years. We specialise in the acquisition of religious artefacts: icons, relics, that sort of thing. The vast majority tend to be Christian in origin but, occasionally, we come across non-Christian materials that we feel a moral obligation to protect. These are mostly Asian or South American but we also have some beautiful Babylonian artefacts – which of course we intend to return once the national authorities have been re-established to an internationally recognised standard.

'We've amassed quite a sizeable collection over the last few decades. Our headquarters here in London house one of the most substantial private collections of Western religious relics outside of the Vatican. It's also one of the few that are freely accessible to the public. That's a key principle of our organisation.'

He emphasised the latter remark by tapping the table sternly with his index finger. Nevertheless, Mos had the growing impression this was a homily he had delivered before. Although he was an articulate speaker, Quinn's words had a certain air of practised repetition about them, attributable no doubt to his leadership role with the organisation.

Mos had a sudden mental image of the formidable cleric on a raised podium before his browbeaten staff, delivering regular, morale-boosting sermons. He coughed into his hand to disguise the curl of his lips and made a renewed effort to listen more attentively.

'We work hard, with pride in our accomplishments. We operate to the highest ethical standards and over the years we've built an international reputation for integrity. For that reason, you might well ask why you've never heard of us.'

The Reverend paused meaningfully. Understanding that he was now expected to ask a question, Mos made a point of not doing so. Undaunted, after a moment's silence, the Reverend responded to his own query.

'The reason you've never heard of us is because the objects we retrieve are of great artistic and religious value. People of faith hold these items in great reverence and draw emotional and spiritual succour from them. Naturally, this creates great sensitivities with respect to their retrieval. While we're doing our best to conserve them for future generations, we also have to work around the fact that they're physical manifestations of contemporary faith.'

He paused and his lips formed into a thin line.

'Given their emotional and spiritual value, you can imagine that many religious artefacts also have an immense financial value, particularly among the more unscrupulous private collectors, treasure seekers and opportunists – a whole range of avarice-driven individuals on the lookout for a quick buck. These people operate to a transient morality. They have no love of history. They can't see beyond their own petty greed and have no qualms about destroying or exploiting something for short-term gain or gratification. We find ourselves constantly monitored by these people, more assiduously than celebrities by the gutter press.'

'Why would they be monitoring you?'

'I beg your pardon?' Quinn scowled but it was unclear if his annoyance was a result of the subject matter or the fact that he'd been interrupted in mid-flow.

'Why would they be monitoring you?'

'Well, obviously, if I'm seen travelling to some location outside of London, they'll know I'm there for a reason; most likely to negotiate the recovery of an artefact. These people have surprisingly well-resourced networks, Mr O'Súilleabháin. As soon as they hear I'm in negotiations somewhere they set local agents to follow me and, if possible, to locate the object I'm attempting to retrieve so that they can approach the holder with a more generous counteroffer.'

Quinn frowned, visibly changined by the topic.

'Given that they have access to far deeper pockets than ours, it's not usually one we can equal. In the last financial year alone, we've had to cancel three recovery projects because certain parties got wind of our discoveries and rushed in and obtain the artefacts before us. Hence, our preference for operating behind the scenes and operating the way we do, with –' he waved a hand at what Mos assumed was the communications equipment in his office, '–technology like this.'

The Reverend exhaled deeply and sat back in his chair.

'Mr O'Súilleabháin, you've substantial experience in the historic and archaeological sector. You must have seen the destruction, the irreparable archaeological damage wrought by those people. You know such artefacts rarely see the light of day beyond the display cabinet of the private collectors who've obtained them.'

'You don't try to recover them?'

For a moment, the strained expression on Quinn's face went blank. Then he laughed out loud.

'We're conservators, Mr O'Súilleabháin. Historians and administrators. What do you expect us to do? Pull on a balaclava and raid the homes of people we suspect of dealing in stolen properly?'

'I was talking about official channels.'

'Ah! Official channels.'

Quinn gave a tight little smile.

'I'm sure you know as well as I do that official channels are just as susceptible to corruption as unofficial ones. Particularly in the third world. Government officials in some countries can make a year's salary from looking the other way at the appropriate time.'

He paused and rubbed his eyes with the palms of his hands. When he looked back at the camera he appeared worn out, although when he spoke again there was no give in him.

'At the end of the day, Mr O'Súilleabháin, like most important things, it all comes down to the integrity of individuals. Some people have a lower asking price than others when it comes to avoiding the right thing to do.'

Mos, reminded of his recent experiences with Milo, could only agree.

'I'm sorry.' Quinn smiled, but it was the sad smile of a man who had had a lifetime's experience of human behaviour and, for the most part, had been disappointed by it. 'I've become a bit of a cynic over the years. I shouldn't burden you with that. It's hardly a Christian thought, but I sometimes think it'd be nice if someone did go in, guns blazing, to defend the undefended. That's never going to happen in our lifetime, of course. We'll just continue to operate the way we do, in secrecy and avoiding controversy wherever possible.'

'These individuals who monitor you, Reverend Quinn. Would they have any reason to be checking up on me?'

From his expression, the Reverend evidently found the question an odd one.

'I can't imagine why. The artefact we want your assistance with is already in our possession here in London so it's too late for them to try and obtain it. Besides, although your name's been mentioned internally, this is the first time we've actually met or spoken. Why do you ask?'

'No reason. Just checking.'

He refrained from making mention of the Subaru or the stranger in Carraig Dubh. There appeared to be no legitimate basis to link either event with his presence here. For that reason alone, the Opus Foundation didn't need to know.

'Well, I suppose that brings us neatly to the next stage of our conversation. The motivation for asking you here today.'

He took a deep breath and gave Mos his most meaningful stare. This was, he seemed keen to emphasise, a matter of some consequence.

'I'm sure you've worked out by now that we've come into possession of an antiquity of Irish origin. Our evaluation suggests that although this particular item is an extraordinary find in its own right, it could also have an exceptional secondary value. We have a problem, however, in that should this secondary association become common knowledge, public interest will be so overwhelming it could threaten our ability to derive that secondary value.'

Jesus! What the hell have they found? Brian Boru's cock ring?

Quinn glanced towards his compatriot. 'Do you have the paper, David?'

On cue, Coffey pulled a plastic document holder from one of the folders on the table and slid it smoothly across the polished surface. Mos picked it up, opened it and read quickly through the three-page document it contained. It took him only two minutes. When he was finished, he placed it on the table and considered the Reverend Quinn in silence.

'Before we begin, I'd ask that you sign that confidentiality agreement. By signing and accepting the agreed sum for the outlined advisory services, you also consent to reveal nothing that is discussed in this room today: not the questions asked, the topics alluded to or the advice provided. I apologise for the heavy-handed approach but as you can understand we have to take this seriously. I'm also obliged to inform you that any breach in the confidentiality conditions will be followed up with legal action.'

'Fuck that,' said Mos.

Both men gaped, visibly taken aback by the response. Coffey, in particular, looked as though he had been slapped across the face.

'What?' he croaked.

'I said, fuck that. Seriously lads, I came here in good faith to provide a professional service. Nobody mentioned anything about a confidentiality agreement and you're really pissing up the wrong blackthorn bush if you think I'm going to sign this crock of shite. Jesus!'

With this last exclamation, he pushed his chair back from the table and got to his feet.

'If it's really that important for you to have a confidentiality agreement, I suggest you find someone else who meets your criteria.'

He looked meaningfully at the screen where Reverend Quinn was staring back at him.

'Good luck with that.'

Coffey, red-faced, surged to his feet, all previous bonhomie evaporated in the heat of his outrage.

'How dare you talk to the Reverend Quinn like—'

'David!'

The Reverend's voice cracked from the speakers like a whip. Startled, Coffey turned to face the screen where his employer was glaring down at him.

'But—'

'It's all right, David. Calm down. I don't need you to defend me.'

He redirected his attention at Mos.

'Mr O'Súilleabháin, it appears we've seriously misjudged you. For that I'm genuinely sorry. After so many years of dealing with charlatans, I'm sorry to say I'm no longer capable of recognising a man of principle when I see one.'

He spread his hands in a pleading manner.

'If you're still willing to work with us and give me your word that you won't reveal anything we discuss today, I'd be more than happy to accept that.'

Mos hid his astonishment at the unexpected back down behind an impassive stare.

What the fuck is going on here? Their conditions were obviously a total bluff.

'Would the original deal still hold?'

'Of course.'

'Very well. In that case you have my word. I'll reveal nothing discussed with you here today.'

'Thank you.'

The Reverend hid his relief well, but it was obvious he was shaken. Coffey, pinch-faced and fuming, was struggling to contain his temper as he returned the confidentiality agreement to its folder and slipped it back into his briefcase. Quinn was quick to move the discussion along.

'Perhaps we can make a fresh start and just move straight into the questions. Would that work for you?'

Mos nodded but refrained from comment.

'Very well.' The cleric glanced down at a sheet of paper lying on the desk before him. 'I suppose our first question is the most fundamental one. Naturally, we've read Professor Hegarty's excellent introductory paper but, given your expertise, did the Fianna actually exist?'

Mos took a deep breath. Although tempted to express his true opinion on Hegarty's paper, he reckoned they'd had enough of his volatile peculiarities for a little while, at least.

'Which one?' he asked.

The subsequent silence was highlighted by the quiet background hum of the electronic equipment. Coffey looked confused and glanced at the screen, where Reverend Quinn raised one heavy eyebrow in response.

'There was more than one?'

'Of course. "*Fianna*" is the plural noun of "*fian*", a Latin word that was adopted in Ireland. Originally, it meant "pursuing" or "hunting" but over time the meaning changed to refer to a band of warriors on the warpath.'

He paused to verify that they were still with him.

'Please, go on,' said the Reverend.

'The historical literature indicates that a "*fian*" was made up of warriors outside of the tribal systems – landless men, or simply individuals out to avenge some private grievance. From the commentary of the time, it seems that the Church wasn't particularly fond of them, but they obviously held a far greater societal status than that of simple marauders. The little information we do have suggests that they weren't a standing military force but one that came together for a common purpose on occasion. It's unlikely they remained in the field as a cohesive unit for any lengthy periods of time once that purpose was fulfilled.'

Mos coughed and cleared his throat, which was raw and itchy from the excesses of the previous night. He poured himself a glass of water from the decanter and swallowed half of it before continuing.

'Each member of a *fian* was called a *fénid*. The leader was called the *rígfénid*. The various *fianna* appear to have taken their names from their leader so, for example, "*fian Maicc Cais*" would refer to the battle-group or action-group of Maic Cais.'

Coffey held up his hand.

'So Fionn mac Cumhaill's group would have been called "*fian Fionn mac Cumhaill*".'

'No. His group would have been called "*fian Find*" or "*fian Find ua Baoiscne*". "*Find*" was the earliest form of the name Fionn. The latter didn't actually develop until several centuries later.'

'And Baoiscne?'

'That's a false precursor for some hypothetical ancestor. Some narratives suggest Fionn was "*ua Baoiscne* – a descendent of Baoiscne. "Baoiscne" is an old word meaning "a great tree" but the general consensus is that the name was simply made up for fictional purposes.'

'I see.' The Reverend nodded. Coffey, whose body language betrayed his unease, listened with interest but remained silent. His glance flicked repeatedly from one man to the other as they spoke.

'As late as the tenth century,' Mos continued, '*fian Find* was just one of a number of *fianna* and Fionn was just one of the *rígfénid* mentioned in the surviving manuscripts. The Annals of Ulster, for example, has an entry for an individual by the name of *Máelcíaráin Mac Rónáin* who led a *fian* in a number of engagements against the Norse. The Annals of Tighernach record the death of another *rígfénid* – *Máelumai Mac Báitáin* – charmingly known as "Garg the Fierce". What's interesting, though, is that although there are numerous references to different *fianna* in the earlier documents, from the ninth century onwards the stories and literary references become increasingly dominated by *fian Find*. By the twelfth century, which was when many of the oral stories were collated and put in literary form, all reference to other *fianna* has been completely eroded and their adventures subsumed into those of *fian Find*. The original meaning of the word *fian* also appears to have been almost completely lost by that time, to the point that where the term *fianna* is used, there's an automatic assumption that it's a reference to that particular group of warriors headed by Fionn mac Cumhaill.'

Mos swallowed the remaining water and put the glass aside.

Reverend Quinn cleared his throat.

'I realise I'm revealing my complete ignorance here, Mr O'Súilleabháin, but perhaps I should amend my original question.' He paused and took a deep breath. 'Did Fionn mac Cumhaill actually exist?'

He frowned as a wry smile crept up one side of Mos' face.

'The question amuses you.'

'It's not that it amuses me …'

Mos hesitated before continuing.

'There's something inherently fascinating about Fionn mac Cumhaill. The stories surrounding him have survived in relatively intact form for more than a thousand years, which is quite astounding in itself. I suppose what does amuse me is the degree to which the character has intrigued people over the centuries. Historians and historical writers have been asking themselves whether Fionn is based on a real historical figure since the tenth century.'

'And do you have a personal opinion on the matter?'

Mos pursed his lips and tapped them thoughtfully with his left index finger. 'I'd probably have to go with the general consensus.'

'Which is?'

'That he never existed. Certainly not in the way we think of him today.'

'But Professor Hegarty's report clearly states that the Annals of Tighernach have a record of his death in 283 AD.' Quinn glanced towards Coffey. 'At the battle of Gabhra. Isn't that right?'

Coffey confirmed this with a nod.

'Ah, that.' Mos gave a wry smile. 'The Fenian stories are pretty inconsistent when it comes to Fionn's death. The two moist common causes attributed are either beheading during a battle or falling from a height as a result of a great leap. The 283 AD reference is often cited as the "official" record by amateurs who haven't done their research properly. Its veracity is unlikely in any case. Several other, independent, sources also refer to the battle of Gabhra but make absolutely no mention at all of the *fianna Find*. Given the status that such a *rígfénid* would have, it's inconceivable that his name wouldn't have been mentioned if he'd been present, particularly if he was killed during the fighting.'

Mos shook his head.

'No, it's more likely that some pre-eleventh-century writer saw the entry in the earlier annals about the death of Caibre Lifeachair at Gabhra and decided to link this with Fionn's reputed death for a contemporary work of fiction. Later, another individual who compiled the Tighernach Annals added in the 283 AD reference for consistency's sake.'

The Reverend Quinn exhaled heavily and said nothing but his exasperation at the shortcomings in Hegarty's report was obvious. In the ensuing silence, Mos reached down and removed a hardcover notebook from the satchel beside his chair. Placing it flat on the table he flipped through several pages until he'd located what he was looking for: a white slip of paper with several lines of handwriting inserted between two leaves.

'This is a segment from the *Leabhar Laighneach*, the Book of Leinster. It's a medieval manuscript compiled about 1160 but it refers to a seventh-century poem by Senchán Torpéist that's the earliest known literary reference to the character Find ua Baoiscne. Naturally, it was written in Old Irish but the translation goes something like this:

"From Nuada Necht, one of the four sons of Seta Setback, is the origin of the men of Leinster, and he was King of Tara. By him at Alenn (Knockawlin) fell Etarsceela the Great, son of Iar, King of Ireland, a deed which Nuadu performed on behalf of Lugaid of the Red Stripes. Lugaid seized the kinship of Ireland. And the famous Find ua Baoiscne and Cailte were grandsons of this Nuadu Necht."

He paused and glanced up before continuing. 'Here's the relevant bit.'

"As Senchán Torpéist has declared in the "Great Compilation" dicens: Find, Tulcha and Caílte, a tribe of hosts, shook the warlike … with barks from waves. Three descendents of Baoiscne, a victorious company …"

Mos closed the notebook and replaced it in his satchel. 'That's it. With respect to the other two other members of the "victorious company", Caílte is a reference to the character Caoilte Mac Ronáin, a warrior of *fian Find* who was famous for his agility and speed. As for Tulcha, the only other reference to him in the remaining manuscripts is a much later twelfth-century text where he's introduced as Fionn's half-brother.'

He coughed once to clear his throat. 'From the Senchán Torpéist reference, we know that at least one Leinster dynasty in the sixth or seventh century was portraying Fionn not only as a real, historical figure, but as one of their ancestors.'

'But surely that contradicts your argument that he wasn't a historical figure', said Reverend Quinn.

'Ah, but you've got to take that claim in context. This text would have been written by someone in the employ of that particular Leinster dynasty. It's highly likely he was instructed to make the claim.'

Reverend Quinn looked at him, bewildered. 'But why would they do that?'

'There were probably several reasons but the most likely would have been to strengthen the justification of that dynasty's rule. Life was extremely precarious in the sixth and seventh century and it took relentless effort, both political and military, for the ruling families to retain their authority. By linking their pedigree to a legendary character like Find, the Leinster rulers were using his name as propaganda to bolster their prestige. In a sense, it's a kind of celebrity fraud, the equivalent of claiming to be a descendent of, say, Elvis, and then getting your family genealogist to tinker around with the family tree to support your claim and impress your constituents.'

Reverend Quinn sighed. Even through the camera lens, Mos could see the slight sagging of his shoulders. To some extent, he had anticipated this reaction. When it came to history, people tended to interpret the past through their own personal experiences and aspirations rather than through historical fact. When they were confronted with a reality that did not align with scenarios of their own construction, they were almost invariably disappointed.

'So you don't think it's possible that he existed?'

'Oh, anything's possible!' Mos conceded. 'It's possible Fionn mac Cumhaill existed, it's possible he led a *fian* back in the early third or fourth century, it's even possible some of the recorded adventures are true.'

'But—' Quinn prompted.

'But there simply isn't enough evidence to support his existence. All references in the historical literature – well, they come from a period several hundred years after the time he was supposed to exist. As for physical evidence, there simply isn't any. The earliest artefact believed to have any potential connection with the Fenian cycle only dates as far back as the eighth century. Before that there's nothing. No evidence whatsoever.'

Then again, you're a religious man. You're probably used to operating in that environment.

'There is alternative school of thought, however.'

Quinn raised his eyes and regarded him cautiously but said nothing.

'Some elements of folklore suggest that Fionn mac Cumhaill didn't actually die. There are some Fenian tales, particularly within Scotland and up around Sheebeg in County Leitrim, where Fionn is said to be hidden away and sleeping in a cave, ready to arise again when Ireland needs him most.'

'Really?' asked Quinn. You could tell he knew such an event was highly unlikely, but he could not resist exploring the possibility.

'Yes. It was a common conceit in Europe after the great political upheavals towards the end of the Middle Ages. Supporters of many defeated political leaders refused to accept their demise. For years afterwards, they spread stories that their heroes hadn't really died but were asleep with their armies in some great cavern or trapped like King Arthur or Charlemagne in some Otherworld territory, unable to return to save their country until certain conditions had been fulfilled.'

'What do you think?'

Mos looked at him and grinned. 'Well, given all the shit this country's experienced, I figure the bastard's overslept by at least 400 years.'

***

The discussion continued in a similar vein for another three hours. Mos did most of the talking, responding predominantly to subject matter dictated by the Reverend's questions or requests for clarification. Sometimes, these veered well beyond the scope of the *Fianagecht* and a significant amount of time was spent on explanations of related background topics such as the influence of Roman Britain on Irish culture or the rise of the *Ulaid* tribal confederation. Unaccustomed to speaking for such an extended period, he was relieved when the Reverend Quinn finally brought the meeting to a close.

'Thank you, Mr O'Súilleabháin. I'd like to take some time to reflect on what you've told us today. You've certainly provided food for thought.'

The cleric stood and flexed his arms, sending the oversensitive webcam into a paroxysm of frenzied autofocussing. The creak of stretching bones sounded surprisingly clearly though the speakers.

'David, perhaps you'd be good enough to organise Mr O'Súilleabháin's fee.'

'Of course, Reverend.'

Coffey departed, leaving them alone as he passed through the double doors to fulfil his errand. Mos retrieved his satchel from beneath the table, stood up and stretched.

'Mr O'Súilleabháin, would you be willing to let us call on your expertise a little further?'

Mos turned to look at the screen where the Reverend was observing him intently.

'In what capacity?'

The Reverend 'hmmmed' thoughtfully before responding.

'We've been very fortunate to secure someone of Professor Hegarty's experience to assist with the artefact's authentication, but—'

He glanced towards the edge of the screen as though checking that Coffey had, indeed, left the room.

'Sometimes, it's good to have a second, independent, perspective.'

He coughed delicately.

'I suppose it's best to be up-front. I'm in a bit of a fix. As I mentioned earlier, our main work is conservation. Normally, we focus on nothing more substantial than the retrieval of authenticated, validated objects that meet our criteria and ensuring their conservation.'

He frowned and rubbed his chin.

'The artefact we need your help with is a bit more complicated. We lack experience with Irish artefacts, which was why Professor Hegarty was called in. Unfortunately, over the last few weeks, I've lost confidence in his ability to deliver on the project. As far as I'm concerned, he's consistently overpromised and under-delivered. For that reason, I was wondering whether you'd be interested in taking over the assessment process.'

Mos listened in silence, intrigued by the direction the conversation had taken. He wasn't surprised by Quinn's disappointment with Hegarty. Although an adequate theorist and lecturer, Hegarty's lack of meaningful experience in the practical assessment of manuscripts meant he was insufficiently qualified for the job. Desperate for professional kudos, he'd obviously manipulated his friendship with Coffey and made some outrageous claims which, because of their lack of expertise, the Opus Foundation had been unable to verify. It was now clear that he'd hoped to utilise Mos' expertise to disguise the fact that he was in completely over his head. It was also likely he'd have claimed any of Mos' findings as his own. Unfortunately for Hegarty, the Reverend had seen through that ploy.

'Won't Hegarty have something to say about that?'

'I'm afraid I don't have the time to pander to Professor Hegarty's feelings. I realise he's a good friend of Coffey's, but this project has limited funding and needs to be completed by the end of next month. As far as I'm concerned, we have no chance of achieving that timeline while Hegarty's running it. Our contract with him can be terminated if I have any concerns with his service delivery and right now, I have plenty of those.'

He paused and regarded Mos with quiet intent.

'Mr O'Súilleabháin, you've demonstrated your expertise to my satisfaction over the last few hours. I understand you also have some knowledge of ancient linguistics that could be useful. Will you do it?'

'I'm afraid you'll have to be a little more specific. What exactly would you want me to do?'

'That's a fair question. Essentially, there are two tasks. First, replace Professor Hegarty. Take over the assessment and verification of the artefact and ensure it's completed by December.

'Sure, but what does that actually mean? I've no idea what the artefact is. Given Hegarty's involvement, I'm assuming it's a manuscript of some kind.'

He watched as the Reverend considered how much he could comfortably reveal.

'Yes,' he admitted grudgingly. 'It is a manuscript. Carbon dating places it before 1400 AD. According to the previous owner – a private collector – it was sourced from another private collection in Munich but he believes it originally came from somewhere else in Germany, possibly Regensberg.'

Mos nodded thoughtfully. That made sense. Irish monks had been prodigious missionaries on the European Continent from the end of the sixth century. One group had established a mission at Regensberg towards the end of the eleventh century that had flourished and expanded to include a number of subsidiary monasteries in Wurzburg, Nuremburg, Vienna and several other locations which, together, formed the famous congregation of German *Schottenklöster*. This had all been managed as one congregation under the Abbot of St. Jacob at Regensberg.

In the earlier stages of the mission, the *Schottenklöster* had been renowned for the quality of the manuscripts and writings they produced. In later centuries, however, when the mission began to crumble from lack of funds and personnel from Ireland, many of these treasures had been sold off, stolen or ended up in other libraries. Other *Schottenklöster* manuscripts had been discovered over the years so it was possible – theoretically, at least – that the Foundation's manuscript was similar to one of these.

'Has it been translated?'

'To a degree. The original owner provided us with an initial translation, but he admitted it wasn't a particularly accurate one. Professor Hegarty was working on a new one but despite several weeks of promises we've yet to receive it.'

'Hmm. You mentioned a second task.'

'Yes, I did. That concerns the associated secondary value I referred to earlier. Again, according to the previous owner, the manuscript contains some obscure reference to the location of another object that has a connection with the Fenian tales. We'd like you to evaluate whether there's any substance to these claims and, if so, whether it's possible to locate it.'

'What's the object?'

'The grave of Fionn mac Cumhaill.'

Mos stared at him wordlessly, his face as blank as stone. After several seconds of extended silence under that steely gaze, the Reverend grew increasingly uncomfortable.

'Yes, yes. I understand your scepticism, particularly after everything you've just told me. All the same, I also recall your comment that there was no evidence to support his existence.'

He paused and regarded Mos with almost melodramatic intensity.

'I believe we may have found this evidence.'

Mos' response was a cryptic smile.

'That's unlikely. You said your manuscript only dated back to 1400. Even if he ever existed at all, Fionn's associated with a period of time before the second or third century, certainly well before the fifth. Any claims that manuscript is making have got to be dubious at best.'

'Yes. I admit the chances are slim. I also recognise we may be grasping at straws, but I'd still ask you to consider the offer. If anything, your scepticism would be a welcome reality check for the rest of us.'

Reverend Quinn leaned forward, placing both hands on the desk as he stared into the camera.

'Would you be interested? Any valid advice you can give us – positive or negative – will be well rewarded.'

Mos regarded the screen quietly then abruptly turned away. Leaving the table, he approached the window and stood there staring in silence at the skyline outside. Despite his outer calm, his equilibrium had been ruffled by Quinn's astounding offer. Over the years he'd been working with Fenian lore, he had encountered many extravagant claims but never one as outrageous as the location of Fionn's burial site. Despite this, he found himself experiencing an almost irrational sense of excitement.

He took a deep breath and released it slowly, his eyes following a stream of cumulus clouds blowing in over the city. Indirectly, their aimlessness reminded him of his own predicament. He had been drifting for years, driven by vague plans and unclear resolutions.

He bit his lower lip for several seconds then turned once more to face the screen. 'Why?' he asked.

'Why?'

The Reverend's puzzlement was reflected in his features.

'I don't understand. Why what?'

'Why are you so interested in Fionn mac Cumhaill? He's a Gaelic or pre-Gaelic legend. Your organisation's an Anglo-American entity that specialises in Christian western religious relics. The Fenian stories and their associations have no real Christian connection. If anything, they're probably the antithesis of organised religions – an anarchistic, nature-based belief system.'

'That's true. Although I also said we acquired non-Christian materials from time to time. Mind you, I admit we're stepping well outside our comfort zone on this particular subject. It's unlike anything we've done before.'

'So, again, to repeat the question. Why?'

The Reverend paused to think about that for a surprisingly long time. When he finally answered he appeared genuinely amused by his own uncertainty.

'You know, I've never actually considered my own motivations with this matter before. Speaking for myself, I suppose my interest is driven by my own personal infatuation with the character. Fionn mac Cumhaill was my childhood hero. I told you my grandparents moved to the States but even there they brought their stories and traditions along with them. I was raised on a heady diet of Fenian tales. I had all the books, I heard all the stories – and I didn't have any siblings, so when I was young I used to spend hours by myself, imagining that I was Fionn and acting out his adventures.'

The cleric paused suddenly and looked sheepish, embarrassed at letting such personal details slip. He moved quickly to change the subject.

'Not all my colleagues on the Board support this particular endeavour, needless to say. In fact, one of them has opposed it strongly from the very start. Still, two of them have an Irish background and share my interest. A third has a strong intellectual interest in the subject of early community theology so we have the necessary support to research the possibilities further.

'I realise, of course, that we should probably pass this on to the Irish government and, to be fair, we intend to do so. But for the moment …' he held out his hands. 'We just want to know if it could possibly be true.'

Mos stared at Quinn but did not know what to say. The unexpected honesty of the cleric's response had thrown him. From the start of the conversation, he hadn't particularly liked the man and had looked forward to the termination of their brief encounter. Now, to his great surprise, he found they shared a common intellectual and emotional fascination with Fionn mac Cumhaill.

When he looked up to face the screen again, he saw that the Reverend was observing him with a mixture of concern and expectation. He coughed, cleared his throat, and until he had actually opened his mouth to speak he was still unsure of what he was about to say.

'Ah, what the fuck!' he said. 'All right, then. I'll do it.'

Chapter Nine

West Cork, Early 1960s

Friday night was rabbit stew night. Just as Thursday night had been. And the Wednesday and Tuesday before that. Although his taste buds were weary from the recurring flavour, Diarmuid couldn't help but feel a little sense of triumph at the success of his snares.

Clean out them little feckers yet.

Saturday brought a welcome respite from the culinary delights of rabbit flesh. Around two in the afternoon, Pat Harrington called in with two fresh mackerel, the outcome of a successful day's fishing with his nephew Liam. There had been an unseasonal shoaling at Smig an Chailleach – the Witch's Chin – a fishing spot renowned more for the snagging of fishing lines and the loss of tackle than the actual catching of fish. Pat claimed they'd been pulling the fish up faster than they could unhook them and sink the line again. It was, no doubt, a typical fishing exaggeration. Nevertheless, the change from rabbit stew would be welcome.

Pat was a weather-hardened old-timer with all the gentleness and patience of a man whose rough edges had been sanded and tempered by time. A small, wiry individual with a frame shrunken in on itself, his gnome-like face was a hanging post for wrinkles. Even as a child, Diarmuid always remembered him as looking ancient. For all that, he remained a canny man, a competent farmer, and there were few in the district who knew the area and the history of the land as well as he did.

'Will you stay for a bite, Pat?'

'No, boyeen. I'll be on my way home after this. I have a game of cards tonight.'

Diarmuid hid his smile and poured his visitor a glass of *poitín* from the brandy bottle he kept hidden at the bottom of the kitchen cupboard. Despite the fact that Diarmuid himself was no spring chicken, Pat still addressed him as though he was talking to a child.

Pat sipped at the *poitín* and his eyes lingered over Demne, who was sitting quietly at the table on the far side of the room, arranging a battered deck of playing cards. Diarmuid had introduced his nephew earlier and had been disappointed to discover that the old farmer was already well aware who he was. He had hoped the child might be spared the rumours and tittle-tattle spreading through the community. In reality, he knew it was inevitable in such a small area where the *greas cardála* – the chat – was still the greatest form of social entertainment.

'He has his father's face.'

'Do you think so?'

'I do.'

''Twould be a worry if he had the postman's.'

The old man looked at him askew then a smile split like a widening crack across his face.

'You always were the cheeky fecker, Diarmuid.'

'No. Shamie was the cheeky fecker, Pat. I was the quiet fecker.'

'Ah, ye were a pair of feckin' feckers. I'll never forget that day you burned my haystack down.'

'Jaysus, never forget is right. That was over fifty years ago. Will ye not let it go.'

Pat gave a nonplussed shrug. 'Sure, I'm like one of them elliphants. I never forget.' He raised his glass and clinked it against that of his host. '*Sláinte!*'

His gaze settled back on the child playing quietly by himself, oblivious to the old men's conversation. 'Isn't he the great little fella, playing away there and minding his own business.'

'He's a good lad, Tadhg. Mind you, he's a wee thingeen.'

'Ah you know what they say: *is minic a bhain dealg beag braon.*' It's often the small thorn that draws blood.

The farmer's face took on a serious expression. 'You did a good thing to take in your nephew, Diarmuid, but you can tell the boyeen has a soul sickness on him. It's written across his face as plain as the ace of spades. You won't have a moment's rest in the house until you deal to that.'

He looked up at his host.

Diarmuid's morale plummeted as it always did when he regarded the child. 'I know,' he said at last. 'And, I will.'

***

Pat did not tarry once he'd finished his drink. Daylight was fading and he was keen to get home to prepare for his weekly bridge session with his nephews and nieces. Although a spinster himself, his brother had several children and Pat was a favourite with them all.

Diarmuid waved the old man off as he trudged across the field in the direction of his cottage further up the coast. In the waning light, the withered figure looked frail and appeared to be moving at a more laboured pace than usual. Diarmuid felt a sudden pulse of concern. Pat was one of the last of the *Seandaoine* – the Old People – in the local area, a dying breed that would be missed when they were gone. One day, he knew, the old man's body would be discovered in the fields around his house after passing away in the middle of his daily chores. Pat was not the type to stay abed even when he was feeling poorly. The world would be a sadder place for his passing.

Shaking his shoulders to dispel such gloomy thoughts, he went inside to prepare the tea.

He gutted the fish easily in a cold bucket of water and fried the fillets in butter and herbs using the same saucepan that his parents had used. It was blackened and battered but it still did the job more effectively than many of the newer models they were selling in the town. When the food was ready, he placed it on the table with soda bread and buttermilk and called Demne from his play.

As usual, they ate in silence. Over four weeks had passed since the child had been unceremoniously deposited into his care and although they were still not entirely comfortable in each other's company, a tenuous routine had developed between them. For the most part, Demne remained solemn and introspective, but he seemed to have accepted that he'd be remaining with his uncle for the time being. He had proven more approachable since the discovery that he spoke Irish, although communication remained a passive rather than a proactive exercise. In general, the boy was happy enough to respond to a direct inquiry – provided one refrained from broaching certain topics – but volunteered nothing of his own accord. Of his time in Glonnyhust or his parents he made absolutely no mention and Diarmuid did not force the issue, although he appeared happy enough to listen when Diarmuid spoke of Séamus in the context of his own childhood.

His uncle had also noticed a loose association between the boy's temperament and the time of day. Demne was most at ease in the mornings when, fresh from bed, he arose ready to play with the dog or to assist his uncle. As the day wore on, however, and the sunlight darkened, so too did the boy's mood. By mid-afternoon, he could usually be observed staring gloomily into space or brooding in silence as though weighed down by some unspoken burden. As the dusk drew in, he would grow tense and withdraw even further into his shell.

The nights were still the worst, for the nightmares continued unabated. For a short period after settling down, the boy would mutter and shuffle around on his mattress before drifting off into a deep sleep. Within four or five hours, however, the nightmares would recommence. Over the previous sleep-deprived fortnight, Diarmuid had found it was most effective to sit up with the child in order to wake him before they took hold and drove him hysterical with fear. Dozing in his rocking chair until late into the night or the early morning, he would wait until the first mutterings began. Before the nightmares got any worse, he'd wake the boy and reassure him that he was safe until, exhausted, he fell asleep once more and remained comatose till morning.

Despite its relative success, the process was not sustainable and lack of sleep had also been taking its toll on Diarmuid. The previous afternoon, completely exhausted, he'd dozed off in the chair while reading and for the first time in his life had missed the second milking of the day.

After dinner, Demne laid the straw mattress by the fire and went straight to bed, worn out from the day's activities. Over the last week, he'd been rising with his uncle at six in the morning, and today had done a full day's work. He had milked the cows, taken the churn out to the road for collection, fed the hens and carried out numerous other useful errands. He may not have been the best conversationalist but he was a hard worker, listened to everything he was told and followed instruction well. Diarmuid, accustomed to doing everything on the farm himself, was pleasantly surprised at how helpful it was to have an extra pair of hands around.

Within minutes the boy was out like a light. Diarmuid watched him as he snored softly into his pillow, seeing his brother's features reproduced on the sleeping face. The terrible ache of Séamus' death still lingered like an ember in the ashes, stirred to life each time he looked at the boy. It had dulled somewhat since their visit to Na hAoraí and the ceremony in the graveyard but not as much as he'd hoped. He suspected that the child sensed his pain, and took it as a form of disapproval.

Moving carefully so as not to disturb him, Diarmuid put the dishes in the sink to soak in hot water and retired to his rocking chair by the fire. Before sitting down, he put on his reading glasses and pulled the collection of papers obtained at Daingean an Poncán from the top of a small shelf set into the wall. His visit to the American's folly and the retrieval of the papers had, it turned out, been fortuitous. Two weeks earlier, his old friend and current man of the cloth Tadhg Mac Carthy had called in with the gravestone for Séamus. Over a cup of black tea, he had informed Diarmuid that the eccentric construction up in the mountains had caught fire and burned down. By all accounts the blaze had been substantial, for little remained of the building apart from the outer shell of blackened stone. Everything else was gone.

Because of its isolation, it had been several days before the destruction had become public knowledge. Word had finally seeped into Na hAoraí from one of the mountainy men, who had heard it from one of his own. Everyone in the village simply assumed it was arson. In a community where millennia-old pre-Chritsian tradition still lingered hand-in-hand with Christian beliefs, it was not unusual for sites of ignominious reputation to be unofficially 'cleansed'. In any case, the event had served only to increase the rumours throughout the parish.

Diarmuid had suppressed a frisson of disquiet as the priest recounted his news. On the long drive back from the far side of the peninsula, neither Dinny nor he had spoken of their experiences up in that isolated valley. He had not seen his friend since that trip, but images of shadowy figures on mountaintop ridges had plagued his sleep for several nights afterwards.

With a sigh, Diarmuid settled his aching frame into the rocking chair and began to browse through the papers. As he read, he rocked himself back and forth, maintaining the movement by pushing against the cabinet with the tip of his foot. The recovered documents seemed to cover a twelve-year period, the most recent item dating from some eighteen months earlier. They consisted of newspaper clippings, pictures, invoices, formal and personal letters (in Gaelic), various illegible writings, academic papers and so on. There were also a large number of handwritten notes in Séamus' tidy hand – mostly summaries of various adventures from the Fenian stoires, many of them versions of stories their own father had told them as children. In all, there were about forty pages of these, spread throughout the pile. They appeared to have no particular association with any of the other papers; at least none that he was able to decipher.

Two particularly intriguing items amongst the collection had drawn his attention. The first, a crumpled graduation certificate from Cork City University, conferred his brother with a Master's Degree in 'Celtic Studies'. From the scraps of information he was able to cobble together, it appeared that Séamus had obtained his degree in Cork before going on to teach at a Dublin University for more than seven years. About five years earlier, he had abruptly resigned from that position and returned to West Cork to work on an item of research that he seemed to believe was of critical importance. Diarmuid hadn't been able to work out what the research entailed but the decision had evidently surprised and dismayed his colleagues, three of whom wrote to him and urged him to reconsider.

The second item of interest was a black and white photograph that had been sealed in a faded brown envelope with the word 'Macnas' written across the front. It was a strange title, for the subject of the enclosed picture was an attractive woman walking along a deserted country road. Apparently, the photographer had caught her unawares; she was looking back over her shoulder with a blank, almost enigmatic expression on her face. She had large eyes, a sensuous mouth and her long, dark hair seemed to be flowing freely in a passing breeze. She was barefoot and a light-coloured overcoat covered her slim figure but obscured any other clothing that she might have been wearing.

Diarmuid picked up the photo and studied it. He had no idea who the woman was. A colleague? A friend? A lover?

It was even possible that she was Demne's mother. There were certainly similarities in the form of the chin and the eyes although most of the boy's facial features seemed to be dominated by his father's genes.

The view of the surrounding landscape provided little assistance. It was impossible to tell where the photo had been taken for the road looked like any country road in Ireland. It had stone walls and there was a field with a few scattered haystacks in the background but there were no definitive distinguishing features or landmarks.

With a sigh, he put the papers aside. Although they went some way to explaining Séamus' activities over the last few years, they shed no real light on why he had returned to Na hAoraí or why he had based himself in seclusion in Glonnyhust. Neither did they help to clarify the events leading up to what he could not accept as an accidental and therefore pointless death.

Diarmuid flicked a guilty glance in the direction of the sleeping child as he opened a different envelope containing the Consent for Adoption forms Pádraig had left with him. Since Demne's arrival, he'd read them through every night before going to bed, hand poised over the signature line but incapable of placing the pen to paper. On each occasion he had flipped through the five-page document, he'd never failed to notice the blank space for the mother's name, an absence matched on the other side of the page for the relative granting consent. Diarmuid had told Dinny that he'd hoped to find some contact details for the boy's mother within his brother's belongings, ostensibly to return him to his rightful family. If he had been honest he'd have admitted that his true motivation had been to divest himself of responsibility for a child he did not know.

He continued to stare at the empty space for over a minute, then impulsively signed his name with a flourish. Holding up the form, he considered the signature. It was done. The boy could now be placed under the care of the State and become someone else's responsibility. He had filled one of Pádraig's big, gaping holes. He just wasn't quite sure how true a fit it was.

Over on the far side of the room, the boy murmured something incomprehensible. Diarmuid sighed as he replaced the papers in the envelope. It was still early. It would be another two to three hours at least before he'd be obliged to wake the child from his sleep and calm him of his personal demons.

Pat's words returned to him at that point and he remembered how startled he'd been by his neighbour's astute diagnosis of Demne's condition. The *seanduine* had recognised it straight off, the troubling spiritual distress that permeated his nephew's dreams and tainted his waking hours. It was unfortunate indeed that Pádraig had been unable to extend such insight to suggest an appropriate remedy.

Diarmuid frowned. In the old days, his father would have known what to do. He would have simply approached the local *bean feasa* and sought her advice. Following Independence and the subsequent collusion of the Church and the State, however, the *bean feasa* were no longer to be found. In their wisdom, thin-faced men with big hats in the big city had decided that all guidance of a spiritual nature for the nation would now be dictated by the Catholic Church and its upstanding, celibate clergymen.

Diarmuid spat into the fire and was rewarded with a satisfying hiss that appropriately reflected his mood. He had little faith in the ability of the local priest – a fanatical little *seargánach* with fuck-all life experience – to advise him in a meaningful manner. He would, therefore, have to come up with an alternative solution to relieve his nephew. Diarmuid looked at the sleeping boy and tried to ignore the creeping sense of shame. He owed him that much at least.

***

Demne was woken earlier than usual on the following morning. Roused from sleep by a rough hand on his shoulder, he struggled up from the mattress, wiped the sleep from his eyes and quickly shuffled into his clothes.

The fire had died out during the night and the temperature inside the house had dropped dramatically. Diarmuid was standing at the table eating his breakfast. He handed the boy a cup of tea and a bowl of steaming porridge to counteract the cold.

'*Druid isteach agus bí ag ithe. Tá orainn siúlóid a dhéanamh.* Shove in and eat. We're going for a walk.

'Where are we going?' the boy wanted to know.

Diarmuid shrugged.

'Eat up. You'll see.'

Daylight was a distant glow over An tOileán Mór when they left the house. The grass, white and brittle from a thick hoar frost, glowed eerily in the gloom, crunching beneath their boots as they crossed An Páirc Mór. The air was bitterly cold and pinched the exposed skin on their faces. Vapour clouds from their breath trailed in their wake like reluctant ghosts. The dog whined, put out by the freezing sensation beneath its paws.

Diarmuid set a brisk pace as he led the way across the fields, following the worn track to Párc an Cnoic. By the time they reached the hill field, the sun had made its appearance, a faint red glow filtering through the low mist in the eastern sky. They drew to a halt at a spot overlooking the bay. A steep incline rolled down before them to a small field bordered on one side by dense woodland, one of the few patches still remaining in the area.

Diarmuid paused and looked at the boy. Although he was tired and smothering a yawn, his nephew was eyeing him suspiciously, wondering why he'd been dragged out to the isolated hill at such an hour of the morning. To his amusement, Diarmuid noticed that the boy had subtly widened the distance between them, laying the groundwork for a quick escape should his uncle make any kind of threatening move.

'Can you guess why I brought you here?'

Demne shook his head.

'Because of your secret.'

The boy gave him a guarded look.

'You have a *galar rúin*, Demne. A black secret that's poisoning your sleep and making you sick. If you don't deal to it, it'll get worse. It won't be obvious at first, but over time you'll wither away.' He stopped and scratched his nose. 'Instinctively, I think you know that I'm telling the truth.'

'*A Uncail, ní féidir …*' Demne stopped. He was breathing with difficulty, obviously close to tears. 'I can't …' Unable to continue, he turned his eyes to the ground.

'That's okay, *a bhuachaill*. I understand you can't tell me what it is. Sometimes emotions are just so big they jam you up inside and you can't get the words of them out.'

Too upset to say anything, the boy simply nodded.

Diarmuid approached to put his hand on the boy's shoulder and was relieved when he did not back away.

'Demne, I understand you've little reason to trust me but you need to hear me out and make your own judgement on the matter. The only way to cure a bad secret is to release it. If you can't free it by telling someone, then you have to find another way to do it.'

He pointed at a faint track that weaved its way down the incline and ended up in the lower field.

'If you follow that track, it'll lead you down to the woods at the bottom of the hill. There's an opening there with a narrow path that cuts through the trees. That'll bring you into a small clearing with an old ruin in the centre. To the left of the ruin you'll see a well set in a crevice under a big, black rock. An Carraig Dubh. That's where this piece of land gets its name from. There's a tiny stream running out from underneath the rock and there's a big old willow tree towering over it.'

He stopped for a moment to make sure the boy was taking everything on board before he continued again.

'Demne, when you get to the clearing, kneel down at the pool and take some water in your hands. Drink some of it and when you're finished, move over to the old willow tree. About four feet up, you'll find a bole hole on the eastern side of the trunk.'

He paused.

'Now, Demne, this is the important part. The willow can help cure the *galar rúin* but you need to follow my instructions exactly. Do you understand?'

The boy nodded.

'Good. I want you to get your lips as close to the hole as you can and then I want you to whisper this spell into it:

Is duitse táim á innsint
A phuill an chrainn,
A phuill an chrainn

'After that, tell the tree all the bad things you've been holding up inside you. Whisper it out of you and into the tree and it'll keep your secret safe, the way you won't have to.'

He looked at the boy.

'Can you repeat that?'

Diarmuid made the boy repeat his words twice more until he was satisfied that he had them off by heart.

'If you don't manage to get the spell right on the first go, just go through it again. Repeat it until you've told the tree everything.'

He nodded.

'Right, so. Off you go, *a bhuachaill*. Take as long as you need – even if it takes all day. I'll be waiting here for you. However long it takes.'

A cold breeze fluttered across the hill and the boy shivered. He looked up at his uncle but saw that there was no give in the old man. With evident reluctance, he began the descent to the trail.

The dog jumped up as he started to walk away and started off after him but Diarmuid called him back.

'No, Dog. This time you stay with me.'

The dog stared forlornly at the departing child but remained where he was, as instructed. Half-way down the hill, Demne stopped and looked back uncertainly.

'Go on,' shouted Diarmuid. 'Keep going. I won't leave without you.'

Despite his obvious lack of enthusiasm, Demne continued down to the field and approached the woods. With a final glance back at his uncle, he stepped into the trees and disappeared from sight.

***

As the trees closed in around him, Demne halted and looked around nervously. He'd never been in a large wood or seen so many trees in one place before. Although many were denuded of their summer greenery, there were enough evergreens clumped together to make him feel claustrophobic.

The path before him – little more than a rabbit trail – was barely visible in what little light permeated the canopy. He followed it through the trees and scrub, occasionally ducking under damp boughs coated with moss and dripping deadwood. The ground was spongy from two days of rain but the wood was protected from the rigour of frost by a slight, salt-tainted breeze.

Demne negotiated the winding path for two or three minutes before emerging into a clearing that looked just as his uncle had described. High slabs of grey rock, muffled with moss, occupied the southern and eastern edges. The remainder of the glade formed a rough oval shape, hemmed in by the trees. In the centre of the open area, the foundations and fallen walls of some ancient stone building were barely visible beneath a layer of dead fern.

The well was half obscured in the shadow of the high black rock that overhung it. A silver rivulet of water spilled from a cut and flowed down into the wood. Beside the rock was a large tree of a variety that Demne hadn't seen before. Its upper branches spread upwards and outwards for several feet and although the tangled boughs were winter-bare, the starkness was softened by a carpet of lichen that coated the trunk and lower sections.

He approached the well to find the water perfectly clear, the sand-coated bed visible three or four feet below the surface. Kneeling, he cupped a cool handful of water in his palm, raised it to his mouth and drank. The liquid was cold but left an invigorating after-bite. Wiping his mouth with the back of his hand, he rose to his feet, approached the willow tree and began to search for the hole as his uncle had instructed.

He located it almost immediately on the eastern side and found he could reach it comfortably in a standing position. He leaned forward into it and put his lips as close as possible.

> *Is duitse táim á innsint*
> *A phuill an crainn,*
> *A phuill an crainn …*

For several seconds, he found he was unable to say any more. He paused, frozen in indecision, the bark of the trunk rough against the skin of his cheek, unsure what to expect or what to do next. Finally, it came to him in a wave of clarity and he almost sighed in relief at the simple rightness of it.

Leaning forward with renewed confidence, he placed his lips against the tree and whispered into the hole.

'*Demne is ainm dom,*' he began. Demne is my name.

***

Diarmuid remained standing in the same position for several minutes after Demne had disappeared from view. The wind blowing in from the sea had a bitter edge to it and he shivered, tugging the collar of his coat up around his neck. Pulling his cloth cap down tighter around his forehead, he consoled himself with the fact that it wasn't raining.

He strolled in small circles for a while, shaking his legs and stamping the earth to regain some sensation in his frozen toes. The effort only served to exacerbate the ache in his knee joints.

Feckin' old bones!

He hated growing old. Not for any particular philosophical opposition reason but simply because of the sheer inconvenience of it, the restrictions it placed on his ability to achieve the things he wanted to achieve in the time he wanted to.

Mallacht ort a chinneachain!

Diarmuid had been thinking about death and dying over the last few days and, although it wasn't a subject he'd given much thought to in the past, he understood that these reflections on his own mortality had been prompted by recent events. Whatever the reason, the truth of the matter was that he could disappear off the face of the world any day now without warning and, unlike the Pats or the Dinnys of this world, he had no family to remember him, no one to mourn his passing.

B'fhéidir an buachaill. Maybe the boy.

He dismissed that idea with a snort. No. Any impression he left on the planet would have all the duration of a footprint on the bed of a fast-flowing river.

Fortunately, the reality of his existence did not particularly disturb him. A pragmatist at heart, he lacked the anxiety of those who obsessed with leaving a legacy behind – a kind of memorial to their own insecurity.

He had regrets of course: paths he might have taken, words he could have spoken, actions he should have avoided. Overall, however, he was sufficiently realistic to recognise that his life experience had made him the man he was and there was little point in regrets.

He gave a sour laugh.

Mind you, if he'd known then what he knew now, he'd certainly have chosen to do some things differently.

Things like Séamus.

Frowning, he crouched by the dog and absently patted it on the head. The dog looked at him, surprised by the uncharacteristic gesture of affection from its master.

'What about you, Dog? Do you have any regrets?'

The dog raised two large, brown eyes and Diarmuid found himself momentarily touched by the complete absence of self-interest or guile in that regard.

'Any lost bones you'd love to get those mangy teeth into? Any puppies you regret never rearing?'

The dog barked.

Diarmuid gave a gruff laugh. 'Ach, I didn't think so.' He shook his head. 'Yerra, I'm going quare in the head. Talking to dogs!'

Standing once more, he strolled over in the direction of his parents' graves, clambered over the fence and remained there for several minutes to pay his respects.

Maybe one day, someone will lay me down here with you. I think I'd like that.

He raised his eyes towards Cnoc Daod, unmoved to find the summit still obscured, its upper bulk enclosed in a thick wad of impenetrable cloud. There'd be no let-up of the clouds today, then.

With a grunt, he left the little graveyard and returned to roll a cigarette while looking out over the bay. The sun was noticeably higher now, casting a greasy film of subdued grey light over the harbour that gave the sea a limp and listless appearance.

The lighthouse on Roan Carraig was a white splotch against the colourless backdrop. Further up to the northeast, across a bleak stretch of dishwater-coloured sea, An tOileán Mór was a gaunt charcoal shape against an ash backdrop. Despite the melancholy chill he could not help but feel warmed by the familiar contrasts of grey upon grey upon grey.

Closing his eyes, Diarmuid relaxed and listened to the sound of breakers along the shore, the mournful fragments of seagull cry, the distant chug of a boat making its way to Baile Chaisleáin Bhéarra.

He remained at his post, soaking up the view, for almost an hour. Although he did wonder occasionally about the boy, he wasn't overly concerned. The location of the well was a safe place and the task would take as long as it would take. There was no point in worrying about it.

It was the dog's whimper that finally alerted him to movement down among the trees. At first he could only make out a vague blur of shadow between the branches. A moment later his nephew emerged from the scrub and started his way uphill. When he reached the top and approached, his uncle took note of the stains on the knees of his trousers and the dried tear streaks on his cheeks.

'*Ceart go leor?*' he asked. All right?

'*Ceart go leor,*' confirmed his nephew.

The old man nodded in satisfaction.

'*Abhaile linn, mar sin.*' Let's go home, so.

***

Diarmuid had finished milking the last of the cows when Dinny's familiar shadow fell across the doorstep of the milking shed. He glanced up in surprise from where he was crouched, loosening the stall rope looped around Rua's neck, then smiled. Although he would have been the first to

152

deny it, he missed the *craic* and companionship of his neighbour's company.

'Is it yourself, Dinny? We've not seen hide nor hair of you for ages. Were you off somewhere getting me a nice present?'

'Sure, what would I be doing bringing you presents? Isn't my presence present enough for ye!'

'Aah, typical. Always turning up with one hand as long as the other.'

The two old men chuckled. Diarmuid picked up the metal cap of the milk churn, sealed the lid and escorted his friend back to the house. Dinny took his usual spot by the fire and started filling the pipes while his host put the kettle on. When Diarmuid returned with two mugs of creamy tea, the bowls were filled to the brim with tobacco.

'*Cén scéal, mar sin?*' he asked, placing the two mugs on the hearth before them. So, what news?

'Yerra, we had a bit of a family crisis. Last week meself and Margaret found out that Máire, my eldest, is going to be in the family way herself, soon.'

Dinny breathed out deeply, completing the extended exhalation with a gentle sigh.

'Only twenty years of age. Unmarried. Father Byrne says she's a complete disgrace.'

'Ah, Dinny, when did you ever give a flying fuck about what Father Byrne says?'

His neighbour's smile cracked through the weathered wrinkles on his face.

'Ah, sure, it never hurts to keep in with the priests. Besides, aren't you always saying yourself: "Keep 'em happy and the feckers'll stay out of your hair."'

'Ah, sure, I know. But Máire ...'

'Ah, Máire.'

Dinny puffed thoughtfully on the pipe for a moment.

'Well, Máire's grand, to be honest. She knows as well as I do that gobshite Father Byrne can go feck off. She's my daughter and I think she'll be a great mammy.'

'Do ye know who the father is, at all?'

'Well, I'm pretty certain Máire knows who the fecker is, Diarmuid, but she sure as shit knows better than to tell me at the moment.'

He gave a low growl and clamped his teeth around the ebony stem of the pipe.

Diarmuid remained silent as he puffed a fine white circle of smoke that hung in the air for several seconds before dispersing.

'Well congratulations, *Dadó*,' he said brightly.

'Ah fuck off, you oul bollix!'

Diarmuid roared with laughter at his neighbour's sour reaction. His good humour slowly softened into a chuckle and faded as his nephew entered the house with the dog at his heels. Demne glanced over at the two men as he went to the kitchen, nodding politely to Dinny. He returned a few seconds later, drinking some water from a chipped enamel mug.

'Demne, will you ever be a good boyeen and take the churn out to the road. Seán'll be passing by in a while to pick it up.'

The boy nodded, put the mug down and left, whistling at the dog to follow him.

'Still quiet as ever,' commented Dinny.

'He's no feckin' Lord Haw Haw, that's for sure.'

'He looks different, though.'

'What do you mean?'

Dinny paused and thought about this for a moment. 'I'm not sure,' he admitted at last. 'It just strikes me that he looks – different.'

They sipped at their tea.

'Did you make any decision on the young fella then?'

'I did. I signed the papers.'

'Oh.' Although he did his best to disguise it, the disapproval was audible in his neighbour's voice.

'I signed them,' continued Diarmuid, 'and put them in an envelope with a stamp.' He paused. 'And then I threw them in the fire.'

Startled, Dinny turned to consider him with an appreciative expression. Diarmuid shrugged.

'I got to thinking. What with the young fella hanging around all the time, it was like having Séamus' ghost back on the farm.'

'He's the spit of his father, sure enough.'

'Anyway, I figured out that it wasn't having Demne around that was upsetting me. It was the fact that I'd never squared things off with Séamus. I still feel bad about that.'

He took a deep breath.

'Over forty years ago, Dinny, I made a terrible mistake. And it cost me my brother. A few days ago I decided that I didn't want to repeat the same mistake again.'

His neighbour leaned over and gave him a slap on the back but said nothing. They continued to smoke quietly, staring into the fire. After a few minutes, Diarmuid picked up a metal poker and used it to shift the smouldering turf, rearranging the burning sods to build the flames again.

'You know,' he said suddenly. 'In all these years, you've never once asked me about my falling out with Séamus. You knew him well but you've never once questioned me about it.'

'Sure, I figured if you wanted to tell me you'd tell me and if you didn't, you wouldn't.'

Diarmuid grunted. 'You're a singular man, Dinny Murphy.'

Laying the pipe aside, he picked up the mug of tea and blew, his breath rippling the surface of the steaming liquid. He took a tentative sip.

'You were only a tiny snip of a thing when it happened. A few weeks after Tadhg Mac Carthy was called up to Dublin, the local Volunteers received a message to meet up on Cnoc Mór. When we assembled on the hill that afternoon we found a strange woman waiting with the Battalion Commander.'

He sighed then and lapsed into silence as the years rolled away and he was a young man again, striding across the steep slopes of Cnoc Mór.

'God, but she was beautiful, Dinny. I'd never before seen a woman like the one I saw that day. And I've never seen her like since. Standing up straight she was, dressed in some fancy green coat, bronze hair billowing out behind her like some great orange sunset against the sky. Carried herself like a queen, she did. There wasn't one of us that didn't stop and wonder at the possibilities.'

He paused to knock his pipe against the side of the fireplace, scattering the charred tobacco onto the grey stone beneath.

'Turned out it was Tadhg's sister, Muireann. I'd heard of her before then although I'd never actually met her. She'd been away working in England since she was ten but word had it she got mixed up with the Fenians in London when the Troubles started getting serious. Afterwards, we heard she'd come home to help out with organising some *Cumman na mBan* groups in West Cork or to act as a messenger for the more important dispatches. The Tans were always less likely to search a woman — particularly one as charming as Muireann.'

He put the tea aside and blew carefully through the stem of his pipe before filling it with a fresh plug of tobacco.

'Anyway, I fell for her hard. And Séamus fell for her just as hard. A few nights later at the dance in Eadargóil, he plucked up the courage to ask her out and from there it became obvious that she liked him better than me. I cursed my luck but at the same time I wished him luck and walked away. That was that.

'Or so I thought.

'A few weeks later, the Commander asked me to drive Muireann up to Galway. Naturally, I wasn't in the know as to why, but it was obvious she was carrying an important message for the Volunteers there. I got the job because the usual driver had been picked up by the Constabulary and the Commander was in a bind. He knew I'd some experience of driving a lorry for a creamery job in Baile Chaisleáin Bhéarra. I hadn't driven a car before, and the distance was further than I was comfortable with but he just told me to drive it slow and stay calm if I saw the military.'

Diarmuid glanced over at Dinny and smiled. His friend was sitting upright on his stool, tense as a post as he listened to the story.

'Anyways, we left Beara late in the morning and I drove it slow. So slow we had to stop to spend the night at a hotel in Limerick. There were some British military types staying there as well so to be left to our own company we let on to be a young couple off on our honeymoon.

'Later, when we were having dinner in the hotel, we just seemed to fall into the roles. We got to talking, the drink got to flowing. One thing led to another and …'

He grimaced.

'Didn't you realise she was doing a line with Séamus?' Dinny interrupted, completely caught up in the tale.

'Of course, I did. But I was young and full of *teaspaí* and, truth be told, for that night I was a selfish fecker. Caught up in the moment. I just pushed all thought of Séamus from my mind.'

He raised the mug of tea again and exhaled slowly, staring into the milky liquid.

'But, by God, he was back in there again the following morning! We were the both of us ashamed of ourselves when we left the next day. Young things that we were, neither of us had the wherewithal to know what to say. We didn't speak the whole trip and when I dropped her off in the centre of Galway, she walked away from the car without a word.'

He scratched the stubble at the end of his chin.

'Jaysus, 'twas the longest trip in my whole life, taking that road back to Beara. My heart was heavy the whole way and I had no idea what I was going to do.'

'Yerra the fault was with her. She shouldn't have led you along.'

Diarmuid shook his head. 'No, Dinny, the fault was mine. She led me a merry dance but I knew the tune and the steps well enough. I could have put a stop to it at any time I wanted to. But I suppose I didn't want to.'

He stopped then, surprised to discover a long-forgotten emotion swelling up at the back of his throat, choking him and making it difficult to breathe. Disguising his disarray with a long swallow of tea, he continued his story.

'When I got home I couldn't live with the thought of Séamus finding out from someone else so I told him meself.' He paused. 'He didn't take it well.'

He stopped talking then and just sat staring into the fire, puffing an occasional cloud of blue smoke from the corner of his mouth.

'Things were never the same between us after that. Séamus wouldn't speak to me and after a while I got the hump from feeling guilty and being unable to get him to talk to me. You can imagine what it was like on the farm. By then, my own father, God bless him, was bedridden, so we practically had the place to ourselves. We spent three full weeks trying to avoid each other and manage the work on the farm at the same time. Apart from some brief conversations with the Oul Fella, there wasn't a word passed within these walls from the crowing of the cock to the setting of the sun. Seamus' heart had turned black against me.'

'That's a terrible story, Diarmuid.'

'Yerra, that isn't the worst of it, *a chara*. After a few weeks of that you can imagine my relief when the Commander called me up and sent me off to collect some rifles that'd been smuggled in by boat. The lads had unloaded them and hid them in a small rock cave down on the Tuorish peninsula. However they did it, though, the feckin' Auxiliaries got word of the cache and came a running. Fortunately, a couple of our boys spotted them east along the road and got word to Séamus to go ahead to warn me.'

The old man sighed.

'I never saw any sign of him, though.'

Dinny peered at him aghast. 'You don't mean ...'

'I don't know. The only thing I do know was that when I came out of the cave, I found myself cut off by the shoreline with soldiers beating the bushes all around me. I managed to hide myself away in a clump of ferns off to the side but one of them – a big, ugly brute – found me. He gave a great snarl and lifted his rifle so I let him have it with my pistol. Bang. Bang. Bang. Three rounds. That's all the ammunition I had, and the bastard was welcome to it.'

'What? Did you kill him?'

'I did for he'd surely have killed me if he'd had the chance. I was lucky, though. I was fast, I knew the lay of the land and I managed to give his friends the slip. But it was a close thing. Needless to say, we lost all the rifles. The Auxiliaries were angry about losing one of their own and I was away in hiding over at Tadhg's for a week. Eventually, things settled down and they went away again.

'I heard from Tadhg that the Commander had taken Séamus to task for not getting the message to me and losing the guns, but he said he'd been delayed trying to avoid another patrol. I could never tell if he was lying or not. Sometimes I still wonder about that. And how the Brits knew where the cache was hidden in the first place.'

He saw the surprise on his friend's face but offered no further speculation on that particular subject.

'After that, things just seemed to get away on us as we got caught up in other events. Séamus was drafted off to Cork City to fight with the Volunteers there. I stayed at home on the farm to take care of our Da. To be honest, I was glad to see the back of him for the guilt was still heavy on me and I was suspicious after the events at Tuorish.

'Da died a few weeks later. Séamus turned up and helped us to bury him but then he disappeared without a word. He never came back.'

'Did you not hear from him again?'

'Not a word. Now and again, I'd hear talk of him from other people, but I never heard from him. The last time I heard from anyone in his regard was just after the end of the Civil War. I was here at home fixing the wall when a car arrived down the lane with two strangers in it and I knew straight off there was something unsavoury about them. They were hard looking feckers. Two big men, one with a long scar down his cheek.

'They made their way up the lane to where I was working and demanded to know – arrogant as you please – if I was Séamus O'Súilleabháin. Well fuck it, says I. I won't be taking any chances with the likes of you. If it's not me you're after, it's my brother.'

I clattered the nearest one on the skull with the hammer I was using on the wall. He fell to the ground. The other one tried to pull a pistol from inside his jacket but, by Christ, I broke his arm with the next blow.

Well, the two of them were lying down there *ollogóning* and giving out and, to be honest, I felt a bit sorry for them. Not so much that I was going to turn my back on them, though. Fortunately for them, Pat Harrington was passing by and agreed to go off and call an ambulance. While I was waiting, I went through their pockets and that's when I found their identity papers. They were coppers: two Cork-based detectives from the new national police force. Apparently, they'd received an anonymous tip that Séamus was an Éamon De Valera sympathiser, and that he'd a stock of weapons hidden here at the farm. Actually, that part about the weapons was true, but they were mine and I sure wasn't keeping them for the Long Fella.'

'I suppose the bigwigs weren't too happy with you beating the shite out of their detectives.'

'You could say that. The cops swore blind that I'd attacked them without provocation and their word was taken over mine. I ended up in prison for over a year. If it hadn't been for Tadhg Mac Carthy and his connections, I'd still be there.

'I was finally released but I had to swear I'd keep quiet about what had happened. The feckers kept a file open on me, though. Technically, I'm still on probation, as Pádraig's always happy to remind me. If I ever get into any more trouble, I could potentially end up back inside. Even after all this time.'

He gave a sour laugh.

'So that's the story, Dinny. I'm not proud, but that's the way of it.'

They settled into a mutual silence. After all that had been said, there remained little else to say. The fire crackled as they smoked their pipes and the peace was only broken some minutes later when Dinny coughed and put his pipe aside.

'Diarmuid, do you mind if I ask you a question?'

'Jaysus, you've lasted thirty years without even asking me one and now you've got a feckin' ton of them. What do you want to know?'

'I was just thinking about Tadhg's sister. Did you ever see her again?'

Diarmuid gave him an odd look.

'Is it a romantic you are, Dinny?'

Despite his sardonic response, a thoughtful expression came over Diarmuid's face.

'You know, time puts a strange perspective on things. When I look back all them years ago and think of her, I can still remember that fluttering sensation in my stomach, the hot pulse of blood through my veins. I truly thought the sun shone out of that girl's arse, Dinny. I'd have ridden the wind for her. I'd have climbed a mountain and risked my own arse sliding back down on a rainbow. Back then, I'd have done heroic deeds if she'd as much as asked.'

He picked up the mug but was disappointed to discover he'd already drunk its contents.

'When I look back at those days, it's like I'm seeing everything through a sheet of dirty plastic, as though I was under some great fever when it all happened. Sometimes it feels as though all those emotions belonged to someone else, that I'm remembering someone else's life.'

He shook his head, struggling to make sense of it.

'I can still remember the passion, though. Just as strong but these days I have the experience to put it in perspective. I understand, now, that I was simply infatuated with Muireann. She was attractive, sure enough. And beautiful. But at the end of the day, she was just a normal person with a normal person's drives and a normal person's weaknesses.'

'So, whatever happened to her?'

'Ach, she married a butcher, a Volunteer from Dublin. They ended up living in Drogheda. No doubt they're cutting sausages and steak for the locals to this day, regaling them with tales of their heroic service freeing Ireland from the Crown.'

He gave a wry laugh. 'Tadhg had a photo of her when he visited here the other day. He asked me if I wanted to see it, but I said I didn't.'

He saw the surprise on his friend's face.

'I suppose that's how you know when you're old, Dinny. The experience has been lived but the passion's all run out of steam. Besides, she's no longer the person I knew, just like I'm no longer the person she knew. That's all history now and we'd be nothing to each other but strangers.'

Dinny was clearly disappointed with the response to his question. He pulled his cap off and scratched the flattened patch of wiry grey hair.

'And you've never considered taking another woman, raising a family of your own?'

Diarmuid turned and looked at his old friend with a sad smile.

'Sure, why would I do that. It's all too late now, Dinny. I've not really had any interest since my experiences with Muireann. I don't want love or romance any more. I just want my brother back.'

Chapter Ten

Cork City, 2008

Mos arose to a sky devoid of sunshine and a street devoid of blue Subarus. For over a minute he observed the armour-plated cloud cover from an upstairs window then, with a sigh of resignation, proceeded downstairs.

The phone rang twice during his habitual routine of grinding coffee beans. He made a point of ignoring it on both occasions and let it ring out. When it rang a third time, he reached over and switched the power off.

He returned upstairs to sip the coffee at his observation post by the corner window, a location that provided the best view of O'Donovan's Road and the street in front of his house. Despite the absence of anything out of the ordinary, he was unable to suppress the feeling that critical events were unfolding unseen around him.

He frowned.

Although wary and suspicious by nature, such expressions of foreboding were uncharacteristic and prompted, he suspected, by a poor night's sleep and disturbing dreams of shadows lurking on the outskirts of Carraig Dubh. The nightmares had left him exhausted and on waking their unpleasant residue still lingered at the back of his mind, tainting his mood.

Sod this! May as well do something useful!

Putting his empty coffee cup aside, he took a seat at the nearest computer and spent half an hour browsing the internet for some background information on the Opus Foundation. His search returned a base response of approximately fifty documents, mostly media releases sourced from the organisation itself, as well as several links from the websites of other conservation authorities and NGOs where mention – consistently favourable – was made of the Foundation.

For the most part, the online material confirmed everything Reverend Quinn had told him. The Foundation had been established in the late 1970s; its headquarters and principal repository were located in London. It also appeared to have links with several representatives or partner organisations – it was not clear which –throughout the world.

The official website of the Foundation was tastefully designed with a muted blue and white palette scheme and bore several striking images of relics from their extensive collection. In most respects, however, it was a typical corporate site, a slick marketing tool designed to encourage visits to the museum or donations to 'continue the good work of the Foundation'.

Donations, Mos discovered, formed a significant proportion of the organisation's income. Although the Foundation received financial support through grants from reputable international heritage agencies and American and European government departments, the most recent Annual Report indicated that almost twenty per cent of its annual budget was derived from the collective donations of visitors to the London repository. This was further supported by substantial individual contributions from well-known international companies and unidentified private donors.

The governance documents on the website stated that the Opus Foundation was overseen by a Board of five directors that included Reverend Quinn. Mos was interested to note that, as well as holding the role of Chair, Reverend Quinn also acted as the official spokesperson on all matters pertaining to publicity and media.

Each board member had a full bio page dedicated to them. These outlined their experience and qualifications and laboriously underlined how terribly important they were. Four members, including Reverend Quinn, were male. Of these, Paul O'Leary, a Dublin-born businessman, was the only name he recognised. According to coverage he'd read in the national press, O'Leary was a successful building developer although, apart from his obvious commercial acumen, it was unclear what other attributes he brought to the organisation.

The blurb on the two remaining men – Dr Klaus Hessman and Professor Peter Boyle – indicated that the former, an Austrian theologian, lectured at a well-known German university while the latter held the role of an American Christian organisation.

Sarah Smith, the only female member of the board, was surprisingly young to hold such a position. Thirty-five years old, she had amassed an impressive amount of experience: her curriculum vitae outlined a number of senior management roles held in Christian-based humanitarian organisations across Europe. The attached photo showed an attractive woman with short black hair staring stonily at the camera.

On impulse, Mos clicked on an image of Reverend Quinn which dated from several years earlier. The photo, in black and white, showed him with longer and darker hair, smiling benevolently and shaking hands with a local Member of Parliament at the official opening of the Foundation's London office. Mos leaned back in his seat and stared at the beaming face of the Opus Foundation's Chairman, recalling how the man had almost instantaneously switched from convivial geniality to ruthless assertiveness.

Congratulations, Mos. That's your new boss!

He switched off the computer with a sigh and rubbed the back of his neck. It was now becoming increasingly tender to the touch. From experience, he knew he had less than twenty-four hours to address the condition before it progressed through to more serious stages: headaches, seizures and, ultimately, memory loss.

Pulling his diary from the desk, he studied his timetable for the rest of March. During his conversation with Reverend Quinn, he'd reluctantly agreed to travel to London on Friday to meet the conservation team and examine the manuscript in detail. This, essentially, gave him two nights back in West Cork to deal with his condition before it got any worse.

He sighed.

No choice, then.

He was going home to Carraig Dubh.

***

Mos was packing an overnight bag when the doorbell resonated from the hallway below. Unaccustomed to visitors, he stiffened in surprise and approached the window. He peered cautiously down through a gap in the curtains, grimacing as he recognised a familiar shape below.

The doorbell chimed again.

Muttering under his breath, he descended to the hall and opened the front door.

'Desmond.'

'Hello, Muiris.'

'What are you doing here?'

'I'm looking for you.' The portly professor shuffled nervously and Mos noticed he was holding a padded envelope under one arm. 'I tried ringing.'

'Ah, right. Problem with the phone.'

Hegarty eyed him dubiously.

'I thought you might be out. You always seem to be out.'

There wasn't a clear response to that so Mos said nothing. Hegarty, a man uncomfortable with silence at the best of times, was quick to offset the looming hush.

'Actually, it's probably a good job you didn't go out. I don't know if you've heard the news, but poor O'Donoghue was mugged in McCarthy's Bar. The very night we were there!'

He shook his head in apparent incomprehension at the depths to which Irish society had sunk.

'Honestly! It's a terrible state of affairs. Terrible.'

'Terrible,' agreed Mos.

Hegarty stepped onto the front doorstep, paused, then stepped back again when Mos didn't move aside.

'Well, aren't you going to invite me in?'

Mos shook his head. 'No.'

'Why ever not?'

'I don't like you.'

'For God's sake, Muiris!'

Mos shrugged.

'What can I say? You bring out the worst in me. Anyway, what the fuck do you want?'

Hegarty stared at him in a mixture of shock and indignation. With visible effort, he straightened up and slowly pressed the tips of his fingers together.

'I spoke to David Coffey last night. He told me to give this to you.'

Hegarty removed the envelope from beneath his arm and passed it to Mos, who hefted it in one hand.

What the hell is this?

'He indicated that you'd be helping out with the artefact's evaluation.' Hegarty regarded Mos with a glacial expression. 'Leading it, in fact.'

'Uh-huh.'

Desmond glowered. 'Muiris, I'm disappointed. I know I might have made some mistakes in the past, but I didn't think you were the kind of man to bear a grudge and betray me like that. I worked bloody hard to get this project up and running. I also went out of my way to offer you a once-in–a-lifetime opportunity. Then you repay me by doing your best to undermine my professional reputation.'

Hegarty had slowly been building himself up to a crescendo of fury. By the time his tirade had reached its climax, his face had taken on a disturbing shade of scarlet. He stood, gasping for breath and glaring petulantly at his old student.

Mos returned the glare for a moment then, without a word, closed the door in his visitor's face.

There was a startled silence as he strolled back down the hallway, followed by a squawk of outrage and some agitated yelling. He was pleased to find that when he entered the kitchen and shut the door behind him, he was no longer able to hear it.

He sat at the kitchen table and fumed in silence for a minute or two before turning his attention to the envelope Hegarty had given him. Ripping the seal, he upended it and tipped a single sheet of A4 paper and several glossy photographs of an illustrated manuscript onto the table. It was a moment before he understood what he was looking at.

The Fragments!

He grasped the nearest photo, which bore a sticky label identifying it as 'Folio One' and examined it closely. At first glance, the folio reminded him of *An Cathach* – a sixth century manuscript psalter – for it was laid out in a similar pattern of four paragraphs, each consisting of what appeared to be a single psalm. Again, like *An Cathach*, the initial letter of the first word in each paragraph was historiated in the form of an animal. The remaining letters in the first words were oversized to a lesser extent but gradually diminished as they moved to the right until they matched the body of the text. A relatively simple decoration, it lacked the complicated triskeles and geometric ornamentation of later illustrated manuscripts but was no less impressive for this.

The text was Latin and although he was insufficiently skilled in the language to decipher it completely, Mos recognised enough of the words to confirm that the paragraphs were, indeed, psalms. The letters – typical insular script – were inscribed in a bold, flowing hand. Despite the document's age the writing flowed clearly: like most early manuscripts, it had been designed for easy legibility and to be recited aloud.

Mos briefly scanned the remaining photographs, then put them aside and picked up the piece of A4. This contained a short summary of Hegarty's analysis and was entitled 'The Guttmann Fragments':

> *The "Guttmann Fragments" consist of four folios that, originally, formed part of an early medieval manuscript – most likely a Psalter or 'Pocket Gospel' which contained any of the 150 sacred songs, lyric poems, and prayers collectively known as 'the Psalms'. Psalters were developed by the Roman Christian church from the early 8th century. They were one of the most popular types of illuminated manuscripts available to the learned classes – predominantly ecclesiastical – during the Middle Ages and were often used for recitation at different parts of the liturgy.*

Mos glanced over at the six photographs and frowned. Four double-sided leaves should mean eight photos, but only six had been included.

So, where are the other two?

He continued reading.

Provenance:

> *According to Dr Heinrich Guttmann, the Fragments were discovered within the leather cover of a seventeenth-century book of hymns obtained from another private collector, who originally sourced the document from the Universität Wien library in Vienna. Certification confirming this provenance has been received and assessed as genuine. It is not known why the Fragments ended up within the book of hymns; however, given the relative rarity and cost of parchment at that time, it was not unusual for older – 'superfluous' – parchment to be recycled as a strengthening or support material for more recent tomes.*

Physical:

> *The 'Fragments' are rectangular vellum sheets with Latin text. Each sheet measures approximately 18 cm by 16 cm. The physical condition of the vellum on three sheets is excellent (although there is some minor crinkling) with no moisture damage. Extensive damage, however, exists on the lower right-hand quarter of the fourth sheet (Folio 4). Much of this parchment is missing and the edge is marked*

by a ragged tear and a dark stain. A number of smaller holes and stains are spread throughout the remainder of Folio 4.

All sheets display evidence of having been cut from a centre fold with a very sharp object. There is no trace of the original binding.

Text:

The text is written in Latin with a vocabulary consistent with that used between the sixth and tenth centuries.

The text on three sheets (Folio 2, 3 and 4) is laid out in two columns and written in a fine pointed insular minuscule. The text on the first sheet (Folio 1) contains four historiated initials in the left margin, one representing each of the Four Evangelists' symbols. All of these letters have been decorated with a selection of red, yellow, black and green inks. The impressive, simplistic style of the large initials is typical of the illustrated manuscripts produced within the monastery scriptorium of Irish monastic or missionary scriptoriums from the sixth to ninth century.

Folio 1 also includes a hand-written gloss in the upper left-hand quarter margin. The language of the gloss is Old Irish (sixth–tenth century). The letters are of moderate size and written in small, delicate characters but due to minor damage (described above) several words are missing or illegible. A translation of the glossary has been provided by Dr Guttmann.

Mos checked though the pile of photos and checked again, but there was no sign of the translation or of the Folio 4 referred to.

The gloss bears the signature of one Christianus Mac Carthy, believed to be an abbot of Regensberg in the early twelfth century. This individual is known to have died prior to 1158 during a visit to Ireland raising funds for the Regensberg mission. Given the signature, it is possible – and even likely – that the original manuscript was a personal possession of Abbot Mac Carthy.

That's it?

Mos double-checked the text on the photos again but, so far as he could tell, there was nothing in the Fragments that bore any relation to the *Fianaigecht.* Given that they appeared to be a reproduction of the Psalms, this was hardly surprising. This also tended to suggest that any association to the Fenian works had to be in the gloss of the remaining folio.

Which, of course, hasn't been included. What are you up to now, Hegarty?

Mos sighed as he replaced the papers in the envelope. It was frustrating but he would have to deal with it later in the week, during his visit to the Opus Foundation in London. He had other issues to focus on right now.

Mos packed an overnight bag and prepared to leave. Returning to the front door, he was pleased to find no trace of Hegarty, who had evidently given up and moved on. The sky, however, had taken on an even more intimidating appearance and the air temperature had dropped dramatically.

He initiated the house's security system then slung the bag over his shoulder as he strolled out to his car, a battered, green Citroen parked against the kerb in front of the house. As he unlocked the driver's door, he caught himself whistling quietly and realised that, despite the attempted intrusions into his personal affairs, Hegarty's unpleasant visit, his worsening physical condition and the consistently shite weather, his mood had improved.

Ar fheabhas! It can only get better from here on in.

The sky caved in as Mos left the city. The initial dump of rain smeared the windscreen, almost completely obscuring his view as the wipers struggled to cope with the downpour. To his immense relief, after several minutes of being obliged to drive at a snail's pace, the inundation eased to a sustained drizzle.

Traffic was light and he made good time through the suburbs of Wilton and Curraheen. As he emerged through the cluttered tangle of the outer suburbs, the dark, skeletal structures of half-completed residential developments rose up out from the gloom on either side. Mos frowned as he took in the rows of identical, half-completed buildings. Each time he took this route, he had the impression that the construction had expanded further. It wasn't really so long ago that the place had consisted of green fields and woodland and the city had been little more than a blur against the horizon.

Intensive construction in the area had taken off over the previous eight years, following decades of a stagnant economy. The desire for more modern accommodation was easy enough to understand, even if a lack of sustainable planning and mind-numbing house designs had left some residential estates with the aesthetic appeal of a fast-food outlet.

The higher cost, Mos felt, was that there had been no recognition of the cultural heritage the developments obliterated. Historical community sites had been replaced by a collection of uniform housing units where neighbours did not know each other, and age-old local place names had been replaced by meaningless English substitutes ascribed by developers with no allegiance to the area. Over the previous decade there had been a creeping eradication of local history and a severing of familial and personal ties to the land. Children born in the housing estates were inheriting a topographical amnesia, a memory-starved landscape from which all heritage had been scooped up and thrown away with the topsoil.

With mounting irritation, Mos pressed his foot on the accelerator. The car surged forward as the road opened out before him.

Towards the West.

***

For the first half hour or so the car ate up the miles, plunging through a landscape of sodden, gently rolling countryside. As the vehicle travelled further from the city, the rain cleared, although it remained overcast and a forlorn shadow hung over the increasingly rugged farmland. Dairy pasture gradually gave way to smaller, rougher fields where the hills were steeper, the farmland overrun by briars or gorse. Buttresses of sharp, grey rock erupted through the thinning soil and the roads became narrower, forcing Mos to reduce his speed.

Several miles outside of Gleann Garbh, he pulled into a lay-by that offered a view of Cuan Baoi, a grey stretch of water hemmed in on either side by a long peninsula and, to the south-west, by a cold slab of cumulonimbus spilling in from the Atlantic. In the distance, the island Oileán Faoide was a vague green-black blur and the lonely slice of Rinn Mhuintir Bháire was faint against the incoming mist. The gigantic granite spine of the Caha mountains running down the Beara peninsula could still be seen.

Mos got out of the car and stretched to release the stiffness in his neck and shoulders. He shivered as he took in the terrain around him. It was a hard land, this particular part of West Cork. Desolately beautiful on a sunny day, on any other day it could be a grim and unforgiving place with few natural resources besides an infinite supply of rock. Some claimed that the nature of the land was reflected in the character of the people that inhabited it: hardy, fiercely independent individuals who resented outside interference in their lives. Mos held no particular opinion on such generalisations but the extent of military activity in the county during the War of Independence spoke for itself. West Cork had been at the heart of the most vigorous republican conflict outside of the capital. At the height of the fighting, over 12,000 British soldiers had been stationed across the region to deal with a guerrilla insurgency that had never consisted of more than a few hundred poorly armed and part-time Volunteers. Michael Collins, a key instigator of modern guerrilla warfare, had also met his end in his native West Cork, struck down at Béal na mBlath by a bullet from a disillusioned veteran who'd been trained to fight in the style Collins himself had promoted.

To this day, the citizens of Cork City still referred to West Cork as 'Indian Country'.

A fresh shower drove Mos back to the car. The mist closed in as he started the engine and nudged the vehicle back onto the coast road. As he neared the Beara peninsula, the vegetation diminished, reduced to scattered clumps of conifers and the occasional windswept oak or holly tree standing solitary on some isolated promontory. The sparse vegetation gave the land a harsh, alien aspect and it was difficult to believe that the peninsula had once been covered in a green canopy so thick that squirrels were said to be able to travel from one end to the other without touching the ground. That was all gone now, of course. Following the disastrous Irish defeat at Kinsale in 1601, the forests had been systematically plundered by English colonists, the huge trunks reduced to barrel staves and masts for Spanish shipping or charcoal for local iron works. Enormous swathes of forest had been clear-felled without any form of coppicing to reduce the destruction – a policy encouraged by the English Crown to deprive Papist rebels of refuge.

Gleann Garbh appeared unusually dark and subdued as he drove through, hunkered down against the inclement weather. On the far side of the village, the road wove up through the steep hills from which it had derived its name: Gleann Garbh – Rough Glen. Rock dominated the view as he followed a coastline that increasingly resembled a frozen lunar landscape.

After fifteen minutes or so, the familiar *botharín* leading down to the sea came into view. Mos turned off the main road and let the car freewheel downhill, his heart tightening in anticipation as he turned off into the entrance to Carraig Dubh. The driveway was an unsealed lane, half overgrown with weeds that had shrivelled back over the winter months. Resilient reeds in the centre of the lane scraped the underside of the car as he negotiated a tight curve, passed between thick hedgerows of fuchsia and blackthorn and drew to a halt before an ancient iron gate sealed shut by a rusted padlock. Switching off the engine, he rolled the driver's window down. The salt tang of the sea mingled with the scent of wet grass and earth flooded his nostrils.

He was home.

***

Like the driveway, the narrow lane leading towards the house was overgrown. Poor drainage had resulted in several muddy puddles and he was obliged to negotiate his way with the assistance of a flashlight. The eastern gable of the house, barely visible through the denuded fuchsia bushes, was layered with a thick mat of ivy.

Mos circled the building twice. He tried to check the lower windows for any signs of disturbance but in the failing light it was difficult to see if any attempt at a forced entry had been made. Deciding that it was a waste of time, he returned to the front of the house where a small porch shaded a thick oak door. Withdrawing an old key from his pocket, he twisted it in the ancient lock, grinning as a satisfying metallic click rang out loud in the evening quiet.

The interior of the house was dark and cold and the air was stale but at least it was dry. The curtains were drawn but from the dim light seeping through the doorway behind him, he could just make out the hearth and mantelpiece. Kindling that he had laid down more than a year before sat in the grate, coated with a dusty spider-web. He pulled a box of matches from a stone shelf over the fireplace, lit one and the brittle twigs erupted into flame as soon as it came into contact. As it flared and took hold, he added one of two larger pieces of wood and a few scraps of turf from the nearby fuel bucket.

He settled back onto his haunches and waited for the fire to build. The growing flames revealed a room that was approximately six metres by four and simply furnished. At the far end, facing the fireplace, two doors opened into a toilet and a small kitchen. To the right of the kitchen doorway, a narrow stairwell led to the pokey upstairs level.

The furniture – a rough wooden table and chairs, a narrow wardrobe, a long bookshelf and a scuffed, black leather sofa – was old but sturdy, and had been well maintained. Two square windows were set in the northern wall adjacent to the doorway and there was a third, smaller one in the southern wall.

He lit an old kerosene lantern on the mantelpiece and its soft yellow light slowly brightened the room. The house wasn't wired to the grid and although Mos had considered connecting it he'd never actually committed to doing so. Electricity, he knew, would fundamentally change the character of the house, undermining its rustic atmosphere and diluting deep-rooted memories of his childhood. It was not a price he was prepared to pay for any extra convenience.

Taking the lantern in his hand, he went upstairs and dropped his bag on the floor of the larger of two bedrooms that were separated by a tiny landing. He pulled some fresh linen and a cardboard box from the bag, dressed the queen-size bed with the former and proceeded downstairs with the latter. The fire was burning strongly now, smoky blue and yellow flames emitting a pleasant scent of turf and bathing the room in a warm glow.

He ate dinner – a tin of ravioli – at the table in the flickering illumination of two candle stubs. While he ate, he flicked through a book haphazardly plucked from one of the nearby shelves. It was one of his old schoolbooks, a collection of Fenian tales that opened automatically to a picture of Fionn mac Cumhaill burning his thumb on the Salmon of

Knowledge. Although the coincidence amused Mos, the image triggered fresh thoughts of the task awaiting him with the Guttmann Fragments.

Fionn's resting place. Is it possible?

The question came to him unexpectedly, but he knew it had been lying there, dormant, beneath the surface for some time. He was surprised by the palpable sense of excitement the thought provoked, but it also irked him that his professional detachment could be so easily diverted by what was clearly an outlandish claim.

Mos stared at the black and white illustration of a young boy crouched over a fire, turning the giant fish on a wooden spit. He breathed out slowly.

He understood the appeal of the legend to individuals like Reverend Quinn. For Irish people, the Fenian stories were a fundamental cultural reference, a familiar icon of heritage that evoked fond memories and strong associations with great deeds and heroes. For non-Irish nationals of Irish descent, the pull could often be just as strong, although dominated more by the fantasy and fictional mythical elements of the tales.

Those tales had also inspired Mod' own interest in history and *An Fianaigecht*. With the cynicism of experience, he now knew the simplistic illustrations of handsome, clean-shaven warriors from his schoolbooks were a distilled version of true Fenian lore from which the essential earthiness had been sanitised. Deep down, he knew that his intellectual connection to the tales was matched by a profound emotional connection, something his unbridled enthusiasm had demonstrated all too well. The truth – although he was reluctant to admit it – was that much of that magic remained.

With a sigh, Mos closed the book and returned it to the shelf. He could easily spend hours engaged in the contemplation of the Fenian stories. In the meantime, there were more pressing matters that demanded his attention.

Stripping out of his clothes, he threw several sods of turf on the fire, locked the fire guard in place and spread a bundle of blankets on the ground before it. Naked, he settled into the nest he'd created and opened the cardboard box he'd brought down from the bedroom. From this, he removed a glass bottle containing a clear liquid and a tin cigar-box. Unscrewing the cap on the bottle, he took a whiff, wincing at the powerful scent of *poitín*. He coughed as he put it aside then opened the cigar box. This held several slivers of a black material with an unusual heady aroma.

The *poitín* – acquired from a contact in Carlingford – was an excellent batch, one of the best he had ever tasted. A slight burning sensation on the tongue and the vaguest awareness of alcohol evaporating off the tongue was a good indication of its quality and strength.

The black material – which he had mockingly named *Cáca Cacach*, literally, 'Shitty Cake' – was a chemical concoction of more local provenance. Manufactured from a complex mixture of different herbs, it was his drug of choice from the many formulations he'd experimented with over the years. Of them all, *Cáca Cacach* had been the only one able to release the pressure at the back of his head without the usual significant side effects.

Mos poured himself a shot of *poitín*, swallowed it, then cut a sliver of *Cáca Cacach* and placed it on his tongue. When it'd dissolved to a slick, sour paste, he washed it down with a second shot of *poitín* then stood to replace the box on the mantelpiece.

He was about to sit again when he caught sight of his reflection in a small shaving mirror situated at the far end of the mantelpiece. Although not usually a person to be overly concerned with his appearance, he felt a sudden strange compulsion to examine his features more closely. He considered himself for several seconds – the blue eyes, dark hair, day-old stubble – then raised the glass in ironic toast to himself.

'*Sláinte*, y'oul bastard!'

***

Two glasses of *poitín* and one sliver in.

It started with a slight buzz around his ears, a warm cloudy feeling that filled up the space at the back of his head. He breathed deeply, sitting cross-legged on the blankets as he waited for the drugs to kick in.

The initial descent with *Cáca Cacach* was always enjoyable, invariably accompanied by an agreeable sanguinity that calmed and relaxed him. At this stage of the process, there was no rush. He wasn't going anywhere.

Half an hour in, his metabolism responded to the cocktail of active ingredients fuzzing up his bloodstream. It was at this stage he habitually noted a slight 'speeding up': his heart rate quickening, his intellectual processes gaining an astonishing depth of perception as they built up a momentum that would carry him well past the point of rational thought.

It was also at this stage that he began to lose the concept of time and could no longer figure out if he'd been sitting on the floor for minutes, hours or even days. His vision flickered as his eyes lost focus and he clumsily moved his hands to his face, pressing his index and middle fingers against his temples and massaging his skull in circular motions. He inhaled slowly, taking in deep breaths and growing increasingly aware of the sound of his own breathing, the pulse of his heartbeat, the sense of his body growing heavier. Soon the room was moving in and out of focus, blinkers in his peripheral vision swelling and receding in time with his pulse. A sickly-sweet taste filled his mouth and he felt nauseous. There was a bizarre sense of euphoria when he felt himself fall onto his side and it seemed to take a long time before the side of his head hit the blanket-coated floor.

He heard himself cackle.

There was a blur, then he heard a faint rushing sound as though his head was being invaded by an undetermined horde of unfamiliar notions and foreign concepts. A quiet whispering emanated from one corner of the room and although he concentrated, he could make no sense of the voices, which sounded like a crowd of people all trying to speak at once.

The visions came then. His back arched and his fists clenched as pictures exploded in his mind, abstract forms without meaning or form. The images bombarded his senses, too fast to absorb or make sense of them.

A dark figure silhouetted against a blank canvas; a horizon or a skyline.

A pair of eyes hanging in the air, observing him.

A shocking red spray of blood against a white wall.

Bog water; black and viscous.

Overwhelmed by dizziness, he sank to his knees, leaned forward and vomited. Then followed the long, dark tumble into oblivion.

***

He came to his senses in silence, or rather in the absence of the sounds that would normally have roused him: the cough of a neighbour's car, the background hum of traffic, the flutter of conversations on the street outside his house. From habit, he automatically moved his hand up to the back of his neck, relieved to discover that the pressure there had dissipated.

Tá gach rud ceart go leor arís. Everything's all right again.

He remained on his back for several minutes, staring up at the ceiling of the bedroom. He must have made it upstairs during the night, although he had no recollection of doing so. An industrious spider was spinning a web in one small crack on an otherwise featureless white surface. The silence hung in the air, thick, punctuated intermittently by the keen of seagulls or an occasional surge of waves along the distant coastline. A weak slice of sunlight slid through a parting in the curtains, a golden shaft dotted with dust particles and he felt an immediate lifting of spirits.

Sunlight! A good start.

As usual when he tried to remember, his memory of the visions was scattered, flickering half-sensed images on the edge of his consciousness. Now and again a solitary image would form unbidden, but he lacked any context to make sense of it. All that remained was a vague but lingering sense of menace and unease.

A growing apprehension stirred him and he was suddenly keen to be up. He swung his legs off the bed. The timber floorboards were cool against the soles of his feet. They creaked when he put his full weight on them and crossed the room to a low table by the window with a washbowl and jug of water. He poured some water into the bowl and washed his face and hands before drying them off with a rough, grey towel.

When he'd finished putting on a fresh set of clothing, he stumbled downstairs. Breakfast consisted of a mug of instant coffee that he sipped on the old stone wall overlooking An Páirc Mór. After a week of dismal weather, the climate gods finally appeared to have relented. Mos closed his eyes, enjoying the sensation of sun on his face. When he opened them again he noticed several rabbits, brazen from the extended absence of human activity, moving through withered red fern at the far end of the field. Tossing the dregs of the coffee onto the grass, he returned inside and deposited the cup in the sink.

He locked the house behind him when he left, cleared the wall and started walking, following a muddy path across An Páirc Mór through an opening in the ditch on the far side of the paddock that led to another, smaller field. This was called Páirc na Meara, although he had no idea of the name's derivation.

The path became more overgrown, running between blackthorn bushes and clumps of dead fern. In places, the earth was muddy, pockmarked and beaten from the hooves of the six cattle that Bróna's brother Ciarán maintained on the land to keep the worst of the vegetation under control.

He halted suddenly, bending to – retrieve a slender ash branch that still retained some firmness and then proceeded onwards, striking idly at the grass to send drops of cold liquid dew whipping into the air.

A gap in the holly trees at the end of the field opened onto a grassy clearing that ran down to a rocky shoreline. Off to the right, a narrow band of white sand strewn with rocks and boulders stretched for about three hundred feet, ending at a rocky promontory that poked out into the bay like a knobbly triangle. A large boulder encrusted with lichen lay at the tip of the outcrop and several seagulls, keening plaintively, were whirling in geometric patterns overhead.

Water lapped gently against the shore. It was nearly low tide and clumps of bladder wrack and other sea vegetables lay exposed above the water line. In the past, he was aware, the beach had served as an important food source, an area where people would gather to collect shellfish and harvest the dark brown seaweed that grew there year after year. During the *Gorta Mór* – the Great Famine – the site had held a particular importance; a collection of *sleabhac* with *báirneachs* and other shellfish would have staved off a family's hunger for a day or two.

Making himself comfortable on one of the flatter rocks, Mos rolled a cigarette. He smoked in silence as he stared towards An tOileán Mór. In the early light, the island looked extremely close, like a giant whale lying half submerged offshore. Its bulk stretched up the length of the bay, dominated by two large hills, one capped with an old Martello tower.

He inhaled deeply, pulling the frigid sea air into his lungs and releasing it slowly as the tension eased out of him.

Jesus, it's been too long since I smelled the sea.

He remained on the beach for over half an hour, taking the time to absorb its stark beauty and refamiliarise himself with landmarks and sounds that he'd forgotten after a full year in the city. As always when he returned, he found himself wondering why he'd ever left in the first place.

He was staring at the sea when a round head suddenly popped up from the water about six metres out from where he was sitting. It bobbed there silently, two moist, black eyes watching him without expression.

'*Dia duit, a rón,*' he greeted the seal. '*Cén scéal?*' What's new?

The animal regarded him impassively then, as suddenly as it had appeared, it was gone, sliding beneath the surface without a sound or any trace of a ripple in its wake.

Muiris grinned wryly then stood and brushed a thin layer of the sand from the arse of his jeans.

He followed the rocky foreshore easte for twenty minutes or so until he reached a steep promontory known as Srón an Gabhar, the Goat's Nose. There, he clambered around the lichen-stained rocks and entered a narrow inlet containing a small pier and two rowboats moored to a weather-beaten buoy. A rough track by the pier meandered uphill to a thick hedge where a narrow gap allowed access to a small garden. Passing through the gap, he crossed a neatly manicured lawn that rolled up to the edge of a tidy cottage. The front door was open so he called out as he entered:

'Hello, Hello.'

The sound of cutlery and a chair scraping on a stone floor emerged from a doorway at the end of the hall. A moment later, a boy of around seven years of age peered cautiously around the doorframe.

'Uncle Muiris!'

Throwing his previous caution to the wind, the child rushed down the hall and embraced Mos around the waist.

'*Dia duit, a Dáire. Conas taoi, a bhuachaill?*' Hello, Dáire. How are you?

'I'm good, Uncle Muiris,' the boy answered in Irish.

Dáire led Mos into a snug kitchen and reclaimed his space at the table to continue a breakfast of toast and honey. The southern wall of the house had a wide fireplace that held a blazing turf fire. Sitting beside it, in a leather armchair, was an old woman with pebble spectacles and grey hair tied up in a tight bun. She looked up to study the new arrival with interest.

'Hello Máire. Are you back?'

The old woman peered at Mos even more intensely through the thick glass lenses but said nothing.

Mos shrugged.

'So, a Dáire, where's your Ma?"

'She's gone out the …'

Whatever the boy intended to say was lost as a telephone on the dresser erupted into life. Startled, Mos stepped back. The old woman by the fire glared at the offending irritant, then pointedly turned back to the flames, dismissing herself of any responsibility for it. The child looked at Mos with an expectant expression. Sighing, Mos pressed the phone's speaker button.

'Hello?'

'Good morning!' A heavy American accent boomed across the room. 'This is Martin Sander. Could I speak to the Finance Manager please?'

Muiris looked at the boy and mouthed 'Finance Manager?' The boy rolled his eyes and shrugged. Mos was about to confess his ignorance when a woman with copper-coloured hair brushed in through the doorway, snatched the telephone from its cradle and switched the speaker off in one smooth movement.

'Good morning! Gael-Link. This is Bróna Murphy. How can I help?'

The newcomer was slim, in her late twenties and had a thin face dotted with freckles. Despite the cold, she wore nothing but a pair of jeans, a tee-shirt with a green 'Celtic' symbol and slippers. Under her right arm, she was holding a wide wicker basket that contained a few solitary clothes pegs.

She spoke briefly but authoritatively on the telephone, rattled off an account number then hung up and offered Mos a warm grin.

'Hello, Mos.'

Mos reached over and hugged her.

'Hello, Bróna. What's all this with the Finance Manager stuff?'

'Yerra, I wasn't getting much business so I jazzed up the website. I kinda gave the impression that Gael-Link's a small company of thirty staff. Martin Zander's an American supplier so I could hardly admit the Finance Manager, CEO and chief tea lady was hanging out clothes in the garden.'

'Dem fecking Yanks!'

Over by the fire, the old woman leaned forwards and spat a gob of phlegm into the flames. A searing hiss filled the room and she sat back in devilish satisfaction.

'Jesus wept, a Aintín!'

Bróna, appalled, glared at the old woman.

'*Tóg go bog é!*' Take it easy!

She inclined her head towards Mos and muttered quietly from the corner of her mouth.

'She's never liked Americans since they landed on the moon.'

'The moon?'

'Traipsing around up there with their big, fecking *cábógs!*' spat Máire, who it appeared had exceptional hearing for her age. 'Haven't they the harvests destroyed on us, the feckers!'

Bróna grimaced then shook her head.

'Dáire, keep an eye on Aintín Máire, will ye? I've got to talk to Mos.'

'Righto, Mam.'

She poured two cups of black coffee from a pot on the table, handed one to Mos and led him through to a small conservatory. When the door was closed behind them, they settled down and Bróna turned to Mos.

'You look like shit, Mos.'

'Thanks. I always try to make an effort for the ladies.'

'You've been hitting that shite you take again, haven't you? I can see it in your eyes. They still look glassy.'

'Yes,' he admitted. 'I have.'

'You'll kill yourself if you keep doing that.'

'No, I'll kill myself if I don't.'

Bróna huffed and gave him a look of disapproval but let the matter go.

'Are you down long?'

'Came in last night. I needed some time out to deal with …'

With a cynical grin he pointed at his 'glassy' eyes.

'I also wanted to check the house. I suppose there's been no sign of that "visitor" since …?'

'Not in a physical sense.'

'Meaning?'

'Meaning he hasn't actually returned to the area. Just to be on the safe side, though, I scanned your home network in Cork and there's been at least three attempts at cyber infiltration up there over the last week.'

'What!'

'Relax, Mos.' Bróna made a placating gesture with her right hand.

'The firewalls I set up prevented anything from getting through. Besides, you're hardly ever online so it's hardly the easiest system to break into unless someone's got physical access to the computers.'

'Nah. I've been there consistently since …'

He paused with sudden insight.

'Are you suggesting I initiate a scan when I get back?'

Bróna shrugged.

'I can remotely monitor any activity from here but, yeah, you should.'

She put her cup down on the table and gave him a pensive look. 'You know, to be honest, I always thought you were being overly paranoid. As it turns out, you might have been right. Someone's certainly going to a lot of trouble to get something on you. Do you have any idea who?'

Mos frowned as he ran though the possibilities that came to mind.

Hegarty? Someone linked to the Opus Foundation? Milo from Ros na Rian?

'Haven't a feckin' clue,' he admitted at last.

'Is the house secure?'

'I set the security system before I left. The windows on the ground floor are all locked up, the front and back doors are shut with dead bolts.'

'Any idea why they'd target your computers?'

'Not really. There's nothing in there but work reports and various projects I'm working on. Nothing anybody else would find of value.'

'Hmmm.'

Bróna picked up a pen and repeatedly pressed the nib, the regular plastic clicks punctuating her thought processes for several seconds. Mos maintained a respectful silence. This was very much her area of expertise.

'In that case, the only thing that makes any sense is that they're trying to access some personal information.'

She stopped clicking the pen and looked at him.

'Does somebody know?' she asked quietly.

'Fuck knows how. I've been pretty good at covering my tracks.'

'Maybe someone worked it out.'

'Then I'm damned if I know how. Or, more importantly, why.'

Mos fumed quietly for several seconds.

'Fuck this,' he said at last. 'I don't like sitting back on the defensive. Isn't there some way you can track down whoever's carrying out the cyber attacks and hack them back?'

'Just like that?'

'That's a problem?'

'Of course that's a feckin' problem. Hacking doesn't work like that.'

'I thought you were the ace hacker, West Cork's Lisbeth Salander.'

'Ten years ago, maybe, but those days are done. Now I do more baking and cleaning than hacking. Besides, the IT work I do these days is completely legit. I have Dáire to look after now.'

'I'm sorry. Bróna. I didn't even think. It was …'

Mos paused and shook his head.

'A fucking stupid idea. Please forget I even suggested it.'

Bróna reached across the table and placed a hand on his.

'Mos, sometimes I think you're an idiot, but I've never once thought anything you said was stupid.'

She grinned weakly in an attempt to lighten the mood.

'Look, I'll tell you what. I've got a meeting in Mallow tomorrow, so I'll go back with you and do a scan on your systems while I'm there. In the meantime, though, I wouldn't invite anyone back to the house for a while.'

'Thanks, Bróna.'

'Not that that's likely to happen.'

She responded to his glower with a wider grin.

Mos mulled over a mouthful of lukewarm coffee. 'Did I mention that my place in Cork's being watched?'

'What? By whom?'

'Someone in a blue Subaru. Having a right old gawk he was.'

She frowned. 'Shit! What the fuck's going on, Mos?'

'I don't know Bróna. I really don't know.'

Chapter Eleven

West Cork, Early 1960s

Three days after *Lá Fhéile Bríde* – St Brigit's Day – word reached Diarmuid of Pat Harrington's passing.

The first indication of anything amiss had been the old man's absence from the weekly poker game. Concerned, one of his nephews had gone round to the farm on the following morning and found his uncle stretched out in the barn, a pitchfork full of hay still clutched tightly in his hand. Coming so soon on the shirttails of his brother's death, the news lay heavily on Diarmuid, intensifying a growing sense that the world was changing faster than he could keep up with.

It was a full week before he could shake off the dark thoughts that were troubling him, but he finally dismissed them with his habitual stoicism.

Mallacht ortsa. Is e sin an aois ag caint. A curse on you. That's just age talkin.

As his closest neighbours and longest surviving friends, Diarmuid and Dinny were asked to help Pat's brother dress the body for the wake. It was a man's work to help lift old Pat, to shave him, dress him in his best clothes and lay him out on the table of his home for the final resting. The wake, however, organised by Pat's young nephews, was a restrained affair: plenty of food and tobacco, but little craic and few enough of the other old timers present. There were no songs, no games or dancing and the disapproving presence of Father Byrne ensured there was no excess of spirits, emotional or alcoholic.

Diarmuid sipped a mildewed whiskey from a flask hidden in the folds of his coat sleeve and watched the muted conversations with a jaundiced eye. The proceedings were a far cry from some of the send-offs he'd attended as a young fella and for Pat's sake he regretted the subdued nature of the gathering. Even in his old age, he'd been a vivacious character and would have appreciated a little excess or, at the very least, a *caoiner*'s haunting *ollogón* to escort his spirit from the physical world.

Despite his dissatisfaction, Diarmuid could feel no ill will towards the nephews. They were a product of their time, after all: conservative, respectable, churchgoing members of society. Unfamiliar with the old traditions, they had simply done what they thought was best.

The subsequent – and more clerically acceptable – funeral in Eadargóil was a more crowded affair. The church was filled to the rafters with flowers, wreaths, family and well-wishers dressed in black. Diarmuid, observing the large number of mourners gathered, felt an unexpected pang of jealousy at the turnout. His own departure, he knew, was unlikely to be so well attended.

With this thought, he turned to his nephew, who was staring wide-eyed at the church service. He was unable to repress a sudden swell of disappointment. On his own demise, it would probably fall to Demne – as his only surviving relative – to take care of the final arrangements. In his heart, he did not feel the boy had the wherewithal to ensure it was carried out the way he would want it.

He admonished himself almost immediately for the thought. It was hardly Demne's fault he was the way he was. Raised in complete isolation, he had been deprived of a normal childhood and although he hated to admit it, Diarmuid knew his brother bore a significant responsibility for that. God alone knew how many other stressful circumstances Demne had experienced in his short life but with his mother's disappearance and his father's inexplicable death, it was a minor miracle he had any kind of social competence. Even now, after six months with his uncle under his belt, he remained as introspective as ever, refusing to be drawn on his father or his earlier life at Daingean an Poncán. On those occasions when he had been confronted with his uncle's questions, he'd retreated into impenetrable silence.

On a more positive note, Diarmuid conceded, the boy had shown a perceptible improvement, in terms of his overall comportment, since his visit to the willow tree grotto. The nightmares and coma states had diminished in frequency and apart from the occasional relapse the boy was sleeping soundly.

Demne also appeared to have grown more comfortable around other people, although it still took a long time for him to warm to them. He had established a close relationship with Dinny and Margaret and although initially cool to their daughters' attempts at friendship, he'd eventually consented to talk to them. Nowadays, he got along like a house on fire with Aisling, Niamh, and Úna, the youngest three. Diarmuid often came across them at play together in the fields around Carraig Dubh or the Murphy house, the dog barking in their wake.

It was due to this limited but undeniable progress that Diarmuid judged it time for his nephew to enter the national education system. On a Monday morning in mid-February, therefore, the old man approached the local school.

Mr Cassidy, the teacher, more commonly known by his title *An Máistir*, was a well-educated man with a reputation for a slightly tyrannical teaching style. Although his refusal to mollycoddle the children in his care was generally accepted within the community, there had been some less tolerant whispers that the man had an irrational dislike for any of his charges who were in any way out of the ordinary. These whispers lay heavy on Diarmuid when he met with the teacher and he made a point of explaining the boy's background in detail.

To his surprise, during their discussion, *An Máistir* revealed himself to be completely ignorant of the rumours circulating about his new pupil and appeared more interested in Demne's complete lack of exposure to the English language. After Diarmuid had explained the situation, *An Máistir* mused silently for a long period of time. Diarmuid watched him stroke his long, black beard as he waited patiently for the teacher's appraisal.

Finally, he spoke and assured Diarmuid that he should have no concerns. His nephew and his surprising lack of English were a rare challenge, but he would take it upon himself to have the child operating effectively *as Béarla* – in English – within three months.

Diarmuid left the school with the sprightly step of a man half his age.

For the next few weeks, with the assistance of Dinny's daughters, Diarmuid began his nephew on an extensive programme of study on the basics of the English language. In almost all respects this represented a significant personal sacrifice, for it went against many of Diarmuid's most fundamental beliefs. Although he recognised that the boy needed the language to operate effectively in an English-dominated world, he smouldered at the injustice of having to teach him the tongue of their historical oppressor. His nephew was unique, one of the few people of his generation for whom Gaelic was a first language and whose mental constructs operated entirely through the medium of Irish. Instruction in English was the first in a series of steps that, over time, would erode his cultural identity and his distinctive way of thinking. Diarmuid's own complicity in this process was something that made him feel even guiltier about it.

When the day finally arrived, Diarmuid prepared a substantial lunch and accompanied Demne to his classroom. He left the grounds with a heavy heart made by the burden of his own reservations and the haunted expression on his nephew's face as he left him.

That afternoon dragged more slowly than Diarmuid could have believed possible. Finally, much later than expected, Demne arrived home, and holding himself stiffly as he stepped through the doorway. Although he attempted to downplay it, it was obvious the boy was in pain and his uncle demanded that he raise his shirt. Reluctantly, he lifted the thin material.

Diarmuid stared silently at the blue welts running down his nephew's back. Without a word, he reached for a heavy blackthorn stick standing beside the doorway and left the house.

It was a good half hour's walk in the fading light to the teacher's residence, a small cottage set in a copse of trees across the road from the school. On Diarmuid's arrival, however, the house was in darkness and there was no response to his hammering on the door.

Stumped, he remained at the doorstep for several frustrating minutes, struggling to decide on his next course of action. He was just on the point of leaving when a neighbouring farmer – a second cousin of his – happened to pass by. Recognising him, the farmer stopped to chat and informed him that *An Máistir* had been taken away to the hospital in Beanntraí with a fractured skull, the result of a rock cast with devastating accuracy by some unidentified assailant.

The subsequent walk back to Carraig Dubh provided ample opportunity for Diarmuid's temper to cool and gave him time to consider the day's events from a number of different angles. He was calm, therefore, when he arrived home to find Demne hovering in nervous anticipation by the fire.

It did not take long to get to the bottom of what had happened. Demne admitted that *An Máistir* had beaten him for not speaking in English, regardless of the fact that he'd lacked the vocabulary to understand what the teacher had been saying to him. He also took full responsibility for throwing the rock. Although he expressed some regret when he confessed to the latter, it seemed to stem more from the prospect of his uncle's displeasure than from any real sense of guilt at his actions.

The old man pondered the situation for a full minute. He couldn't really encourage his nephew to go around throwing rocks, but then neither did he feel any sympathy for *An Máistir* after his assault on the boy. 'Did anyone see you?' he asked at last.

Demne shook his head. 'No.'

'Good. Then keep your trap shut and we'll say nottin'.'

Within the fortnight, a woman by the name of Miss Kelly was appointed to replace *An Máistir* and take over the school's teaching duties. A strict but fair woman, within the community it was generally felt that she was a significant improvement on her predecessor. Of greater importance for Diarmuid however, was the fact she was a *gaelgoir* from the *Corca Dhuibhne Gaeltacht* and took an immediate shine to the young boy who spoke the language so fluently.

When the school reopened, Diarmuid was much more relaxed about releasing his nephew back into its care. Demne's new teacher was kind and supportive and the language barrier was no longer a problem. The full potential of a national education, it appeared, now lay out before him.

Within a week, Diarmuid discovered that his confidence in the national education system had been naively premature. Returning from the fields on a Thursday afternoon, he was astounded to find his nephew sitting stiffly at Carraig Dubh in the company of a red-faced Father Byrne. The old man's initial reaction was one of heartfelt panic. Father Byrne, he knew, was first cousin to *An Máistir* and must somehow have discovered Demne's involvement in his recent hospitalisation.

Before Diarmuid had a chance to leap to his nephew's defence, however, the parish priest leapt to his feet and released a torrent of accusations that were as perplexing as they were vitriolic. Because Father Byrne was practically frothing at the mouth, it took some time to work out what he was complaining about. Slowly it became clear – to Diarmuid's immense relief – that the ecclesiastical outrage was not related to the assault on *An Máistir* but to the less immediate threat of his nephew's eternal soul.

Completing his visit with a warning of severe consequences should the issue not be addressed to his satisfaction, Father Byrne wrapped himself in a cloak of religious self-righteousness and stormed from the house.

'Safe home now, Father!' Diarmuid called in his wake, although he could not resist throwing a two-fingered salute at the back of the departing cleric.

Despite the cold, Diarmuid remained outside and smoked a cigarette as he attempted to work through the ramifications of what he had just been told. He was shivering by the time he returned inside but, realising that there was no time like the present, he drew up a stool next to the boy and looked him directly in the eye.

'So, let me get this straight,' he said. 'You don't know who God is.'

There was a brief silence.

'I know the one hanging up on the cross in the church,' the boy admitted. 'And Miss Kelly and Father Byrne were telling me about three other ones, but …' He paused. From his demeanour, Demne seemed unsure as to whether someone was winding him up or not.

'Did yer Da never bring you to …'

Diarmuid stopped abruptly. He had been about to ask whether Demne's father had never taken him to church. On reflection, the answer to that question was patently obvious.

'Did yer Da ever tell you about God and Jesus and all that?' he tried instead.

The boy shook his head.

'*A Dhia na bheart!*' the old farmer exclaimed, throwing his hands in the air. Taking a deep breath, he calmed himself and started again. 'You have to listen to what the priest tells you about the religious stuff, *a bhuachaill*. You have to do what he says and toe the line.'

Demne's lips tightened and his uncle repressed a twinge of frustration. Evidently the boy had inherited the family's gene for stubbornness: the determined expression on Demne's face was identical to the one he remembered on his brother's face as a child.

'But Father Byrne says mad things, *a Uncail*.'

'Sure he does, but he's a man with influence in the community. He's also the Church's local representative and that's a crowd you don't want to mess with. They've a lot of power since the Long Fella did a deal with them and they don't like the faithful getting ideas above their station. If you come to their attention they won't leave off until they've made you submit to their view of the world, one way or the other.'

'But it's not true! That's wrong.'

Diarmuid regarded his nephew with surprise. Clearly, he was going to have his work cut out trying to educate him in the fine tradition of moral hypocrisy.

'It doesn't matter if it's true or not. It's not about right or wrong, it's about survival. The Church love going around telling people how they should live their lives. If you want to stay out of trouble you've got to put up with that. That's why we go to Mass on Sundays. It's not that I believe some big God fella's going to smack me across the arse with a bolt of lightning, it's because it keeps the clergy off our backs. If going out there, bending your head at the right time and mumbling some oul shite is enough to keep them quiet then we're all happy.'

The boy did not seem convinced.

'Demne, people get upset when others don't agree with them or don't believe in the same things they do. If you want to be part of a community, you have to blend in. If you're too different or you stick out, you'll eventually end up turning them against you. Everyone around here goes to Mass or believes in God – or at least they say they do – so you have to follow suit. Stirring the priests up will only make life more difficult.'

'Do you like priests?'

Diarmuid stared at him with genuine astonishment.

'Whatever gave you that idea?'

'You like Father McCarthy.'

'That's different. He's not really a priest. He just thinks he is.'

'Maybe I should throw a stone at Father Byrne.'

'No, you can't throw a feckin' stone at Father Byrne!'

'You didn't mind me throwing a stone at *An Máistir*.'

'Only because you'd already gone and done it. You can't go around lobbing rocks at people in authority. You …' he hesitated momentarily. 'Well, actually, you can, but you wouldn't be long getting caught.'

'I'd be clever, *a Uncail*. They wouldn't get me.'

'You'd have to be very feckin' clever not to get caught eventually, Demne. No, if you go up against the big boys you've got to be able to pick your battles. More importantly, you have to pick your defeats – the way that you can choose the fights you want to win.'

It took another half-hour of intense argument before he finally convinced his nephew to adhere to the priest's teachings – or, more accurately, to pretend to go along with them, keep his head down and get on with his work in school.

This reluctant concession appeared to achieve its objective, however. Within a few weeks, Demne's troubles at school ceased. To his uncle's surprise and immense satisfaction, Demne revealed himself to be an adept and natural scholar – although it still irked him that this had only been revealed through the use of English.

For his own part, Diarmuid too eased into a more mundane routine, dictated by the never-ending responsibilities of farm work and the bitter spring weather. Short, grim days and cold evenings continued to send them scurrying inside for the warmth of the hearth each evening. There, in the flickering light of a blazing fire, Diarmuid would dredge up old stories and poems to pass the time and amuse his nephew. He surprised himself by how many he'd accumulated over the years: tales of the Fenians, of Cú Chulainn and the Red Branch Knights, local legends of Domhnall Cam O'Súilleabháin Bhéara's epic march to Breifne, and the poems of Aogán Ó Rathaille and Eoghan Rua O'Súilleabháin.

Sometimes, for a change of pace, the old man would tell an old-time riddle or stand up to recite one of the *laoidh* he'd learned from his father, releasing the deep chant to roll around the house as Demne looked on from the fireside. Although he showed no great aptitude for contemporary poetry, the boy expressed a fondness for the ancient Irish nature poems and proved insatiable in his demand for tales and legends from the nearby areas.

Much to his own surprise, Diarmuid found that he enjoyed teaching the boy the rituals and traditions and got great satisfaction from guiding and shaping what he now understood would be a clever and quick-minded young man.

They burned a wealth of turf that winter.

It was during this extended period of calm that uncle and nephew constructed a relationship that was as tentative as it was undefined. Both parties privately acknowledged that the other had certain subjects he didn't wish to discuss, secrets concealed in hidden places and occasionally drawn out to be picked at like the jagged scab of a poorly healed wound. There was a shared acceptance that such confidences would not be exchanged, and this was strictly adhered to until one night in early April.

The evening had passed like many before it: an early supper followed by tales in front of the fire. Diarmuid had just finished reciting a *laoidh* and had sat down, feeling surprisingly breathless from the effort of the sustained chant.

'Did you write that one, Uncle?' his nephew asked.

Diarmuid laughed

'I did not. More's the pity for it's a lovely *laoidh*, that one. And quite ancient. They say it was written by Fionn mac Cumhaill himself, you know. No doubt he sat down in a dark cave on some bitter night just like this and composed it.'

His nephew regarded him in surprise. 'Why would he compose it in a cave?'

'Ah, well. That's how the long-ago poets used to compose. They were taught to write their verses lying down in the dark or in some hidden spot, away from the people.'

'That's mad!'

'Well, it is and it isn't.'

The old man paused as he worked out how he was going to explain it.

'You see, the old poets were successors to the druids and the best of them had access to *imbas* – the otherworld wisdom. Like the druids, they'd sometimes go off to some godforsaken spot by a river, on top of a mountain, in a cave or a desrted *ráth* and try to tap into the *imbas* there that would help them write their poems.'

'Is that true?' Demne looked at him with a frown. Over the last few months, and particularly since the Father Byrne incident, his nephew had developed a healthy cynicism of what people claimed to be true.

'Well, that's what my father told me. Mind you, the ones that weren't so good wanted to keep their status, so they started putting on airs, inventing all sorts of complicated feckin' composition rituals to make themselves look important.'

He tapped his pipe against the fireplace, emptying the ash from the wooden bowl.

'There's actually a practical technique to some of their madness. If you ever try to write a poem yourself, you'll find it's easier to compose in the dark, away from distractions, where you can get into a deep meditation and clear your head. They say Fionn himself was great at that kind of thing.'

His nephew 'hmmed' thoughtfully.

'Fionn was very wise, wasn't he, *a Uncail*.'

'That's what they say, *a bhuachaill*.'

'I think I'd like to be wise.'

Diarmuid was amused by his nephew's seriousness, his complete absence of braggadocio. He took care to hide the smile curling at the ends of his lips.

'I'm sure you'll achieve great wisdom, Demne.'

'How do you get wise?'

'Well, the way I see it, wisdom is when you use knowledge in the right way, so the first thing would be to accumulate knowledge. I suppose that's why most wise people tend to be older. It takes a long time for people to get through all the experiences that give you knowledge.'

He blew sharply through the stem of the pipe, clearing it of obstructions, then laid it aside by the fireplace.

'Mind you, some eejits never manage it no matter how feckin' old they get.'

Demne lapsed into silence and they mused separately, staring into the red heat of the fire. A few minutes later, Diarmuid was surprised when his nephew abruptly took up the conversation from where it had left off.

'Would wisdom help to stop *na drochrudaí, a Uncail*?' The bad things.

His uncle looked up from the flames, confused by the question.

'What bad things are these?'

'*An Púca.*'

'*An Púca?*' Diarmuid stared at his nephew. 'Why would you want to stop a *Púca*, Demne?'

'A *Púca* wanted to hurt me.'

'A *Púca*! When did a *Púca* try to hurt you?'

'Back home. Back in Glonnyhust.'

A sudden frisson shivered down the old man's spine. He hadn't forgotten the eerie presence up in the hills on the far side of the peninsula and mention of the legendary entity in the context of that memory made him distinctly uneasy. 'The *Púca*'s just a *piseog*,' he insisted, nevertheless. 'An old maid's tale.'

'People always say something's a *piseog* when they don't know things.'

Diarmuid nodded grudgingly. People were often rediscovering that there was a logic behind the old ways and the old rituals, even when the sense of them in contemporary times had been lost. What sense there might be behind a mythological shape-changing creature like the *Púca*, however, he couldn't even guess.

'I've never seen a *Púca*. Never heard of one hurting anyone either, outside of the old folktales.'

'*Púca* kill sheep,' his nephew continued. 'They kill sheep on the hills at night.'

'That's just dogs, Demne. They get a taste for blood and go mad and then go off after the sheep.'

The boy shook his head.

'*Púca*,' he said firmly. 'Dada told me.'

Diarmuid did his best to disguise the surge of anxiety rising within him. This was the first time his nephew had spoken of his father without being prompted.

'What did your Daddy tell you about the *Púca*, Demne?'

The boy continued to regard him intently, but his expression was unreadable and he volunteered nothing further.

'Did he ...'

As soon as he asked the question, he sensed his nephew's withdrawal, the emotional retreat as the boy closed in on himself. He backed off hurriedly, knowing that further interrogation would stress the child and potentially trigger another of his death-like comas.

'Don't worry about it, *a bhuachaill*,' he managed. 'It's not important.'

With that, the matter was dropped.

For the remainder of the evening, they spoke no more on that subject. Nor on any other.

Demne retired to bed earlier than usual and when he was asleep Diarmuid threw some turf on the fire, folded into his rocking chair and smoked his pipe in silence.

He sat there staring at the flames long into the night.

***

On the following Saturday, Diarmuid was up before the first ghostly fingers of dawn had scraped their nails against the roof slates. As he laid the fire and filled the fireplace with kindling, he considered the last few pieces of turf in the fire bucket. There were more than enough supplies to see them through the last of the cold weather, but he'd nevertheless agreed to accompany Dinny and Seán O'Shea up to the Cruach Mhór hill on the coming weekend. Harvest time for turf was almost upon them but first, the *scráith*, the upper layer of heather stems and roots, would have to be removed.

After completing his regular morning routine, Diarmuid retrieved the two *sleán* – turf spades – he had inherited from his father. The *sleán* had long wooden handles and were tipped with an L-shaped, double-sided steel head that allowed a sod of turf to be cut out of the bog in a vertical direction. He spent half an hour sharpening the tools and doing minor repairs, pausing only when Demne returned from milking the cows and deposited the churn at the entrance to the property.

'Would you ever do a job for me, *a bhuachaill*? I need you to go off and check the snares I put out last night.'

The boy immediately went to retrieve the boots he'd just discarded. As he pulled them on and stood up to go, his uncle saw him grab a heel of soda bread from the table and stuff it in his pocket, a habit he'd noticed on more than a few occasions.

'Why do you always carry a piece of bread around with you, *a bhuachaill*?'

Demne looked at him and raised his eyebrows.

'The one in your pocket.'

'*An féar gorta.*'

Diarmuid grunted, a mixture of surprise and exasperation. You could never really tell what nonsense the boy was going to come out with next.

Féar gorta – literally, 'famine grass' or 'hungry grass' – was an old superstition dating back to An Gorta Mór. According to the old stories, *féar gorta* were small patches of land where people who had died from the famine had been buried. It was said that people who stood on these spots were struck by a sudden hunger, so ferocious that they would collapse and die from hunger pangs if they didn't get food into them immediately.

'Demne, the *féar gorta's* only a …'

The boy grimaced just before he got to the word '*piseog*'.

Ah, fuck! Here we go with that again!

Demne bit his lip and stared at the ground.

Diarmuid sighed. 'Oh, all right! Show me, then. Show me the *féar gorta.*'

A Dhia na bheart! Walking this land for over sixty years and I've never come across any feckin' féar gorta!

Muttering under his breath, he followed the boy outside and allowed himself to be led along the dry-stone wall at the front of the house. Several metres from the door, Demne clambered over the barrier and led his uncle to a raised patch of ground where a large flat, rock occupied a space beneath the branches of an old rowan tree.

'There.'

Demne gestured at the ground in front of the rock.

Diarmuid fought the impulse to roll his eyes. The area the boy was pointing at was his favourite spot for taking his ease from the labour of the day. Over the years, his arse had worn a smooth patch into the rock while he'd sat there, admiring the view or reflecting on the vagaries of life. In all that time he'd never noticed anything amiss.

He kicked apathetically at the scraggly grass underfoot. 'So, this is *féar gorta*. Looks safe enough to me. Why's this *féar gorta* then?'

'There's dead people in the ground. Two dead people.'

'I see. And do …'

'And there.'

The boy pointed to another section of ground at the far end of An Páirc Mór.

'There's one down by the gap in the fence and another down by the blackberry bush. That's a big patch.'

'That's a lot of people dead from An Gorta Mór, *a bhuachaill.*'

The boy shrugged and munched at his piece of soda bread.

'How do you know?'

'I don't know. I just feel them. I just know.'

'Are there any more?'

'Any more what?'

'Dead people.'

His nephew looked at him in surprise.

'They're all over, *a Uncail.*'

Apparently, he didn't seem to think it was anything unusual.

'I see. Right.' Diarmuid coughed diplomatically as he used his fist to cover the grin spreading across his face. 'Well, listen, thanks for that, Demne. Why don't you run off now, over to the Murphy's to play for a few hours.'

'What about the snares?'

'Yerra, *ná bac leo*. They'll be grand. I'll go over after them meself, later.'

It was comical to watch the boy attempting to look disappointed, for it was obvious he was delighted at the prospect of a few hours with his friends, free from the farm work. '*Ar aghaidh leatsa, mar sin,*' urged his uncle. Off you go, so.

When his nephew had departed, Diarmuid returned to the shed beside the house and started rearranging some tools and stores that Dinny had dropped off from town earlier in the week. As he settled into a comfortable pattern of cleaning and stowing away, he found his mind turning to Demne's outrageous claims of *féar gorta*. Laughing off such fanciful stories, he focussed his attention on his labour only to find his thoughts repeatedly drawn back to the subject. With a snort of irritation, he pulled a shovel free from its hook in the wall and headed back towards the rock and the rowan tree.

Only one way to sort this out, once and for all.

Approximately fifteen unproductive minutes of digging and one rolled cigarette later, he'd reached a depth of more than a metre. Amused by his own irrational behaviour, he was just on the point of climbing out of the hole when the shovel, unexpectedly, struck something solid. Tapping the compacted earth, he felt the blade glance off to the side of what looked like a large, round stone. Bending down, he scooped away the dirt with his hand then abruptly jerked upright as he realised that the 'stone' had two eye sockets.

'Jaysus, Mary and Joseph!'

When he had recovered from the shock of his discovery he crouched again, worked the skull loose from the earth and held it up in both hands. It was an adult skull, yellowed from age but he couldn't tell whether it was that of a man or a woman. Sifting a bit further with the blade of his shovel, he found another, smaller skull and several other bones, all human. He sighed then, struck by a sudden poignant vision of a woman and her child being interred together at that spot. Replacing the bones gently where he had found them, Diarmuid stood to crawl out of the hole and slowly began to fill it in.

'You poor *craturs,*' he said. 'I'm fierce sorry for disturbing ye.'

He paused.

'And I won't be smoking over you again.'

His hands were shaking as he flattened the freshly turned soil with his shovel. The presence of the skeletons confounded him for the land had been leased, then subsequently owned, by his family since the late 1800s. He had never heard any mention of anyone being buried here which seemed to suggest that the remains were at least a hundred and fifty years old. He was certain his father would have told him if …

He stiffened suddenly.

So how the feck did Demne know?

With sudden insight he recalled the boy's reaction when he had first brought him to his grandparents' grave.

'*Tá daoine faoi fhód.*'

There's people buried here.

Diarmuid shivered.

His nephew had a gift, although it was one heck of a strange one. Demne had said that he'd 'felt them' – the skeletons. Like a water diviner could detect water, he appeared to be able to detect the presence of human remains, even when they were hundreds of years old.

Diarmuid grunted. In that respect, at least, the boy could be said to have a unique connection with the land. Walking, literally, on the bones of his ancestors.

The old man frowned as he made his way back to the shed to clean the shovel and replace it on the wall. There could be serious ramifications associated with this new revelation, but he was damned if he knew what they were. He blew out his cheeks in frustration. He needed to think about this carefully.

When Demne returned later that morning, Diarmuid made no mention of his discovery by the rowan tree. He waited until after dinner to broach the subject.

Pushing the remains of a freshly cooked rabbit stew to one side, he leaned back in his chair and considered his nephew across the table.

'Demne, you know that way you feel the dead people in the ground.'

Demne looked up from his meal and rubbed a smear of sauce from the side of his chin.

'Yes, *a Uncail?*'

'Are you able to tell how long the dead people have been down there?'

'Only when they're recent, *a Uncail*. The ones that feel …'

He paused.

'The one's that feel fizzy.'

'Fizzy?' Diarmuid was unable to hide his bewilderment.

Demne shuffled awkwardly, as though uncomfortable with his uncle's reaction to something that was so patently obvious.

'Like the fizzy lemonade we get in Baile Chaisleán Bhéarra. Except on the inside. Like the feeling we get at Pat's grave.'

Diarmuid stroked his chin but said nothing for several seconds.

'Do you mean to say that when you're at Pat's grave you feel … fizzy inside?'

'Yes, *a Uncail.* Doesn't everyone?'

Diarmuid stared down at the rough wooded surface of the table. 'No, *a bhuachaill.* No, they don't.'

When he raised his eyes again, they were laden with an uncharacteristic gravity.

'Listen to me now. You must never mention this. Never let on to anyone how you can feel the dead people. Anyone. Do ye hear?'

Demne regarded his uncle with wide eyes, then leaned forward in a conspiratorial manner.

'Is this like the Father Byrne thing, *a Uncail?*'

Surprised by the boy's intuition, Diarmuid nodded in affirmation.

'It's very much like the Father Byrne thing.'

'All right, so,' said the boy and nodded in a serious manner. 'I understand.'

To his uncle's bemusement, this appeared to mark an end to his nephew's interest in the matter. The youngster clearly had no qualms with secrets or subterfuge forming an essential part of his daily life. Dismissing the issue in his stride, he returned his attention to his meal, tearing into it with the ravenous gusto of a healthy young boy.

Although he had many other questions, Diarmuid reluctantly decided to let the matter rest for the time being. More details of his nephew's remarkable ability would, no doubt, come to the fore in the future.

With this, he reached across the table, picked up the last remaining piece of soda bread and held it up to the boy.

'Want to keep this for later?' he asked.

***

A sudden thaw brought a remarkably rapid change to the peninsula. Within a week or two of warmer weather and increasing sunshine hours, the wildflowers were blossoming across the land, infusing the topography with dynamic colour to counteract the remnants of winter's grim backdrop. First to appear were the pious daffodils, *lus an chromchinn,* yellow heads dipped low in penitence. Then the *sabhaircín* and swarms of *cloigín gorm* that layered sheltered pastures and woodland with a speckled blue carpet.

A date was set in early May to harvest the turf up at Na Portaigh, on the hill called Cruach Mhór. The day broke over a low-lying mist that clung to the craggy coast with all the intensity of a departing lover. Before the hour of eight o'clock, however, the sun was already prising the cold grip of winter from the peninsula with the rare promise of a glorious day.

They departed for the bog in two vehicles. Diarmuid and Demne rode in Dinny's car, laden down with the *sleáns* for cutting the turf. Seán O'Shea, with his van, took the larger group: Margaret Murphy, the Murphy girls and Seán's own nephew, Niall, a young man in his early twenties who was handy with the *sleán*. Dinny's car soon overtook the slower-moving van and was the first vehicle, therefore, to reach the base of Cruach Mhór and commence the steep ascent to the bog.

The Volkswagen laboured up the tortuously winding *bothairín*, hedged in on either side by craggy slabs of sandstone rock. The bones of the land were close to the surface around them; the few patches of tussocky grass, dotted with white-tipped bog cotton, draped between the rocks like an afterthought.

'Ah for feck's sake!'

Diarmuid looked up in alarm as the car jolted to a halt. His eyes followed his neighbour's furious gaze onto the road before them, where the barbed-wire gate that normally barred the way had been dumped to one side. It lay on the ground in a loose, prickly heap.

'What feckin' eejit left this open,' roared Dinny. 'The sheep'll have wandered up to the bogs.'

'Ramblers,' suggested Diarmuid. 'City folk.'

'Well, then they're thick feckin' ramblers.'

Muttering under his breath, he pressed down on the accelerator, his anger reflected in the vigorous revving of the engine as the car struggled up the steep slope beyond the gate.

After a short drive, they reached a flat area set within an extended hollow at the side of the hill. Dinny pulled the vehicle over to the side of the track and they all looked across at Na Portaigh. The area where they would harvest the turf was instantly identifiable from the bare patches where the *scraith* had been stripped away.

Piling out of the car, they gathered their gear and started up the rough path.

Their section was a trench cut into part of the larger blanket bog. The exposed patch of brown peat at the front of the bank was scored from previous cuttings, patterned with old *sleán* marks where the turf had been sliced. Further out, the remnants of old and poorly managed cuts were filled with pools of black water, a hazard for the hasty or unwary.

Despite its limited size – the bank was little more than five metres long – Na Portaigh had always been productive. The depth and quality of the turf bank more than made up for its width, the vertical levels sufficiently deep to provide a yield of about six bars a *sleán*. After centuries of harvesting, however, the best of the section had been eaten away and, nestled in the nook of a slight depression, was increasingly prone to drainage problems.

Seán's van arrived fifteen minutes later. When the tools were distributed, the men split into two teams and worked in coordinated pairs from different ends of the bank, carving the sods and tossing them up behind them to Demne and the waiting women. They in turn transported the sodden bricks to a flat area and laid them out in a series of lines on the ground. The sods would be effectively dried by the wind and the sunshine over the coming summer months, particularly when they were stacked into the upright footing. Eventually, the dried sods would be collected, and transported in canvas bags down to the homesteads. At Carraig Dubh, Diarmuid would stack his share against the eastern gable of the house, protected from the prevailing westerly wind and rain.

After three hours of hard labour, they paused for lunch, settling down on some blankets spread out over a wide section of flat rock. Margaret Murphy distributed the food. A short, attractive woman with long, auburn hair, she had a well-established reputation for her cooking and the workers were eager to grab the tin plates she handed out.

Diarmuid was more relieved than usual to take a break for the work had left him breathless and shaking, and his heart was still fair pounding from the effort.

Mallacht ort, a chinneachain. Getting too old for this oul shite. This is a young lad's game.

Munching on a piece of apple pie, he stared discontentedly down at the trench. Water was pooling inside the hole, which meant that the digging work would only get harder. By the time they got back to it, they would be working in bog water above their ankles. The deeper the cut, the worse the seepage became; each year's harvest brought the end of the reek's useful life closer.

Irritated, Diarmuid turned his gaze down to the expanse of Cuan Baoi stretched out below them and took a deep breath through his nostrils.

A trace of sea air. A taint of marsh gas. A tang of sweat.

That'd be mine, I suppose.

He grinned then, his good humour regained. Despite the exhausting and monotonous nature of turf cutting, he had always enjoyed his time up on the bog. The solitude of the bog lands appealed to the loner in him. Up here on the isolated hillside, you could be alone with your thoughts for there was no one to bother you and no noise to be heard apart from the whisper of a soft breeze or the lazy drone of a passing horsefly.

Except when you had a work gang of cutters around you, of course.

The happy chatter of the children interrupted his reflections, and he switched his gaze to Demne, who was also staring silently over the bleak expanse.

'What are you thinking, Demne?'

'I'm thinking it looks like home, *a Uncail.*'

'Yes,' he admitted. 'I suppose it does. 'Twas rough country up in your old place.'

'*A Dhaid*, can I go down on the flat?' A plaintive wheedling made them both look up to where Úna Murphy was standing defiantly beside her father.

'No, Úna. Stay here. The ground here isn't like back home. It's fierce dangerous.'

The girl looked around in exasperation.

'But there's nothing scary there, *a Dhaid*. It's a desert!'

Everyone laughed at this outraged outburst, but it was easy to see where she was coming from. The bog land was a desert, albeit a wet one. Exposed and damp, the lack of any shelter or nutrients meant that there was little animal or birdlife to be found apart from the odd curlew or snipe.

'There's nothing out there that you can see, Úna.' Dinny paused. 'But the place is littered with bog holes. If you fall into one of them you'll find it feckin' scary when you sink like a stone and never come out again.'

Úna, however, remained adamant. 'What about the sheep, then?' she wailed.

Her father looked at her curiously. 'What feckin' sheep?'

'The ones down there!'

They all looked to where Úna was pointing, about a hundred metres downhill. Sure enough, several sheep were clustered in a rough circle around an old turf cutting, red-dyed arses a series of psychedelic blotches against the stark brown landscape.

'That's fierce quare behaviour.' Seán, a big man with an even bigger streak of curiosity, got to his feet and peered down the incline. After a moment or two, he started off down the rocky course towards the beasts.

Diarmuid and Dinny looked at each other then rose as one, levering themselves stiffly off the ground. Diarmuid groaned as his bones creaked, but followed his friend without complaint, Demne and Úna quietly tagging along behind them.

The animals scattered as they approached the flat, retreating to a safe distance to watch the newcomers with dull eyes. As they got closer, a dark pool of bog water came into view, its smooth surface glistening in the sunshine. Floating in the pool was the corpse of a sheep, the saturated curve of its back bobbing like a woolly iceberg in the water.

The men stared wordlessly into the hole.

'Well, didn't I feckin' know it!' exclaimed Dinny with bitter satisfaction. 'Feckin' ramblers.'

'Someone's lost a fine ewe,' agreed Seán.

Diarmuid put a hand on his nephew's shoulder.

'That's why we keep to the beaten path, Demne.'

He shook his head.

'Not a nice way to die.'

'The worst,' said Dinny, eager to add his tuppence worth, 'is that the bog preserves the bodies for thousands of years. Someday some unsuspecting fools like us will turn up to cut the turf and find that sheep stuck in the middle of it.'

'Didn't my own grandfather find a man's body up on the north bog years ago while he was cutting turf,' said Seán.

'Go way!' exclaimed Diarmuid.

'He did! He said the fella looked like he'd just curled up for a sleep, though he was all folded up in quare shapes because he didn't have any bones. They say the bog water eats away all the bones.'

'Fair go!' Dinny, too, was impressed by this gem of knowledge.

'What did he do with the body, Seán?' asked Demne, staring at the tall farmer with the morbid fascination of a child.

'Yerra, boyeen, he said a prayer and covered him up again. Believe me, there's plenty of corpses in those black pools, clumps of heather or small sticks still clutched in their hands from trying to haul themselves out.'

'Oh,' said Demne, unable to keep the deep tone of disappointment out of his voice. He scraped at a piece of yellow lichen on the surface of a nearby rock with the heel of his boot then leaned over surreptitiously to his uncle.

'Actually, I don't think there's any bodies around here, *a Uncail.*'

'Er ... that's good, Demne.'

Diarmuid coughed and cleared his throat.

'Shall we get back to it, lads?' he added, anxious to change the subject.

'No rest for the wicked! "Once more onto the beach" and all that other Shakespearian stuff.'

***

They continued to harvest the turf until late afternoon. By then the weather was starting to turn and the trench had filled to the level of the cutters' knees. The men halted work and grouped together, looking down into the dark water.

'I think that's it, boys,' said Seán. 'There'll be no more turf cut here today.'

An ominous noise rumbled through the gathering cloud cover as though corroborating this declaration. The men looked up as one and scanned the sky.

'Someone's telling us to feck off out of it,' said Diarmuid, although there was no bitterness in his voice. Between the lot of them, they'd harvested a fair amount of turf over the course of the day.

With that, they began to assemble their gear and, fifteen minutes later, gathered down by the side of the *botharín* to load the vehicles. It was at this point that Niall, much to his uncle Seán's exasperation, informed him he needed to be back in Baile Chaisleán Bhéarra to meet his girlfriend.

'For feck's sake, you could have told me that earlier, ye gombeen!'

Mortified, his nephew stared at the ground in embarrassment.

Diarmuid felt a surge of sympathy for the young man.

'Yerra, leave the young fella alone, Seán. Didn't he do fierce work today and he deserves the reward. Why don't you go away now and take him back to town. Dinny can drop the womenfolk home.'

'And what about you and Demne?'

'Yerra, we'll just walk our way down. When Dinny's dropped off Margaret and the girls he can come back and get us.'

Seán considered that for a moment.

'Fair enough so,' he conceded at last. 'The lad has done fine work today. 'Twould be a shame to finish that on a sour note.'

Diarmuid and Demne watched as the rest of the group climbed aboard the van. With a wave, Seán headed off down the road. Before he started off after him, Dinny rolled down the window and poked his head out.

'Don't be dawdling now, Diarmuid. There'll be a heavy rain coming.'

'You just worry about yourself, y'oul eejit. With your feckin' eyesight you'll have to be careful you don't drive off a cliff on yer way down.'

'I'll be waiting down there for ye, y'oul bollix.'

'We'll give you a head start but we'll still bate ye down to the bottom of the hill.'

Dinny responded with a great laugh and pressed down on the accelerator. The car lurched forwards and started off downhill. The Murphy girls waved out the back window until it had turned a corner and disappeared from sight.

Diarmuid looked at his nephew.

'*Ar aghaidh linn, mar sin.*' Off we go, so.

The walk downhill was pleasant although Diarmuid was repeatedly obliged to pull Demne up from racing ahead in his enthusiasm to beat Dinny to the meeting point.

'It's a long way down,' he pointed out. 'And the trail is slippery. No point burning yerself out or tripping up and hurting yerself in the first five minutes.'

'But look, *a Uncail.*' His nephew pointed excitedly at the dark cloud coming in fast off the horizon. 'It's getting dark and there's a storm gathering in.'

The old man shrugged.

Five minutes later they reached the barbed wire gateway, which Diarmuid intentionally left open behind them, knowing that the storm would drive the sheep down from the bog. The weather was closing in fast, the temperature plummeting and the first spatters of rain falling on them.

They made another several hundred metres downhill and had reached an ancient stone bridge traversing a wide gully when the rain started to fall in earnest.

'Right so, *a bhuachaill!* Time to take shelter.'

Demne looked around at the exposed expanse of rock.

'Where can we go?' he cried in frustration. 'There's nowhere to go.'

'Down here.'

His uncle grabbed him by the wrist and dragged him down onto a small path leading off the road. This circled back in a descending arc to the wide stone arch at the base of the bridge. To the boy's surprise, the ground beneath the arch was dry.

'We'll sit the worst of it out under here until Dinny finds us.' Diarmuid pulled him in out of the rain. 'The old stream was diverted by a rock fall years ago. There's no water flowing under this bridge any more.'

'But Dinny will never know we're down here!'

'Course he will. This isn't the first time we've been caught up on this hill in a storm.'

They sat there in a silence punctuated by the drip and splash of rainwater from either side of the arch. Demne shivered and his teeth began to chatter. Diarmuid shuffled out of his coat, pulled it over his shoulders then drew his nephew in close so that it wrapped around the two of them.

'Did I ever tell you the story of Eoghan Rua O'Súilleabháin?' he said.

'No, *a Uncail.*'

Diarmuid reached into his pocket for this pipe, belatedly remembering that it was sitting up on the mantelpiece back in Carraig Dubh.

He sighed.

'Ah, well! Eoghan Rua was a famous poet who lived over the way there in Kerry, way back in the day. He was the greatest poet of all time but, by all accounts, he was a bit of a rogue as well. They say he had a great fondness for the drink. And a stream of *plámás* from that silver tongue of his when there was a maid in the vicinity.'

He smiled cryptically at the boy.

'But that's neither here nor there. Anyway, he was such a talented poet that people said he used to recite poetry as a baby.'

Demne looked at him sceptically.

'It's true. They say he lisped out poetry when he was still in his cradle and if you just bent down and listened carefully you'd hear the most beautiful poetry in the world.'

'Is that really true?'

'Aren't I just after saying it's true!' he huffed. 'Anyway, one day a neighbour dropped in to visit for the chat and d'oul *cupán tae*. The mother was away at the time so didn't the neighbour call in through the door, "*Dia duit, Bean Uí Súilleabháin. An siúlann Eoghan fós?'"* Hello, Mrs O'Sullivan. Is Eoghan walking yet?

Diarmuid paused to adjust his position on the stone, so the rough edge wasn't taking a bite out of his arse.

Demne rustled agitatedly beside him.

'So, what happened?'

'Hmmm?'

'What happened in the house? In your story.'

'Oh well, like I said, the mother was out of the house so it was the baby that answered her.'

'The baby?'

'That's right. he called out:

> *'Ní shiúlann, mo bhrón,*
> *Ach siúlann le stól*
> *No siúlann lena thóin!*

He's not walking, alas.
But walking with a stool
or walking with his arse.'

There was complete silence for one or two seconds then Demne's laughter erupted within the confines of the archway, striking off the ancient stone and echoing out into the rain-stained, darkening sky.

Diarmuid stared at his nephew, fascinated and oddly moved by the rare expression of such unbridled good humour. A sudden softness welled up inside him. Over the past year, despite all his reservations, the unanswered questions and half-formed suspicions, the quare behaviour and the constant stream of serious fecking weirdness, a bond of warmth had somehow formed between him and his nephew.

With that completely unexpected insight, he experienced a sudden and profound sense of responsibility. At that moment, he realised, he would never, ever, let anybody hurt the child again.

By then, Demne had stopped laughing and grown silent, somehow sensing the change in him.

'An bhfuil tú ceart go leor, a Uncail?' Are you all right, Uncle?

'The rain's easing off,' he growled.

'It is.'

'Ar aghaidh linn anois.' Off we go, now. 'I'll build a big fire when we get back to the house. Put some heat back in those oul bones.'

The boy looked out at the sky and nodded enthusiastically. 'If we hurry, maybe we'll beat Dinny to the bottom of the hill after all.'

Diarmuid smiled.

'Maybe we will, *a bhuachaill.* Maybe we will.'

✶✶✶✶✶

Thank you for taking the time to read **Beara: Dark Legends - Book 1** and I hope you enjoyed it. The story comes to a close in **Beara: Dark Legends - Book 2**.

If you'd like an update on when the next Irish Imbas book is released, you're curious about upcoming projects, my creative processes, and other bits and pieces, please feel free to sign up to my **monthly newsletter Vóg** at the Irish Imbas Substack. This goes out 10/11 times a year and, naturally, you can unsubscribe at any time.

Other Books by Brian O'Sullivan

Beara: Dark Legends - Book Two

A 'Gaelic Noir' mystery with Ireland's Greatest Mythological Detective.'

In the rugged 1960's Beara peninsula, a terrifying Púca is haunting the Slieve Miskish Mountains. Retired farmer, Diarmuid O'Súilleabháin however, has issues of his own to contend with, mostly involving the behaviour of his strange, Gaelic speaking nephew.

Or dark revelations from his brother's death that might best be kept concealed.

Meanwhile, Muiris (Mos) O'Súilleabháin's search for the final resting place of Irish hero Fionn mac Cumhaill has been complicated by a mysterious circus performer who's too implausible to be true, and a deadly rival who'll brook no competition.

As the two investigations delve deeper into the fabric of fact and legend, it becomes ever more difficult to tell the difference between them.

Beara: Dark Legends is a gripping tale of mystery and suspense, steeped in the rich tapestry of Irish culture and 'mythology'. With its 'Gaelic Noir' atmosphere and pulse-pounding action, this is not the Ireland you thought you knew.

Fionn: Defence of Ráth Bládhma:

[The Fionn mac Cumhaill Series: Book 1]

Ireland: 1st century A.D. A time of strife and treachery. Political ambition and inter-tribal conflict has set the country on edge, testing the strength of long-established alliances.

Following their victory at the battle of Cnucha, Clann Morna are hungry for power. Meanwhile, a mysterious war party roams the 'Great Wild' and a ruthless magician is intent on murder.

In the secluded valley of Glenn Ceoch, a disgraced druide and a battlescarred woman warrior have successfully avoided the bloodshed for many years. Now, the arrival of a pregnant refugee threatens the peace they have created together. Run or fight, the odds are overwhelming.

And death stalks on every side.

Based on the ancient Fenian texts, the Fionn mac Cumhaill Series is a **gritty and authentic retelling** of the birth and early adventures of Ireland's greatest hero, Fionn mac Cumhaill. Gripping, insightful and utterly action-packed, this is **Irish mythological fiction** as you've never read it before.

9 781067 063719